Showdown
and other stories

Michael Brondoli

North Point Press · San Francisco · 1984

The author salutes the following for first publication of
stories in this collection: *Shenandoah* ("Showdown"), *Gargoyle*
("Borrowing"), *ISBN 0–943568–01–3* ("Coldbeer at the Only"),
Paycock Press ("The Love Letter Hack," as a chapbook).
"Showdown" was reprinted in *The Pushcart Prize V: Best of the
Small Presses*. "The Love Letter Hack" is for Tom Ahern.
Special long-term thanks to Bruce McPherson and
Richard Peabody.
The characters in these stories could hardly be, and should
never be, mistaken for real.

For Mary Beath

Contents

Showdown
and other stories

Showdown

Nobody helped. The night Cammie Lewis quit the Only Bar not a soul helped. Her boyfriend who wasn't supposed to be there swaggered in at 9:30, a day early but they had their two hundred bags of Yankee scallops. He wanted her to kiss him, wanted to show her his hundred-dollar bills, wanted to show everybody what he'd come home to, what he'd been calling on the radio every night.

The pay phone rang but whoever called hung up—probably wanted to talk to Tish, who looked over from the other end of the bar, her face hot with expectation.

Ange Buthrell, Tish's husband, owner of the place, signalled for another round at the back table, where he and his friends were anteing for Nan Ervin to change blouses in front of them. She was prolonging negotiations.

Dressed to kill, Tish was drinking and talking up a storm. In the bar, and there alone, Ange let her go.

The Duke checked another half gallon of Beefeater's—this was North Carolina, you checked your liquor—for him and Dallas Alice, who was singing as loud as she could, which was loud. The Nunemaker brothers borrowed Cammie's screwdriver to crank up the jukebox. Already Conway Twitty sounded like soul music and the buzz of the bass notes made the wineglasses tremble foot to foot. Chas (the Razz) Rollins was weep-

ing at the bar over getting in early to find his woman gone,
down fucking that wop in Drum.

Then Tish left, answered the phone herself this time, told
Cammie, "Take care of things a while," flashed a bright, tricky
smile and left. Usually Cammie could handle a weeknight but
the trawlboats were in and besides this was the dead of winter.

Nan changed, for fifty dollars, into an old blouse of Tish's
from the office. Ange ordered a round for the house and asked
her to travel to Bermuda with him, departure tonight. He asked
Cammie to turn the rheostat to zero, leaving in all the bulbs in
the place nineteen watts, and these negated by smoke. Nobody would have given Cammie trouble. Anybody would have
killed for her or tried to. Still it would be a long night if Tish
didn't return.

Cammie's boyfriend R.L. Caffrey, half heifer, half Popeye—
he needed his big shoulders for all the chips he carried—stood
by the first booth checking things out, checking her out, trying
to get easy with people. Cammie bore marks from his last trip
in, a couple of which might scar, temporarily anyway. At least
with R.L. there Chas quit asking her to wipe his tears with her
lovely hands, gaze with her eyes of wisdom and so forth.

"Let's go back to the office, catch a buzz," R.L. said as she
passed with two armloads.

"Yea, okay." She went to ask Ange to watch the bar, knowing
full well he would not, would simply let people take what they
needed. He justified his inability to accept money from people
he knew as a form of public relations. Tish on the other hand
refused the employee discount to her own sister.

"Hell, I missed you all the time," R.L. said in the office, a faint
chunky rhythm going in his body. He removed his cap; the
yoke of curly hair over his collar remained. "I almost caught my
hand in the winch thinking about you." To his mind she was
the prettiest woman on earth, the earth he'd seen, Water
County, Cape May and Rhode Island. She might not have
much of a figure but she carried herself with a nice cool style,

good posture, knew how to dress—tonight she was wearing a corduroy skirt, a ruffly top, a thin silver necklace and dark stockings—and had these large eyes, the only part of her face she made up. And had this hair, so thick, so deep a red. When she tied it back for work it hung like grapes the size of eggs. Every time he saw her hair was as if somebody took a redwood log and split it open before his eyes.

"I really am getting varicose veins," she said, fingering a small bulge.

"That's not a varicose vein, that's muscle from carrying beer. My mother, now she's got some varicose veins." On Cammie the veins had nowhere to lie except close to the surface and the skin was so tight even her breasts felt like muscle.

"I hope you're right."

"I'm right. I've been at sea two weeks."

"R.L.," she said: a warning.

Sometimes, like now, she could look like an old maid on a farm. Other times, she could look warm, she could look cold, she could look innocent, she could look hard, she could look like a little girl who loved her daddy. "You want me to come back at one, help you clean?"

"R.L. We've been through this a million times. I've got to go back out front."

"Serve me another Bud."

She raised her eyebrows to show it didn't matter to her, it was his business, and lit a Marlboro from the desk drawer.

Sitting at the bar was a newcomer, a stranger to Cammie and whom nobody was talking to. In her judgment he seemed a tad too handsome and hip, might even be a narc. Then she wondered if she hadn't been seeing nothing but crabbers and carpenters for way too long.

Ange was on the phone, hurting. Not everyone could have detected his mood, since he kept his face calm under any conditions, his voice low, but Cammie recognized trouble in him quicker than in herself. He never forgot his courtesies. Trouble in him rose like a hungry fish, never quite to the surface but causing a disturbance if you knew how to look. He dialed another number.

R.L. deck-walked out the door, pulling his cap down his nose, pulling his black coat around to hide the beer in his hand. He walked out thinking of her shoulders still dark with freckles from summer.

The regulars at the table with Nan called for beer but Ange wanted her to stay and talk first. He leaned against the backbar, thin and quiet, let his arms hang, looked at the floor, mumbled, "Cammie, I guess it comes to my having to ask you—I apologize, but I have to ask where she went, if you know."

"I have no idea, Ange. Don't go jumping to conclusions though."

"The situation is such—I mean what other damn conclusion can I jump to?"

The Duke ordered gin and tonics, two-thirds and one-third in twelve-ounce mugs for himself, Alice and her cousin Cecelia Thumb at the middle booth, and a pack of Winstons.

"I don't know, Ange. She said something earlier about Cloth Barn Road." Without having to think she pulled out three Schlitzes, two Blues, a Bud, a Miller Lite and a red Malt Duck.

"Right, visiting my mother. Cammie, don't try to—" He didn't finish. He appreciated the difficulty of her position and never would have faulted her for anything anyway. "I'm riding up there, carrying Warren to his grandmomma's, then riding up to Norfolk and I guess taking my gun. Just, you know, close whenever your opinion—no more food starting now, no barbecue buns or nothing."

She delivered the drinks and went back to the office. Ange had put on his sportcoat, was mixing a thermos of Blue Hawaiis, using rum somebody had checked and forgotten the night before. "I know you're upset but really you could be wrong." She didn't think he was wrong.

"Who's that guy at the bar wearing a necklace?"

"I was wondering."

"He looks like a narc, do you reckon?"

"Maybe he's an A.B.C. officer."

"I don't believe so."

"Anyway you should sort of clean up a little."

This he was already doing, slipping baggies out of the adding machine, from behind the clock, from a case of Collins mix, from the spiral of the Only Bar Halloween photograph album. For all his skill at hiding his real self he was pathetically inept at keeping his other self under wraps. His debts, his schemes, his liking for a new drug became public overnight. A five-year-old could have walked in and uncovered every bit of stash in two minutes. He took a handful of ones from the cash box, put on his sunglasses, a good sign he meant to go. Day or night he wore them whenever he left, sometimes in, the bar, thinking they hid the redness.

"Don't take the gun at least."

"It's kept in the car."

"Don't *leave*." She ran to the front and pleaded with his closest friend Slue Swain to talk Ange out of this desperation.

"Just right," Slue said, his voicebox full of sand. He tipped his Blue Ribbon straight up. "Just right, he should have done this two years ago. But no, kept letting it slide and letting it slide, that's the way the man operates, tying himself in knots instead of hauling in the slack on anybody else."

One of the Nunemakers, Acey, came up from behind, rested his chin on Cammie's head. Booths and tables needed drinks. The jukebox stuck on the chorus of a Kenny Rogers song. "Talk to him."

"Hell, I've tried to talk him into it for two years."

She waited.

"I'll talk."

He didn't have to leave the table. Ange was returning to make the rounds, shake his friends' hands, tell them he'd see them tomorrow and to give and take a look with each. "Riding up to Norfolk to pick up our cruise boat tickets, first boat out," he said to Nan Ervin.

"You take care of yourself," she said.

"Slue," Cammie said.

Slue nodded and followed his friend out the door. When he came back he cried out, "Drinks for everybody and put it on my tab and I don't care if my engine stays laid up for a month!"

Cammie was out the door in time to see Ange's cream-color Lincoln pull onto the causeway road, which led across the bridge to the beach bypass to the upper bridge, which led back across the sound and north. He didn't peel out, he eased out, a worse sign, the tires not popping but squeezing gravel.

With close timing Police Chief Omie Marr rolled into the lot from the other direction and parked in Ange's space. Accompanied by a man whose suit and metal-rimmed glasses announced State A.B.C. Board, he ambled toward the entrance. "Got anybody watching the inside?" he asked Cammie.

"Me."

"Well now Ange has installed remote control. Is that in the manual, remote control?" he asked the A.B.C. man, who didn't respond.

The wind had shifted to south-southwest and blowing up the sound and across the marsh and the road smelled of oyster mud, bad fishing and false spring. For the how manyeth time, Cammie wondered, am I wishing I had a boat tied out back to a willow? She stayed at the Only Bar only because of Tish and Ange, who couldn't run the place without her and were her best friends.

Ange's Lincoln always gave Cammie the impression of riding in a space capsule. The quiet and casualness of handling, particularly in comparison with her Dodge van, approached no gravity. The radio tuned itself, its little eye bopping from station to station, its speakers turning guitars to harps. When she had her house, she wanted a living room as cozy as the Lincoln, as ideal for getting stoned in. Nearly every night Ange would say, "Let's go for a ride-around." They'd crawl up and down the beach road, pull off back of a dune, roll down the windows with the touch of a button, light up, listen to the waves. Ford Motor Company sold a line of automobiles whose purpose was to provide the rich with mobile living rooms to get stoned in.

"Yea they're stoned all the time," Ange had agreed. He was. It suited his physiology, his gait and manner, his hospitableness, his chalky voice. On alcohol he used to wreck cars. On dope he glided, miles below the speed limit. They'd smoke, he'd talk about Tish and Del Benoit because if there was anybody he let inside anymore it was Cammie.

He wasn't rich, he just lived rich, in constant danger of being gill-netted by crisscrossing lines of credit in and out of town. The Only Bar—he despised the name, a result of his own neglect—was so in fact in winter aside from the Ramada Inn on the beach. The amount of cash spilling through screened him when he walked into a bank. People tended to believe in him, weak voice included. He'd taken a decomposing crabhouse, doubled the size, made tables and booths out of hatchcovers and sawed-up church pews, paneled it with barnwood, framed old pictures in rope—redneck, but tasteful redneck.

He didn't worry about money thus he was rich. He worried about Tish. Even at nineteen he'd known he would never feel the same for anyone else. He'd tried stray but found it impossible to go more than once, once at night after which he pretended to pass out, once in the morning pretending she was Tish or nothing in the morning if he could sidestep. With her the thing seemed spring-loaded no matter how she treated him.

He wasn't redneck. Time and again he had cut her slack. He'd kept his mind years ahead of the standards of Water County, educated it by dragging it to this and that cosmopolitan spot, ski resorts, San Francisco, Bermuda. People have to believe in each other's best interests, he liked to tell Cammie, who understood, act in good faith, help each other in trouble, talk and deal straight.

But with Del, Tish had fucked with him way beyond any maximum. He sat with his friends in his bar knowing, *knowing* that at that moment she was laying up with Del. Then he felt like a living fish on the gutting board.

On the mainland side of the upper bridge, turning up N.C. 158, he capped the thermos and lit a joint. Omie Marr himself back when they drank together gave him the gun he reached under the seat and slid into his pocket. Though he continued to drive languidly a determination set in, from button-down collar to Hush Puppies, a cement that hardened from the inside out.

"Riding to Norfolk, riding to Norfolk."

"Now where do you suppose Ange's gotten to?" Omie Marr asked, directing his flashlight across the checked liquor bottles to make certain they were labeled with legal names, not Duke but Terence H. Clinton, not Chas or Razz but Charles O. Rollins.

"He went to buy plastic cups," Cammie said. She was keeping tabs on Timmy Spratt, a scrapper whom Ange had barred a dozen times then put on probation a dozen. Omie and the A.B.C. man were going out of their way to avoid noticing the stranger. Normally Omie would have pumped the guy, off-hand style, an art, for some information about himself. Her worst nightmare was of having the bar closed down when she was on alone.

"Tell him I want to sit down with him," the Chief said.

"Oh, what for?" she asked, surprised at herself.

Omie appeared surprised too. It didn't take him long however to come up with, "Hallie across the road's complaining again about parking." Hallie Gaspar, who'd buried three full and some partial husbands—among the latter Ange's daddy—had a fetish about parking, also about not using lights.

The A.B.C. man was fooling with a loose strip of paneling. Ange believed Omie, who held onto grudges tighter than the raffle tickets he preserved years past date of drawing, to be on a new tack. He'd never gotten an alcohol citation to stick, due to common sense and as everybody knew Del Benoit's political connections—no wonder Ange had turned a blind eye, or put Tish up to her affair. But there was no way a drug bust wouldn't stick.

Chas the Razz, having donned his Stetson and moved in on two women tellers from Planters Bank, was acting noticeably drunk, unusual for him, the noticeability. Omie cocked his head. "Girl, you know it's against the law to let anybody get drunk in a bar."

"I'll cut him off. Thanks. Did you gentlemen want anything to drink?"

"Yes ma'am," the Chief said, "two waters."

For these the A.B.C. man dropped fifty cents on the bar and he and Omie proceeded to the door, slow.

Slue's wife called, he refused to talk. Cammie gave him the message his dried-out chicken was going in the setter's bowl, a message intended to enrage him on the subject of a dog's esophagus and chicken bones. Cammie explained once again to Tobacco Ted how to spin quarters into the cigarette machine.

The Duke dragged Chas to the bar, told him to straighten out, right now and in general, ordered drinks and asked Chas if Cammie had ever described the special night they spent. "That was a real special night, wasn't it, darling? You never told Chas about that night, what went down, what kept on going down till the dawn's early light? Wasn't that one special night?"

"I guess it was."

"You know it was, darling, you know it was. Brother," he said to Chas, "brother, we got looned right on out, looned right on out to the *max*." He brought his large, elegant, ruined head, loaded with energy, close to hers. Something about looking at the Duke resembled looking at the jukebox from too close up.

Chas ducked from under the Duke's arm and said, "I don't like you talking that way to my lady, she's too fine for that. She understands." He drew out *understands* to twice its length. "From the moment she stepped off the bus, even when she took up with my raggedy-ass brother, I saw she understood, understood everything, all the towns and the oceans and the winds of the soul, all the hopes and sorrows of the heart."

"Tell it, brother, tell it."

"You cocksucking liar."

"You blind son of a bitch."

"Cammie," Chas said, taking a breath, exhaling smoke, shaking his head as he lifted his eyes to hers and lifted his eyebrows like a hound's or a believer's in church. "Cammie," he said, and had to stop. He reached for her hand, and shut his eyes as he pressed it to his lips.

"I wish I understood a few things."

"Don't give me that bullshit." A native of East Lake, Chas pronounced it boolshit. "Don't try and put that bullshit over on me. You're real. Cammie, you're real." Every time he said her name he shut his eyes.

Loaded with indecision, Budweiser and low-tar nicotine Tish Buthrell was zooming north on N.C. 158 toward Norfolk, empty bottles volleying beneath the pedals. The breeze boosted the horsepower of her 1968 Chevy, although with two warnings on her provisional license, good to and from work, she tried to watch the towns. She slowed to forty through the north end of Grandy, too many shadows under trees. Entering Barco she slammed on the brakes so hard the wheels almost locked—she'd remembered her cousin Nibbie's getting stopped there, past the Sunoco station. Outside town she tapped the brake pedal for stoplights.

She wasn't fooling herself. She knew what she was risking. People accused her of a self-destructive impulse; well now they would have something to go on. At twenty-nine you are too young to spend your life dreading consequences. She wasn't cut out to be the devoted wife and mother three hundred and sixty-five days a year. Every now and then the human organism—she used Del's phrase—needed a little Mardi Gras like in

New Orleans and those people are Catholics. She was risking the house, two years old, the longest brick house in Water County, everything in it, a good living, maybe even Warren though she doubted that. Warren could take care of himself but Ange couldn't take care of Warren.

But it was a fine living, even if she had to kiss a few behinds. She would kiss Omie *Marr's* if that's what it took to make a living. And it was ever her, ever her lips sent on these missions, never Ange's lily-white kisser. He preserved his for preaching the brotherhood of the world. She had to fawn, she had to act gracious, my heavens. She supplied every other form of man-power too seven days a week, eleven A.M. to one A.M., ever there, ever hustling while Ange cut out with his buddies and stayed smoked up all his conscious moments. He supplied the ideas. Great, just great if there wasn't somebody to carry them out, talk to carpenters, talk to salesmen, mop, order, straighten the walk-in, hire and fire in summer, cook pizzas in the eight-thousand-degree oven, collect tabs, return broken bottles for credit, feed a family on the quarters from the jukebox and ciga-rette machines. Right, they went skiing a couple weekends. What about the vacations he took by himself while she handled the bar, her and Cammie? He never finished a thing. Even the sign, the fifteen-hundred-dollar sign saying Causeway Inn had remained in the crate so long the customers had named the bar. In a week Ange spent at the outside ninety minutes in the place when he wasn't blown out. She and Cammie carried the load.

Married at nineteen and seventeen they were supposed to settle each other down, a laugh. Ange hadn't settled, he'd merely gotten slower and stopped punching cops.

She realized she was putting her guilt on him but he messed around, he took money from the register to look at Nan Ervin's puny charms, just because she didn't know jealousy didn't change that fact. She couldn't give up Del, didn't understand why she had to. Ange complained Water was too small for *his* ideas. Every woman loved more than one man but didn't do anything about it or did once or twice on the sly. Why should she care what people who'd bad-mouthed her all her life said? Why should he?

She was no good at giving up. She'd tried with cigarettes, with beer, Lord knows with Del, sometimes going for weeks. Lucky nobody ever gave her heroin.

Ange would go crazy, break furniture and china, bash in the color set, lock her out of the house forever, rip her clothes and throw the shreds out the window, which is why she kept her best things, including her new dress for the Shrine Club dance, in the trunk. But he'd never find strength to give her up. Your nipples are like stethoscopes reading my heart, he had croaked to her once.

How many more opportunities would Water County present her with? Her body was filling out, catching up with her frame. Her complexion aged two years for every one in the cigarette smoke of the bar, that tannery.

She figured she would stop at a filling station before Norfolk to comb her hair, as she drove with the windows wide open.

"Riding to Norfolk." Ange couldn't decide if he wanted to overtake her or not, a far-fetched notion to begin with considering the rate she drove at unless she broke down, a more likely notion, a habit. He didn't know if he could trust his hands once he snatched her out. She'd be swinging at him, as a joke, squealing as if he'd nabbed her in nothing more than hide-and-seek. I knew you'd chase after me, she would say, I wanted you to, she would say. I'm coming home, I was planning to turn around come home if you didn't catch up. She would tilt her head, relax her mouth for him.

Staying laid on back was definitely the right idea. The little eye on the fuel gauge started blinking and while there was plenty to reach Norfolk he turned in at a Sav-Mor self-service filling station, one pump under one light in the middle of nowhere. Fallow tobacco fields all around, a creek to the west flagged by trees. The breeze rustled his flat hair, which hung in

front of his face as he fed bills. Looking toward the creek he
thought he saw flashlights moving between trees, coon hunt-
ers. He'd taken Warren duck-hunting, he and Del had a couple
years back, but never to Stumpy Point after animal.

Steering with a wrist he passed the stores and early-to-bed-
der houses of Succutuck County. Reflecting his headlights in
stale flashes they presented themselves as plywood tomb-
stones.

His heart became a drum, a tub bass, a whole rhythm band
of injury. For long stretches he set his vision on automatic pilot
and went blind to everything but his own separate life, him,
alone, in a space capsule—as Cammie called it—free, white
and thirty-one, money in his pocket, credit cards, dope under
the dash, full talk of gas and no reason to stop short in Norfolk,
no reason not to go on to D.C., N.Y.C., Montreal.

An old pickup passing him brought his attention back to the
road. He was entering Grandy. He entered Grandy as a gentleman but free. No reason was the best reason with a gun.

Coasting out of the north end of town he saw a phone booth,
one phone with one light in the middle of nowhere.

Cindy Spruill flew off the barstool.

"Chas!" Cammie said.

Chas threw his hands up like a basketball player showing he
didn't foul. "I brushed her by accident, I swear. Cammie, you
know I couldn't hurt her back, even a heartsick old man like
me"—he was forty-two—"couldn't injure a little girl"—she
twenty—"who doesn't even comprehend the damage she does
laying up with another man while I'm out on the god-fucking
sea working to where my arms grip the air in *sleep*, who doesn't
even know I can see right through her pretty eyes, right into
her soul when she walks in tells me she's been faithful to me."

The phone rang, wouldn't stop ringing. The Duke, everywhere at once, picked it up and nodded the receiver toward
Cammie.

"I've got news for you," Tobacco Ted was saying, wiping

foam out of his beard at the same time he missed the ashtray. "Damn you're a fine-looking thing, aren't you? What was your name?"

"Ted, how many times have you been in here? Cammie."

"Cammie, I've got news for you."

"How could I be blaming a little girl for failure to comprehend the passion of a man?" Chas asked.

Cindy, accustomed to hearing herself discussed, settled back next to him, straightened the collar of her blouse. "I'd lost my balance."

Cammie took the receiver. "Cammie, this is Ange." He always identified himself over the phone. "I don't suppose— Tish hasn't shown up or anything, has she?"

She considered lying but he'd be able to tell and anyway she couldn't face him were he to return and no Tish. He wouldn't get angry with her, she just could not bear the thought. "Not yet but really you know she could be anywhere."

"That's exactly my assumption I'm operating on. I meant what I said about closing, you know, if it gets too busy, or hell if it doesn't."

"It's already kind of busy. I wish you were here."

"I have to stick to priorities, for once. I guess I'll be seeing you."

"Well all right, Ange."

"You can search the whole world over," Tobacco Ted, retired from the Merchant Marine, was saying. "You can search the whole world over, and you will never find, a man, as sorry, as old Tobacco Ted. I'm telling you truth, you can search the whole world over."

"Aw, you're not so bad."

"I don't blame nobody for not liking old Ted," said Ted. "I hate him myself. But you can search the whole world over, but I've got news for you."

Thirty seconds later Ange called again. "Cammie, this is Ange. I forgot to tell you she's fired. I've fired her. Cross her name off the schedule, you hear me?"

"All right, Ange."

"Hard night, huh?" commented the narc, who insisted on coming on despite her obvious indifference, and nervousness now that R.L. was back, leaning, cap tight, into a group of mates at the middle table, making gestures that fell short.

"Normal," she said. She didn't let him light her cigarette; she lit it herself from a bar candle and moved.

The Duke cleared mugs out of the way and lay across to whisper at the level a bear might whisper, "I've got a little something for you, sugar darling, help you through the evening, little bit of fisherman's friend."

"Just shut up, okay?" She backed off, because of R.L. and because the Duke was liable to just stuff it in her hand in full view.

"Check it out, check it right on out," he urged. He caught up with her emptying ashtrays and no longer pretending to whisper said, "It's some fine toot. My teeth are buzzed."

"The guy at the bar's a narc. Now you take anything you've got out to your truck and you leave it."

"The day anybody has the balls to bust me is the day geese grow balls."

"I'm not worried about you, I'm worried about the bar."

"Let me know when you can slip out and join me over my picture of Jesus."

At the table with Slue, Cal Quinley—once one of Ange's close friends now his blood enemy over rental of the Tourist Office—started chuckling, wheezing through his teeth rather. All Ange's enemies drank at his bar; he wouldn't stand for their not. When Del Benoit came in, Ange paid for his soda mixes, sat down with him, took him back to the office to indulge in the main thing they shared besides Tish, love of bullshit.

Cal pulled Cammie to his side. "One's a fool, the other one's a pure fool and you love them both, don't you, girl?"

"I just want to keep the place open."

Del Benoit was sitting by the window on the fourteenth floor of the Holiday Inn, formerly the Triangle Hotel, his feet up on the air conditioning unit, a bottle of J&B in his crotch, a bucket of

reamed ice cubes at hand. He looked down over the parking
lots and church converted to a memorial for Douglas Mac-
Arthur and philosophized, which meant think about women—
Woman, to be precise.

He maintained an apartment on the beach which nobody
knew the whereabouts of, not his wife, not his men friends,
not Tish. No telephone, only a CB transceiver. Two days a week
in the off-season, or three, he holed up there, with a picture
window out to sea, classical records, cases of J&B, two silk
robes. Once he sent off for the complete Great Books for his
hideaway. Twelve hours after their arrival, however, in the
dead of night he had packed the set in liquor boxes and
dropped it at the door of the county library without identification. "Bequest of the Delbert R. Benoit Memorial," read the
endpapers, which pleased him, the librarian's knowing both
his brand and his liver.

At age fifty he prided himself on having finished with the sex
of life, the ins and outs of making money. He'd sweated blood
to turn his brine-eaten frame inn into the landmark of what
passed for hospitality. The middle class checked into the new
brick places, eating fried oysters. The rich stayed in wood, dining on them raw. He'd knocked down walls, torn up floors,
poured cement—he and the Duke—laid tile, added two wings
in the old style. For fifteen years he'd given up liquor, gone
stone dry, from Memorial to Labor Days inclusive. This season
he could afford to stand pat, didn't need to sacrifice a thing,
except Tish, and she was merely the goal of all philosophy, the
illumination of all liquor, the harmony of the sex not of life but
of sex.

The Norfolk Holiday was the hotel, this the room that had
worked the cure for alcohol fifteen years straight.

His wife couldn't have cared about his philandering nor he
about hers. She saw some guy from Elizabeth City, some travel
agent or arts director—whatever, he always had a mouthful of
Lifesavers, and a pocketful of Del's money, which also he could
have cared about. Maybe if he concentrated on his waitress

from Greensboro College, made a fool of himself, he could transfer his feelings for Tish, not to the girl but to the making of a fool of himself.

Granted he and Tish burned coal in bed. Granted she loved him for the unpredictability, the risk while loving Ange for real. In the beginning this had been his comfort. He'd preferred second fiddle, confirming as it did his theory that Woman is not basically polygamous but a fine tuner of monogamy.

Yet now. Yet now, occasionally, he and Tish would be ambushed in an embrace that sailed and sailed beyond every attempt at philosophy and he wondered if his life hadn't been a lie and if there had not been some moment when he failed to notice a face he was meant to stay very near the rest of his days.

Once or twice he had tipped his hand, exposed his bleary dreams to the laser gun of hers. And she hadn't fired, she'd cried. Then fired.

He considered calling room service to remove his telephone but decided if he could keep liquor around to serve guests when he was on the wagon he could keep a damn phone in his room.

"Cammie, this is Ange."

"Where are you?"

"Coinjock. Sounds busy in there."

"Well I could use some help."

"What that means is she hasn't shown."

By now Cammie thought she could lie once, but never twice—when he asked to speak with Tish she'd have to tell him she was out buying ice at the Fishing Center or something, the ice maker had broken down again: making three lies. "Haven't seen her but I was hoping you'd take the hint. Everybody's in a hassling mood tonight, the Chief's on the prowl, Hallie's hot, Winslow and Eljay waded in and I don't know about this narc."

"Seems to be a long way to Norfolk."

"Are you buzzed?"

"Like a bitch."

"You think you know what you're doing. I hope you don't end hating yourself."

"I'm neutral about myself."

"You're assuming."

"How about it."

Eljay raised two fingers, two one-inch dowels, for him and his partner Winslow, captains out of Swan's Bay, huge, gray, gabardined men who when drunk lost consciousness wide awake without dropping any of their guard. Drunk they became less than animal but more than ordinarily dangerous to other animals. They didn't stagger or slur; they rarely talked. In slow motion they raised Luckies to their lips and barely seemed to drag although the ash burned with amazing evenness. They were like juniper trunks washed up on the shore, with depth charges inside.

"We ain't looking for no trouble," Eljay said when Cammie set the Blue Ribbons down.

"Of course you aren't, Eljay." He hadn't been home as his crew for the most part had, still smelled.

His cigarette took a good ten seconds to describe a perfect arc to the ashtray. "We come in to have a good time."

"That's right, I know you did."

"No trouble."

"Why would there be any trouble?"

"You can search the whole world over, but I've got news for you. Nobody likes old Ted, and I don't blame them. He'll do anything in the world for you but nobody likes him. They know he's no damn good on the inside."

"Shut him up," Eljay said. "We don't want to."

"Ted," Cammie said, wiping around his ashtray, "could you cool it a little while? You're sort of getting on people's nerves."

"See what I tell you. Nobody likes Ted."

"Getting on somebody's nerves doesn't mean they don't like you. People in love get on each other's nerves."

"You can search the whole world over, and you will never find, a person, in love."

"Possibility of getting another Heineken down here?" called the narc.

"Slim."

In the darkness Cammie relied on a sort of radar to track troublespots, an installation in the back of her mind that was constantly scanning, lighting up corners and groupings of bad energy. Tonight the screen had been busy but the blips hadn't come with the timing and density that signalled alarm. With Winslow and Eljay there they brightened, quickened. Ange's departure had left an uneasiness in the back. The first night ashore drew the worst out of men. The Chief, the narc and R. L. added to the strain, hers anyhow, as did the Duke, who never looked for trouble but was careless. Sides wouldn't prove that important, simply the existence of an excuse.

"There's them in here don't like us," Eljay said, or Winslow—she couldn't tell which—causing Ted to turn his head with interest. Eljay or Winslow was referring to Slue and his crew. Winslow had pistol-whipped Slue's fifteen-year-old son off Cape May, leaving him in such shape the mate had had to radio a helicopter to carry the boy to the hospital. Cammie didn't think Slue, hot-headed as he was, would give Winslow the chance to settle the matter outright—he had bided his time for months—but tonight she couldn't tell.

"Everybody's got people who don't like them."

"Ain't looking to start no trouble. You keep trouble clear of us, hear?" She not only couldn't see a mouth move, she couldn't see eyes under the brims of their caps.

The runners on the righthand cooler were getting stickier and stickier. She reached under the register for Crisco.

"That your boyfriend just left?" the narc wanted to know.

"Sort of." She knew exactly why he'd left, so he could sneak back and catch her leaning on the bar talking to the narc or letting the Duke hang on her while he whispered in her ear.

"You ever go out with anybody else?"

She narrowed her suspicion to the guy's fastidiousness, his pressed workshirt with the cuffs rolled back twice, his gold watch, his long hair hanging just so, the way he wiped the condensation off the bar with his napkin. Then she knew his background. It was that air that stayed with a guy forever, that scent he can never bathe, drink or smoke off, the Lysol of the service. She figured Army intelligence. "I try not to go out with anybody."

"You know, that's a crushing damn disappointment. Literally. I was developing this crush on you."

"Anybody develops interest in me's asking for trouble."

"Do you mean you're a heartbreaker or do you mean your boyfriend's a hard customer?"

"I mean I'm fucked up from head to toe."

Startled he spread his arms, and smiled, causing a pendant to swing into view on his chest, a little gold cross.

"Shouldn't you be wearing a pair of those?" Cammie asked. Most nights she possessed stamina to burn but R.L. sucked it out of her. She took a bottle of Visine from her pocketbook. On the job she chain-smoked herself but by eleven the smoke, combined with the effort of keeping her radar focused, put embers in her eyes.

The phone—Del's disguised voice, which he disguised by talking timidly and accenting the wrong syllables of words. "May I please speak to Tish Buthrell?"

"Del, look—" She was sniffling with the Visine.

"Cammie? Cammie, tell Tish I want to speak to her but tell her don't say a word, I can't take the sound of her voice."

"She's not here, she—" Before she could explain he hung up actually moaning.

Taking off from a crossroads where all four directions looked identical, scruffy trees, bumpy pavement, everything a dead shade of blue-gray, Ange was pitying her for her limitations. Every direction was a reflection in the rear-view mirror until the one in front backed down, resumed three dimensions. He hadn't turned, he swore he hadn't. Tish did not know how to insert a split-second of thought between the information and the response. Because she lacked concentration she worked five times as hard as necessary. She had two phases, laziness and craziness, nothing in between, the one as full of deceit as the other.

He pictured her lying across the bar exposing the tops of her breasts, dying for customers, talking to some old drunk like Tobacco Ted, rambling as if falling asleep word by drowsy word. Then in a heartbeat up strongarming some two-hundred-and-fifty-pound sea captain out the door.

Through the years the thing he had longed for was stretches of plain and lingering tenderness. The minute you believed you had one, were safe, it dawned on you she was laughing up her sleeve.

Was that what that lard-ass was able to draw from her, patient attention?

He assumed she'd reached Norfolk by now, was rapping on the door, making some teasing remark. Del might put on a show of turning her away but he enjoyed his weaknesses too much to hold out, especially if he was drinking. No if about it. He'd see her face lit up with beer, he'd see that shiny dress, the highheels she would have changed into in the parking lot—she wore deck shoes to drive—he'd see those eyes making fun of the situation. They were laughing, guzzling booze, going to it. He didn't delude himself that they were laughing specifically at him but they were letting out some kind of giggle that shriveled him.

Try a little tenderness—that's what he'd say as he popped them.

He lit another joint to maintain the cool the job required, the feeling of being just another part of the Lincoln, an interior power accessory registering neither wind nor road. He took an uphill curve, flew across a little bridge. The headlights picked out a pinto pony, a beautiful thing, standing against its shed by the fence. Goddamn, he thought, goddamn beautiful peaceful animal, full of wisdom. It doesn't matter to him, my popping them.

The trees thickened up, met over the road. Branches whipped closer and closer in the slipstream. Maybe he did turn wrong. This wasn't far from skiing, nearly out of control toward the top of one range then sort of waxing into the next speed, the higher the speed the truer the aim. He knew damn well the road lay level here but it seemed to be falling away. He was through the next crossroads before he saw it come, before the flash that lasted in the car for miles like red perfume. The tons of vehicle rode on a single blade, perfectly balanced.

He'd better slow down, he was thinking when he crested a hill and five full pints of blood shunted to his head.

R.L. loved to see her wash mugs, for although not a native or sturdy looking she knew how to work as well as anybody. He wanted to press his face to that spot on her shoulder, get a faceful of both shoulder and hair, the one spot of her she couldn't drain of heat no matter how she tried. "I mean, couldn't we get together after closing and sit down and talk? Here, even, here's fine."

"It would be the same conversation. It's not what we say to each other, it's the sameness that drives me up the wall."

One in each hand, onto the brushes, right, left, she could wash those mugs. "I did wrong last time, but when a man finds his woman—" With her wrist she brushed back a couple of reddish-copper hairs.

"We were *talking*. Damn it, this is what I mean. Never anything different, never the slightest thing changed. That's what'll drive me away from here, not what people do, the sameness of the doing."

"I bought some Thai sticks off Bud Loring. We could sit at the bar after we close."

"No!" She looked around the corner to the front, squinting out of the light over the sink. "You'll drive me right out of Water County."

"Cammie, I'm making a load of money. I'm saving three-fourths. I'll have enough for a down payment, you know? Bud told me about this house on the soundside, you know, we might run by check out some time." His hands had caves in them where her hips were supposed to fit.

"I've got to get change."

Warren was lying on the office floor with sticks of wood, Eveready batteries, strips of bellwire around him, his head on a stack of placemats. He had Ange's straight black hair, Tish's wide mouth and eyes.

"I thought I had a hard road," R.L. said. He spread his coat over him. Cammie admitted there was a sweetness to R.L.'s voice at times, to him, misplaced in this case.

When she shut the door to block out the jukebox, the high notes, Warren woke.

"What are you doing, boy?" R.L. asked.

"R.L., you like World War II?" He copied Ange's muffled tone.

"Yea."

"Look what Hammerhead gave me." He took a khaki tin of C-rations out of his jacket; he'd been sleeping on the thing. "Check this out."

"That's all right."

"Did you read it?"

"Yea, U.S. Army."

"I mean all of it."

"It says what's in it," Cammie put in.

"There's a chicken in here."

"Well not a whole chicken," R.L. said.

"There is."

"They took the bones out."

"Yea of course they took the *bones* out. Hell."

"That's really an all right thing to have."

"How much you give me? It's quite valuable, genuine World War II."

"A thirty-year-old chicken," Cammie said. "Thirty-one."

"It's still good."

"How much you asking?" R.L. said.

"Five dollars."

"Holy Moses."

"Think how much a museum like in Norfolk'd give me."

"I think Hammerhead meant you to keep it for yourself," Cammie said. "He'd be upset if you sold it."

"I can do anything I want with it."

"He'd be upset."

"If he cared he wouldn't give it to me."

"Warren, I'm calling your grandmomma, see if she's home. R.L.'ll run you over there, all right?" She was asking R.L.

"I don't give a shit. I just hitchhiked from there."

"You got some mouth on you," R.L. said.

Warren cocked his head, bobbed it. "You got a ugly fucked-up mouth on you. Your mouth makes me sick to my stomach."

"Warren," Cammie said, "you ready to go back to your grandmomma's?"

"Yea, I'll sleep on the beach. I always sleep on the beach."

"You don't watch your mouth, boy, you'll be sleeping on the bottom of the sound. I'll pitch you out crossing the bridge."

"R.L., for God's sake."

"I like to see you pitch me out, you candyass, you old nerd."

"I better not see that new guy when I get back," R.L. told Cammie, his muscles betraying their bad wiring.

"I've got to get back out front. I'll call from there."

At the bar she lit a Marlboro and pretended she didn't catch anybody gesturing or hear anybody call her name. She took partial consolation from Timmy Spratt's having left, unless he was in the john. Running out from the back, arms full, Warren asked, "You see any extra batteries around here?"

"Nope."

At the door R.L. transmitted a final message to assure her she wasn't putting anything over. At first she thought he was going to give her the finger; then she realized what dredged up wasn't anger but pain, so pure it shone.

Her mother had tried to help her father. A total drunk—Chas the Razz given ten years—visibly yellow, he used to grab her,

and Cammie if handy, around the legs like timber after a ship-
wreck, convincing her mother he would kill himself if she divorced him.

At nineteen Cammie drove trucks for a construction company in Richmond. The practical fact was R.L. didn't do it for
her anymore and knew this but couldn't understand the last
remedy in the world was harder.

Tish, southbound on N.C. 158, experienced a close call passing
a groggy farmer up a hill. It reminded her of the beach when all
the waves stop at once and silence falls heavier than lying underneath surf. She skinned by, thanks to the farmer's diddling,
her reflexes and the Lincoln's wallow at the last moment but
the incident persuaded her virtue didn't pay either. It was over
too fast to fix the color of the Lincoln, yellow, maybe cream. If
Ange *had* pursued her, he wouldn't have gotten this far at his
usual fifty.

She had turned around. She'd stopped at a closed filling station, combed her hair in pump chrome and without fully deciding when she pulled out, pulled out south. She couldn't give
up the work she had put into the bar, not for one night when
Del might spring something like not let her in or let her in to see
a prostitute lounging beside him, dribbling scotch.

From now on she'll be goody-goody for the most part. Three
beers per night, no speed—it wasn't beer, it was those little
doozies when they overshot. Once in a blue moon she'll see
Del. He'll never quit. "Don't talk, just listen," he'd said this
afternoon. "I'm not telling you where I am"—as if everybody
didn't know—"I'm telling you it's got to be over. Next time
we're friends, mutual friends of Ange. We're on his side. I don't
mean to deny nothing, try to prove nothing. We're historical
friends, a couple of damn philosophers." She'd taken a breath.
"Don't be heartless, breathing."

Coming to the bridge north of Grandy her headlights scared
a pony by the side of the road, made him toss and paw.

The spies will carry no tales. She'll keep her legs ever crossed,

her laughter ever low, perch on her twenty-nine-year-old hips
as if they are forty-nine, serve meals of something other than
pizzas heated over. With the customers she'll let herself go a
little but stay this side of the line. No tight clothing. More time
with Warren to prevent him from turning into another mum-
bling conniver. If only their skulls didn't have the same peanut
shape.

She'll phone Cammie from the next booth. What would she
do without that girl? She loved to see her driving her van, with
not an expression on her face, not seeing anybody, not acknowledging a honk or wave, just sitting up there horsing the
wheel, shifting gears, cutting corners, eyes miles down the
road, just flying in that big blue van.

Omie Marr stalked minors, making sure nobody had gone to
the bar, ordered mixed drinks and carried them to a table where
a minor, just off a boat, sat with a warm beer sneaking hard
liquor. Chas had sent Cindy home, sobbing, wailing out the
door, which Cammie knew led to reconciliation, hopefully before the wop from Drum made the mistake of wandering in.
Teresa Ewing was waiting for her ex-husband to wander in
with his girl from College Park, meanwhile staying near
enough a man, any man, to cuddle and lick when he did. Slue,
Quinley, the Nunemakers, Carl Peasley (County Dogcatcher, a
political job thanks to Del) waited. Winslow and Eljay, on their
eighteenth Blue Ribbons—they raised their bottles slow but
had to raise each only once or twice—were waiting and not
waiting. Even the Duke seemed to have entered anticipation,
allowing his women to talk to each other.

Deucy Nunemaker dragged a plastic trash bag of scallops to
the bar and in his best ladies' man style, blond, woozy and
sharp-eyed, asked Cammie to cook.

"Everything's off," she said. She couldn't deny he made her
think how pretty his arms must be, the armpits too, full of
cords and knots. He could dance.

"I want to give some to everybody."

"I can set them in the walk-in till tomorrow."

"I give that little girl, my little niece, two thousand dollars for a car for school and she never come back. I don't blame her for not liking old Ted."

Cammie didn't have to make up her mind about trying to call Del. He called; starting off sounding like a sick old chinaman, one of those you saw coming downstairs to Granby Street in Norfolk whom R.L. always wanted to ask for opium.

"God, Cammie." A native of Beaufort, he pronounced it Gawd. "You're good people, Cammie. Someday you'll turn into the lovely, heartful woman you're meant to be, I have faith you will. Just talk with me and don't put your bosslady on the line."

"Isn't she with you?"

"God no, our race is run. I've wanted to tell you how much I valued your putting up with us so long."

"She left here two hours ago."

"Don't tell me that. Don't tell me the black widow's still on the feed. Do you know why I call her the black widow?"

Her hearing went not long after her sight. She knelt behind the cooler, put a hand to her open ear. "You've told me." A thousand times.

"She doesn't know my room."

"Del, I want to tell you something but you have to give me a double promise. I mean promise for now and for when you're sober."

"I wish I could get drunk."

"You'll never say where you heard."

"If I wasn't true to anybody I'd be true to you. I don't need to promise to promise to you."

"Ange is on his way to the Holiday with his gun."

"Don't tell me that."

Cammie's radar picked up flashes so vivid she stood to look: Thad Colton strolling in with his new wife, a woman Slue had run with prior to the marriage; moreover, Thad was in the fish business with Winslow and Eljay, as his father had been also,

and why was Slue hanging around, why hadn't he gone home
at his usual hour? Was all he was waiting for news of Ange?

"He's got his .32."

"Well that changes the lineup."

She knelt, caught a whiff of the sour beer that collected under
the coolers, the marsh mice's swimming pool, the roaches'
watering hole. She expected crabs to crawl out. "Del, get to
another hotel. Now."

"I don't run scared."

"It's not scared," she began, then realized her mistake in repeating that word with a drunk.

"In my life I've run blind, I've run ragged, I've run one-
legged but I've never run scared. Does the mate of the black
widow spider turn tail? He waits. That is his grace, and honor."

"I want to see you walking in here again."

"I carry a gun."

"Lord."

"I'd best get it out of my Dopp kit. You're good people, Cammie, solid people."

She went to wait on Thad and Ruelle although Thad, the
perfect gentleman—to a point—when out with his wife, his
prize, a woman his daddy would have taken to, always came to
the bar to save her. She determined his and Slue's tables were
ignoring each other, presenting backs and no glances. The Nunemakers showed the extra voltage more than anyone else.
"When you going to cook scallops? We got butter," Slue said.
"We want to share with our neighbors yonder."

"Call for you, sweetheart," the narc said at the bar.

"So how you doing," stated Tish over an excellent connection.

"Where are you, lady?"

"Oh I come over to see this girl who babysits, ask her to sit
for Shriners."

"Warren needs a babysitter now?"

"Well I was sort of on the road to Norfolk. Damn it's dark
outside this booth."

"Ange is driving up with his gun, Del's waiting with his."

"You're kidding me!" She attempted to drop to a somberer note. "When did he leave?"

"Half hour after you did."

"I'd better turn around."

"You'd better get here as fast as you can. If you show up at the Holiday, Ange'll never believe why. Besides I can use some help."

"You don't imagine those two nerds'll do anything!"

"Hurry. Don't stop for beer."

"Where's a place *open*?"

"We'll call from here."

Two fingers from Eljay, one stub—the rest lost to a weeded screw—from Ted. The narc, pouring his third Heineken in two hours, was saying, "You know there's one thing I like as much as I like an attractive woman. You know what that is?"

"I don't care to."

"You'd never guess."

"I hope that's right."

He checked around. "Cocaine," he said. "Co, caine. And when I look at you I understand every toot I've taken had you in it. You know, I seem to come across quite a few passes on the old railroad."

"In your line of work you mean."

That gave him pause. "I've got a lot of lines of work."

The Duke, in full sail after a trip to the john, cut in and swung her away from the bar. "Won't you slip out with me for a minute, sugar darling? It breaks Jesus's heart not to share. Here, just to see you through the next couple hours, turn these ugly faces to angels, turn this bullshit into something you can listen to. Sneak on back to the office, sneak right on back, sugar. I'll handle all aspects out here."

She jammed it back in his pocket, which wasn't easy to locate under his Mexican shirt, his new and only style, comfortable on the belly. The narc was watching and R.L. was watching.

I suppose I've always been an extravagant man, Del Benoit thought, listening for her or his footsteps in the hall, fishing the last cubes from the water. He blamed alcohol, which as scientists claimed and he could substantiate destroyed braincells. What they hadn't discovered was alcohol didn't kill the sex cells of the brain but tumorized them, inflated them.

Any one of those cars . . . footsteps; too far apart to be hers, with her center of gravity, too distinct for Ange. Intent on murder Ange would still shuffle.

He appreciated the effect of suspense on philosophy.

The candle on the back table melted a hole in Deucy's scallop bag and what seemed like gallons of milky juice ran onto the floor, mixing with spilled beer, slippery as snot. Mop in hand, Cammie answered the pay phone.

"God, Cammie, how badly of me do you think for this?"

"If you're still at the Holiday not very highly."

"This is my bed and I'm laying in it, next to it to be precise, slipping shells in my little pistol, ready to frap when Ange noses in the door."

"Catching some long *distance* tonight, aren't you, darling?" the Duke wanted to know.

"Are you clean? I mean it, are you?"

"Everything but my head, and that's where it's all happening."

"I wish."

Slue rushed past, meaning to plug in the deep fat for scallops, unaware Cammie had thrown the circuit breaker.

"You heard us, did you?" Eljay said.

"Riding *in*to Norfolk, *in*to Norfolk"—by Ange's calculation the trip had lasted a half hour overtime. The drizzle continued as the Holiday Inn hove into sight. If there was any flaw to the Lincoln it was that the wipers had picked up a hum, which didn't disturb them in their sweeping, their near vacuuming of droplets but nettled him. In the way he sometimes became paralyzed on a vacation, he worried over action outside of Water County, where the checks and balances of private violence protected you. City laws, with ethnics to control, overlooked human rage and error, washed these into the gutters to keep the streets passable. His friend from boyhood Malcolm Sedgwick was the best lawyer in Water but what if he clutched in a city courtroom? Ange was looking at seven years before parole, seven years without so much as touching a woman.

There was only one woman for him anyway, and no reason to predict his lying down and dying after the act, not with D.C., N.Y.C. and Montreal calling his name, or alias.

He parked on yellow lines by the entrance. He took three or four tokes to clear the brain. With a hundred-dollar bill he took a toot up each nostril to clear the muscles. A sort of electrical current dropped down his spine, electrical but liquid in that it pooled in his balls and sloshed as he got out and swung the door shut. In case he exited in a hurry he didn't lock. He didn't need to cut off the lights, which extinguished themselves after a passage of time. The night air, amazingly thin despite the rain, revealed seaweed and diesel both in one sharp scent.

Across acres of thin carpet he approached and approached the desk, thinking midway that it stood too high, only his head would clear. He was aware he trailed disturbance. Suddenly he had to raise his hands to brake his forward motion. The desk hit belt level, covered his gun pocket. The dropped ceiling and angled wood converged on the blotchy, clever face of the night clerk, like faces Ange recalled from Las Vegas.

"How you doing this evening," Ange said. "Could you please—I'm here to see Del Benoit, friend of mine. What room's he in anyway?" He fingered the rolled-up bill while with his deportment dismissing any difference between monied caller and graveyard shift employee. They were twins, equal princes of night.

"Sir, I'm not permitted to give out the information."

"I forgot to write it down, my own damn fault, as usual."

"We have instructions from the party."

He watched the clerk's hands as he notated cards and the clerk noticed he was watching his hands. They breathed each other, Ange through his iced nose breathing hairspray and a touch of Colombian, thinking the clerk breathed Lincoln heat and the same.

"You know who I'm talking about? Damn, I tell you, do they have freon running in this ceiling? I feel a draft."

"Sir, I understand this interior was stripped from an old wrecked rocketship discovered on Loft Mountain, in the Blue Ridge."

"I believe it. To tell you the truth I decorate with junk myself." He unrolled the bill.

"Please don't try that."

A few white flakes hit the blotter. "Squirrelly little sucker, legs like toothpicks, thick glasses, likes to mess with other men's wives."

The clerk twisted a turquoise ring on his fourth finger. "As I say, I can't give out the information. Obviously he forgot he asked a friend to call. You're free to look around, of course. Perhaps he'll be coming out of his room to go to an ice machine. There's one on the fourteenth floor, for example. Perhaps luck will bring you together."

Ange understood he was to take his money back. He headed for the elevators, a lineup of the straightest faces he'd ever seen. Yessir, one said. "With you in a second," Ange replied, having spotted the phone booths. Five times he got a busy signal before giving up on Cammie.

At the western end of the upper bridge, twenty miles shy of the Only Bar, Tish vowed never take their records off the jukebox. Ange hadn't changed records in so long anyway the new were sliding all over the office, cracking underfoot. Once in a blue moon Del'll mosey over and punch "Try As I Might" or "Leaving You's the Easiest Thing (Since Leaving Town)." She'll mosey back and select "Crazy" or "Torn Between Two Lovers" or "Let's Just Kiss and Say Good-bye." He'll drink another scotch, tell the crew he has business at the courthouse, and wander down to the dock phone, which lacks a booth. She'll answer in the office—not in the first couple calls, Cammie can take those. She'll answer, speaking to the wine man, asking time of delivery. She won't show. Next morning flowers will appear on the backbar. Next afternoon Del'll disappear to catch football practice at the school. She'll answer, whispering, hearing mostly static from his end. With the wind and salt in the wires, these conversations amounted to little more than reading lips over crystal radios.

Ange was locating the door by intuition, strolling up and down the hall waiting for one to communicate. From sitting in blinds together he knew the man's life, breath and sweat (part Ivory soap, part J&B). He'd eliminated two legs of the triangle and the inner wall by assuming Del would choose a view but not the sea—he had one of those from his secret pad up the beach. A view of melancholy, the parking lots, the church. He played the kids' game, You're getting hotter, You're burning up. Sooner or later a door would change from wood to skin to oilskin.

It was probably, but didn't matter, Acey Nunemaker who started chucking scallops. It might have been Slue, but all in all he'd been sitting fairly quietly for him. Whoever, they aimed at selected targets at first, Tobacco Ted, the Duke, R.L. at the middle table, all of whom took it all right, even R.L. It was definitely Acey who upended the bag, got everybody chucking, aiming they claimed for bottles, candles, caps, apologizing for misses. The radar lit up like Christmas. Still, tempers stayed unnaturally cool unnaturally long. The hit threw back, Acey and Slue back and forthed, people threw scallops, ate scallops raw, slipped and fell on scallops until the pile was exhausted and they had to pick them off the floor, which worsened by the second—juice, drinks, boot mud, rain under the door, the leak from the men's room—floated cigarette butts.

"You sorry sucker!" Chas yelled at nobody in particular. "I'll whip all your asses!"

It didn't matter who yelled. People heard what they wanted to from the mouth they wanted to.

"Shut your jellyfish, toadfish, all-mouth mouth!" the Duke yelled.

"Shut it!" Somebody else.

"Goddamn right, I'll shut it tighter than your asshole!" Somebody.

"Come get old Ted! Put Ted out of his misery!"

Cammie wasted no time turning the lights up and getting to the back before scallops hit Thad Colton's table and he and Slue were on their feet and primed.

"I've wanted a piece of you so long I can taste it." Thad's hair spread in fishhooks across his forehead.

"Just because you can't satisfy her after a real man, that's a hard road, ain't it boy?"

"Thad, please," Ruelle pleaded, cracking her rosy makeup with the effort.

"Ready to take this outside, you all?" Cammie said.

Sides chose up. Winslow and Eljay, who'd taken time to finish their twenty-first beers, were moving.

"Watch yourself, Cam, watch yourself," R.L. kept saying. He tried to stand in front of her but she wouldn't let him. She thought her two scraps of authority—that she was a woman and had the power to bar a person from the only actual bar in the county—might save things yet. Too, she counted on Slue to ease back finally, since against these odds to do so would count more as judgment than cowardice among the opinions that mattered. Not a man in the bar could be provoked to go against a black man, for example.

"She made her choice."

"And been regretting it ever since ain't you, Ru?"

The screen blipped the Duke slipping out the back. Teresa hung on Chas; he shook her off. R.L. shed his coat, rolled his sleeves.

Winslow and Eljay moved with the force, the listlessness of

naval cruisers. They flipped tables, kicked chairs to either side without fury, rather as a service, as if clearing for a dance.

Slue climbed up on his chair, Thad up on his upholstered pew, and the air between them changed.

"You been begging to have yourself mangled."

"Damn if that ain't so," said Eljay, whose statement carried as easily as over diesel engines.

Cammie put her left hand to Slue's beltbuckle, her right to Thad's. "Outside," she said. "Omie Marr's shut down every other, you want this bar shut too?"

"I reckon I had her more ways than you ever will," Slue said. Next his chair sloshed out from under, he collapsed, and although the motion was the reverse of attack it was motion itself that triggered Thad. The table see-sawed. Pitchers shattered into icicles. The jukebox swung out from the wall like a toy, smashed into something, a second later sprayed colored glass and choked dead on its own music. Suddenly you could hear the women around the edges cursing. Cammie crawled from under R.L., who'd thrown himself on top of her, and wedged between Thad and Slue. Neither one hit her—they froze at sight of her—but she went down, from a combination of Winslow and Eljay's vanguard and the footing.

When she came up she stopped everything.

Blood ran from her nose and from a gash in her hand—pulsed, didn't gush. She knew she was fine. Her nose bled all the time; the cut was clean, maybe off a wineglass. But working at speed her mind told her she ought to play this up. She rocked her head back so the blood spread over the lower half of her face; she raised her drenched hand in the pose of a prophet or Indian. "I don't mean the parking lot neither! I mean off this property completely!"

"Look at her—shame!"

"I don't care who I start on," R.L. gave notice.

Cammie shoved Slue to the door, slapping his chest, printing her cut hand, knowing he couldn't honorably resist.

"Outside'll go," Eljay said.

"I'm *turning* you inside out." Thad reached over Cammie to swing. She turned and beat on *his* chest.

"I'm waiting!" Slue said. "I guess me and Ange both settle tonight."

"Other side of the bridge!" Cammie yelled. "Beach Police!"

This surprised her: that Slue, dragging one moment the next was hopping out the door, with Acey, Deucy, Peasley, Chas and them bulling their way after him.

"Run, I'm on your tail!"

"Shut up, take care of this girl you injured," Ruelle said.

A ring of black smoke two feet in diameter wobbled in the door, firecrackers went off, and suddenly everybody inside knew what was happening. The Duke had backed his pickup to the door, was peeling out with Slue and the crew aboard.

"God*damn!*"

"This here's a island," Eljay reminded everyone. He and his partners were the only ones not to take off running for the fastest cars in the lot, Quinley's stoked-out Ranchero, Merle Maner's Bonneville.

Cecelia, Teresa and Alice clustered Ruelle, her hair sobbing around her head on the table, her orlon sweater sobbing on her back.

"You all too," Cammie said. She didn't mind showing no mercy. "Party's done."

"You're lightheaded," Alice said.

"I'm riding her over to the clinic," R.L. said, with the same frustration at missing the scuffle as at missing sex. The clinic, the only doctor, was in Grandy.

"You aren't riding me. Go to my house and wait."

"Cammie, damn, you are lightheaded with loss of blood."

"The blood's nearly clotted. I'll be at my house in fifteen minutes. Don't let the cat out. If you don't listen I'll be so long gone you won't ever see, you won't dream of me again."

"Your blouse is soaked red."

"I promise you I won't."

She just wanted to get the door locked and herself out of there before the Chief returned and before she discovered what had happened to the narc. She remembered to cut off the hot dog steamer. Adrenalin ceased filling in for the missing blood. Threading her way out in the dark, slop coming over the tops of her sneakers, she noticed a wooziness, which explained her feeling sorry for Tobacco Ted when she saw him peeing at the edge of the road, raising steam.

"Come on in, Ange, door's unlocked."

"Evening, Del. Wait, I'm—" Positive before, when the door had seemed to go concave at his touch, Ange now thought he was entering the wrong room. The face kept eluding him, kept twisting out of perspective. The details were right, Chinese brocade robe, hairless chest, grinning bifocals, the target pistol in the hand. But the man was too small and flat and distant. Ange pivoted, thinking what he was facing was a mirror but pivoted to a reproduction of boys driving geese through woods and stream. He turned back, his eyes undeceived him. They deceived him, he saw this salesman in town to work a stall at a bathroom fixtures show, hardly somebody who could threaten his very being, hardly somebody who bore that which gave a woman whatever he could not. "Who warned you? Cammie? Hell I don't blame her." He stood at a multiple angle to Del, the bed and the vanity mirror.

"You tell *me*," Del said.

He meant, You tell me if she's been here. If she'd been there Ange could have smelled her, sensed her the way when you're swimming a pocket of warmth will well up around your legs and chest. "She's in another room. I'll find her."

"Stop playing and give us the chance to prove ourselves."

If she'd set foot in that room the light from the polelamp would have changed. Ange gripped the gun so tightly it turned waxy. He could scrape curls of metal off it with his thumbnail. "It don't make much difference she doesn't happen to be in here at the moment, or yet."

"You know what I'm thinking about with you ready to blow my head off? The riddle of the sphinx. What has four legs in the morning, two at noon, three in the evening."

"I've made up my mind, my mind's on ice. It's your prerogative to bullshit a while but why don't you work on what's real? You can empty that little twenty-two and not affect my aim."

Del placed his pistol on the air conditioning unit. "Would you take a drink with me?"

"I guess that's your prerogative. Glad to." He sat on the end of the bed, lifted his gun out and balanced it on his knee, accepted the bottle.

"Simplicity, that's what the riddle is about, the heartbreaking simplicity of the human organism. Did you ever have a dog that didn't want to romp and misbehave and eat and sleep and chase bitches? I ain't nothing but a hound dog. We ain't nothing but hound dogs."

"I never had a dog that married, raised a child for ten years and built things. You never had a dog that bullshat."

"You never had a dog that didn't spend one night a week *howling* bullshit."

"You know what I'm thinking about after popping you? Riding to a brand new town, changing my name and everything, finding people who deal straight and don't deceive and help each other live." He stood the bottle on the mattress in perfect balance.

"I appreciate your allowing me time."

"I'm waiting for a backfire."

After Cammie had locked up, and loosened her hair, she headed straight for her van. When she was two strides from the door the narc, as she'd anticipated, walked out of the shed where they stored beer boxes.

"I've got a confession," he said, zipped up in his leather jacket.

"Make it to the seagulls. I don't enjoy standing in the rain."

"Two confessions. First, I'm a narcotics agent."

"Big surprise."

"Second confession, I want to spend some time with you, ride over to the beach, do a little coke, talk. Just talk. I won't try a single move."

"Let me pass." By the road Ted was warming his hands in his steam.

"Look, I can be heavy but I've got another side. Did you see the papers, five guys shot dead in Raleigh? That was my work in back of it. I'm out here mostly on a little r and r. The job doesn't have to be that important. We'll talk and I'll leave in the morning for Atlanta and that's it."

"Forget it."

"You sure you understand me? You're in the hotbox, baby."

She brushed past him, climbed in and pulled out of there. The narc, who was the one parked in front of Hallie's, pulled out behind her in his plain Plymouth without cutting his lights on.

She pushed to eighty, he stuck as if she was towing him across the bridge. Strut-strut-strut and boo-hoo-hoo, that was all for men, never a glimpse of middle ground and anytime you got beneath their talk all that really mattered was whether their woman fucked anybody else and would you fuck them. She mashed the accelerator, lit a Marlboro, planning her move a mile ahead. Her cut hand glued to the wheel.

The narc fell for it, drawing alongside and gesturing to the shoulder. Side by side they came up on Cuttlebone Junction, where the road split three ways, the bypass and beach roads north, the cape road south, and there was a cement divider. She floored the gas then just as the divider appeared hit the brakes. The narc peeled left but snaked past the divider safely. At one second he was beside her, at two seconds he'd vanished, at three seconds he was in front jamming *his* brakes; his brake lights lit. But now she had momentum and cut by him. He drew alongside again, started tapping the side of her vehicle with his. She jockeyed from gas to brakes but he stuck, tapping, keeping the metal of the van in a shiver. Further up the bypass he began to bang, cinderblocks hitting, booming in the interior. Sand streamed across the road in a low fog, hissed underneath. Then a thunderclap—her right wheel jogged off the pavement and once into sand burrowed. The van knotted around its right front wheel.

She tossed her cigarette into the waxmyrtles and stepped down, bringing the length of radiator hose R.L.'d intended to install. "You're really sick, man." She glanced back to appraise what damage she could in the backglow of the high beams— some paint, a few dents, not too bad.

"You can't afford to stay nasty. We know the whole thing, the whirlybirds flying in from the trawlboats, landing in Ange's daddy's marshland."

"You're sick. That man can't organize the walk-in cooler. He can't decide where to stack Budweiser. You're out of your tree listening to Omie Marr. Ange dumped paint on his face on Water Street, that's the story if you're interested."

"We're doing us a job on Ange and Tish both if you don't reconsider. Come on, let's whiff a little, forget this."

"*Screw* yourself in the nose! You can all screw yourself in the nose!" Her hair, which sponged up the rain, puffed out as she whipped the big, wire-wrapped hose so fast even he, with his experience, couldn't catch hold.

He didn't lose his cool; he protected his face, stayed cool. "Baby, you just screwed your friends."

"I don't have friends."

Also, assuming the van started, she didn't have anywhere to run next—she'd rather face the narc than R.L.—except back to the Only Bar.

Ange told him, "Your mouth keeps shifting from here to here to here. You can't hit ducks, you sorry fool, you can't hit when you talk. Your words slither out and plop." He pictured him all over her, tonguing the sweat she produced in pints. The room felt like a mausoleum already when the door yawned behind him, not a cop, not to release a cop but to give him space to move and fire in.

That the door was unlocked made Cammie wonder but she'd come to no conclusion by the time she was deep in the bar going for the phone, to call Del's room or the State Police, she didn't know anymore. She avoided overturned tables and chairs, she avoided bottles and pitchers, in the pitch blackness she avoided all obstacles until she ran full tilt into something: someone, flesh and arms so familiar yet scary she backed up her mind, retraced her last steps before deciding it was real and ought to be screamed at. Sweat, beer and perfume; rain, blood and shampoo—she and Tish collided, recoiled, collided and held on.

"Lord scare me to death," Tish said. Tugging Cammie's hair she clamped her closer.

"Don't."

"Where are you going? What happened? Why didn't you clean? What's all over this floor?"

"We have to call the Holiday Inn."

Bright blue bats winged one after another through the porthole in the door, followed by hammering.

"Open the damn door!" Omie Marr called.

"Fuck you it's open," Tish said. She cut the lights on.

Omie and the narc strode in like real jackboots, slack-jowled and oiled, wearing muscles off all the cops in the world, mouths stuffed with phrases of all the cops in the world. The narc carried an ax.

With them came Hallie Gaspar in her bathrobe, which her cats slept in. She looked her usual hurricane survivor warmed over, not that they had yanked her from bed. She did two things in life and they were both walk, by day, by night, barefoot, August sun or winter moon. "That's the sleazy bitch right yonder!" she said, Tish.

"I reckon you won't be opening tomorrow," Omie said.

"I reckon I will. Show me a warrant."

He handed it over, a document whose creases perforated. "This lady has reason to believe your husband stole twenty-eight antique telephone insulators from her front room. We're going to have to tear the place apart unless you lead us to them. Or is our report true Ange's on his way to Norfolk to a collector?"

"Shall I start with the office?" the narc asked, asked Cammie.

"Who cares?"

"I care, so do you," Tish said. "You're not doing nothing till I get Malcolm Sedgwick on the phone."

"Don't listen to that thing!"

"Dry up! More! The wind tips your barricades, Hallie!"

"You can leave now, Hallie, we're grateful to you," Omie said.

"I'm not occupied." She regarded Cammie with a kind of sympathy, conveying she held no brief against the simply young or simply drunk but against those who failed to perceive terrors.

"This lady could've saved you trouble," the narc said, and headed back.

"What does he mean? What did you do?" Tish asked.

"I didn't do anything." Instead of taking her slicker off she buttoned it to the neck, and stuck her hand in her pocket.

"I'll follow this prick, you call Malcolm."

"Yea, right." She sat down at a booth where somehow a smudgy glass of chablis stood upright among spillage, breakage and napkin wads, and tried not to let the words bother her. *What did you do?*

"You're staying patient," Omie instructed Tish. With two hundred pounds of body he blocked the way around the bar, with five pounds of right hand pinned the phone receiver.

"At eight in the morning you're out of a job. You'll go to California and not find a job, not security guard in K-mart."

"I believe your influential boyfriend'll be hog-tied on this rig."

"Your name'll be shit."

"Better than being," Hallie said.

Tish's temper was a very warped version of her true self, Cammie knew better than anyone. Yet when she tried to lift the tonearm off, it weighed too many tons. *What did you do? Why didn't you clean?* What had Tish and Ange done except for one thing let her paychecks fall five weeks in arrears through last Friday, less than they blew at Wintergreen, Virginia, on a weekend, not to mention bills out of her pocket like a hundred and forty dollars to the Miller man?

Furniture scuffed and screeched; drawers bounced on the floor; blows, chops reverberated through the walls; wood splintered.

"He's wild in there. Your last chance, Omie."

"Tell me about it."

"Cammie, will you run call *Malcolm*! Go to the dock phone, run call!"

More wood cracking—cedar shingles by the front as an automobile jumped the railroad-tie chock and hit the building, roared, died. R.L. walked in to the sight of Omie Marr and Tish Buthrell spitting at each other, smelly old Hallie twisting her toes in the muck, housewreckers ripping through the backbar and Cammie at a booth facing the door shaking in her coat.

Tish whirled. "R.L., run call Malcolm. We're staying all night, Cammie and I are staying in here all night."

Cammie reclined slightly, opened her eyes full, fluttered her lashes, shrugged, and sipped some wine.

Five times Del had tried to call Cammie without getting through. A quarter hour later he was dialing again when footsteps told him too late, partner, too damn late, the watch's done changed.

The room contracted. He felt something in his gullet or maybe solar plexus spring toward this man who entered hesitantly in shades and a stylish sportjacket that listed. He tasted situations in the back of his throat and this one tasted ripe and, strange to think, intellectual, intellectual in that it was scaly, clean and rang all the tastebuds at one lick.

He struggled to tell the truth but Ange, percolating like a porpoise, kept calling him down, forcing him to approach from every conceivable angle until he was picking through things he had no right to say to Tish's husband and any one of which might prove the triphammer. On the plane underneath this, philosophy flew to pieces.

The creases in Ange's cheeks plumbed to the vertical. Del sensed the rise in velocity in the room. Mentally he strapped himself to his chair. "She devours her mate after fucking," he said. "Were you aware of that? She fucks him, she eats him, every bristle of the poor bastard. He's had what he wanted, life goes on. She chomps him down, not giving a goddamn, stopping to test the web, test the breeze, make a few repairs. Climbs back finishes another leg—leaves one for him to hang with. Climbs back eats his ass. Doesn't occur to her, or him."

"You're telling me about disillusionment?"

"I'm telling you how simple life is."

Not solely as a result of the particular night, though it followed a long dry season, Cammie's reservoir had hit bottom. Tish and Ange irritated her sometimes but not being romantic she wasn't vengeful and would have given anything for her patience not to have run out tonight. At two A.M., at the instant R.L. had appeared, she'd simply gurgled dry. The pouring rain outside turned into a sandstorm. The wine turned to dust on reaching her stomach. She regretted its happening tonight but there was nothing left to tap. Her hand hurt and she might as well leave.

She got up, told R.L., "I said I'd meet you at the house."

For the second time in their lives Tish put her hands on her. "You'll stay with me, won't you?"

"Tish, I don't know, it wouldn't do any good."

"Listen to the child!" Hallie said.

"You can't leave me in this mess."

"Well I sort of have to. R.L. and I are getting up early to househunt."

She avoided whatever expression R.L. flashed, probably one so direct it hurt him. "Yea, we got to get some rest. I haven't slept in two weeks," he said.

"R.L., let her stay tonight."

The narc presented Omie with a roach of marijuana out of the ladies' room and a small crumpled square of plastic. They exchanged a glance remarkable only for its blankness.

"I'll come by in the morning, see how you're making out, okay?"

"God, you can't. I pledge we'll run this place really straight from here out."

"I know. I'll see you in the morning."

Outside, Cammie reiterated her demand that they meet at home but added he could wait in bed.

Ange wanted to parachute, horizontally, use the lobes of his brain in jellyfish propulsion over the lights of the city and on into the black across the sea and jet on.

"We have to learn from her," Del was saying.

Ange realized he'd let his attention wander plenty long enough for Del to have gone for his pistol. "Who do you mean," he asked, "Cammie?"

"Ange, I tell you."

It was the simplest thing, floats. Captain Del used cork or styrofoam floats or old Clorox containers that bobbed and dipped but generally rode high, painted black or orange or in the case of Clorox containers left white. Captain Ange favored glass like those Tish always looked for on the beach and which when Warren took swimming sank more than floated, rolled more than bobbed, swam, barely, in a saltwater the consistency of oil. Ange's lacked any excuse for visibility except what remained from reflecting the fast dead stars all night. He con-

sidered this room in the Holiday Inn to be the Atlantic, saw
blown away floats running down waves in darkness, grouping,
knocking, scattering when the next crest rose. Paying attention
wave by wave he saw them knocking each other to less and less
distance—somebody had put magnets in them, easy enough
in styrofoam, trickier in glass—the pause between knocks
growing shorter, the rebounds closing to a matter of inches
then fractions of an inch, the knocks becoming taps the speed
of a telegraph key then quicker until they were no more than
molecular palpitations. A last wave cleared, the magnets homed
to each other, the floats galvanized into a clump, a litter.

The ratcheting of a heavy-gauge door stories below vibrated
the entire building. A delivery van backfired. Del could have
buried him.

At Cuttlebone Junction Cammie turned south on the cape
road, drove the seven miles to the inlet, crossed the bridge and
drove nine miles south of there despite the front end jittering
and complaining. She eased onto a turn-off of hard sand which
she'd tested before, back to a spot where scrub hid her from the
road. She couldn't see the ocean, certainly didn't step out to.
All she'd find at night was ghost crabs, fish heads and wind; all
she found in the day was seaweed, fish heads and wind.

She cracked the window on the side away from the rain, took
off her shoes, peeled off her blouse and put on a sweatshirt and
after sliding into the sleeping bag in back undid her skirt. The
rain hit in tacks. The breeze shook her, fell to a lipless whistle,
like beer bottles with bad caps. For some reason she thought of
Tish at the beach, never willing to lie flat, ready to leave as soon
as they arrived—then wondering why she didn't tan—every
minute looking around, peering over her shoulder into the
dunes.

More often than in her bed Cammie slept at turnoffs. She did
fine in the cold, didn't mind waking up to sleet on the windshield. Some nights she even had the thought it would be all

right to marry R.L. if they slept in here. Not R.L., not breath in winter, nothing filled the van. Lying in the van made her feel suited to lying in herself, for this was what her heart was like, a metal box forty times the size of a human being and there was no one to help.

The Death
of the Vice Consul

Back in the old days they were in Istanbul looking for a ride south and for each other and for a gynecologist who could speak English. They were staying in a dollar hotel by the square by the Blue Mosque, in the old city. It was early spring. Snow had fallen the week before and though the snow was gone the cold remained, windy and gray. Even Ann didn't really understand Harlee's happiness and he could offer no explanation except his sparse, detached laughter. Her name was Carol but he called her Ann, short for Anthem, he said. They were broke. Still he had the stones, and if he could work a deal with Jack everything would smooth out. There was a chance for the trust to occur, for while in the Turkish navy Jack served time in Norfolk, Virginia, Harlee's hometown. In Norfolk they compared him to Jack in the nursery rhyme. Pull up a chair and have yourself a brew, Mr. Jack B. Nimble. Now he dressed mod, in bells and vests and floppy collars that didn't go with the coal-dust streets. And whether or not they were honorary whelps of the same bitch, as Harlee put it, he kept insisting on her as collateral. "You don't own people," he would explain, ignoring Jack's leer that revulsed Ann because his teeth were stainless steel. "She's not a tape player. You're trying to put something false into something true, and that's a sin, man. Ann is a real person, money isn't."

"You've known her since one week only. Why are you get nervous?" He shrugged and sprang his hand open, palm back, next to his face.

"Yunus, my brother, you've got a long way to go." His name probably was not Yunus. A leftist student from Technical University named Yunus had just been hanged on the Princes' Islands as part of martial law.

Beat-up sheepskin coat and beat-up dungarees and roughout boots gravitating toward him as he huddled on a parkbench in the Hippodrome under the stricken trees. Early morning and Saint Sophia, the wonder of the world, was humped in the mist and he was playing harp pretty badly to a Robert Johnson tune in his head. He'd just noticed that the color of the frost on the grass was exactly the sheeny gray of the pigeons. Now he noticed the paleness of her face and the flat brown of her shoelace hair. Because of the feel of the morning he thought, It's no surprise she's moving toward me. It was too early for her to be the French girl. "I've been trying to play for you," he said, smiling faintly with beat-up romance. "I think my reeds are chapped."

"Excuse me, but can you tell me where I sell my blood?" She asked this in the mocking tone for all worn-out questions. With the pretense of shivering she hunched into the coat.

"Like the sky itself."

"I prefer these days."

"You're stronger than that. Even I'm stronger than that." He told her what number bus to take from Sultanahmet and how to walk to the clinic from the bus stop. He said they made sure the apparatus was sterile, and that she was in luck because the payment had just gone up to ten dollars. This made it a third of what they paid in Kuwait, the highest, so he heard.

Two hours later he was having tea at an enameled table outside Yener's, the tiny cafe by the Cistern. The table was violet, the chair lime. The Cistern was used in the James Bond movie. She walked up and reported what had happened as if complaining about a certain municipal condition to the city manager. "The bitch nurse wouldn't let me. She said I was anemic."

Harlee had to laugh at that, a quiet savoring laugh until she slammed her bag against his face and he laughed a little harder, not in callousness but delight. His laughter was the purest sound of delight. It was warm and hollow together, like sheepbells clatting. "God," he said merrily. "God, where does one go from there? That's about it, isn't it?"

"That's about it." She could not believe doing that.

"Wellp." He was wearing layers of fifty-cent sweaters. He signalled for two more teas and asked her for a piece of paper. He printed this to put up:

Come 2 South Turkey And Mete Momma Univers.
Yellow Yellow Sun and Cleer Cleer Sea and
Delisius Bananas, And The Elaments of Are Other
Lives. Give Us a Ride And W'ell Give You Every
Thing Eles.

Harlee and Ann
Hotel Nurullah

Clouds of steam rose way out of proportion to the surface areas of the teas. "When we get down to that coast, everything's going to be okay, okay, every day."

"Sure, can't wait."

They went into the cafe, seven feet wide, smelling of propane and lamb fat, to post the notice. Harlee had three dollars and with seventy-five cents of it bought her a meal including two servings of spinach for the iron. She ate determinedly. Yet she would switch her fork to her right hand after cutting something and she'd let only her wrists rest on the table. When she finished she leaned back in a kind of careful drowsiness. She hadn't said anything since beginning and now didn't either. Somebody had hung up a painted pumpkin a half year ago. "You can pay me back when your blood count gets up," he said. "All this is just a suggestion."

He took a third of the stones down to the street and showed them to a fellow. "Turquoise and lapis lazuli. I'll sell them to you for twenty dollars. I paid ten in Teheran. In Austria you can sell them to a jeweler for maybe a hundred."

The fellow considered. "Let's talk about something else."

"Wes and I both bought these things," he told her, kneeling in the room, the stones in his hand like eggs in a nest. The light-bulb hurt her eyes to read or even look at anything. He had bloodstains down his village shirt with its formal collar. "I really loved that fellow. All he wanted was to marry a gypsy woman then not learn each other's languages." They could see their breaths. "You should have seen him. In a train station out in the boonies he'd spot some swaddled woman with a kid and step right up. She'd be scared to death. He'd be giving her this big grin. 'Please, please.' He'd just ease the kid out of her arms. He'd be tossing it around, Mom having cardiac arrest. They'd end up rolling on the floor like a bear and cub."

"He and the mother?"

It scares me the way people disappear from my life, she whispered into him, face down half over him. This was the only situation that she ever told him anything from inside in, when they held each other before falling to sleep from their ledge in the boisterous darkness.

As in delirium she heard voices in the hall and watched the light coming through the transom—he'd left. Try a little of this, Antalya. "No, no thanks," he joked. "I'm already about to rocket out of my skin. My soul's on one of those hairtrigger mechanisms they used to have on the radio. I was going down-stairs and I saw this patch of sunlight and just flew to it. The pilot ejected, the airplane crashed. It opened this gash here, bled like a mother. I need the opposite, I need some soul glue."

People's weights shifted on the boards and he opened the

door, trod quietly to the window and kept looking outside as he undressed. The view was only the alley lighted blue by other hotels and a beershop but he seemed to like it and the way he kept gazing induced in her a sheer hysteria.

Her words would come in a rush and be half incomprehensible and then she'd swoon into sleep. Her body on his felt like scattered sticks of firewood. People is people, he claimed. Nobody comes, nobody goes. These outsides, he'd say, slapping his thighs like a car dealer thumping a fender—these outsides, he couldn't finish, he had to laugh. I don't know where you are, she'd say. Right here, right here, the surface is me. I'm easier than an open book. I'm the Reader's Digest Condensed Version of an open book.

He looked at her earnestly as they sat cross-legged on the bunk in the mildewed room with the comic basin and faucet, and took hold of her thighs. His thorax was plated like a crocodile's or a Hershey bar. His neck looked too slender to support the bulk of his bearded head. His head, in fact, looked wider than his shoulders.

She didn't but he did love to be sitting sipping tea from a curvy glass listening to people tell their epics. Talking about trains and buses, about Bali, ripoffs, talking about albums not heard in a long time. The feel of jeans right out of the laundromat dryer! she rhapsodized one drunk moment then cut off as suddenly and thoroughly as the Tulip's jukebox. They interrogated us four days straight. Electric shock. Do you know what falaka is? There aren't any jobs for circuit designers in the states.

At times he'd notice a person grip his shoulder or come toward him with words or something for his hand and he'd hurry back to redeem his frozen bearing. Smoke is the last thing I need right now. I need a bucket of soul glue and a brush that'll get into all the corners.

She was having a clear sticky discharge and pain, no period in three months. I hate to tell you but you look more pregnant every day, he mused. Day by day I can almost see you changing from a young and tender thing to a brood sow. She thought this might mean her period was on the verge, and she had cramps off and on but nothing else except occasionally the dribbling turned pinkish. Your zits are a good sign, Harlee said, because when you're pregnant you get a wonderful complexion like Ivory soap. I've never had a wonderful complexion, she said. She'd never felt pregnant and didn't now but something most definitely was off.

He sold the watch for six dollars to a sweets seller. Six was good enough for the condition, which he explained by holding it up to his ear and shrugging. Broke. He walked over the Galata bridge and up the hill to the U.S. Consulate. The receptionist was Turkish and a real woman, wearing the Jackie Kennedy flip. She scratched a red fingernail down a list of doctors' names.

He returned and gave Ann the six plus the seven from the twenty. They took the bus back across the Golden Horn to the British hospital to the doctor listed there, who was a Turk speaking fair English. He examined her and did a pregnancy test. He explained she probably wasn't pregnant but did have an infection, prescribed antibiotics and told her to check back for the test results. The nurse added she would not improve so long as they stayed in a dollar hotel—they'd had to write its name on the form. The exam cost a little over three dollars, the test the same, the medicine exactly three for four days' supply. They felt reassured having spent time in such an environment.

He fixed a salad in a cookpot, cabbage, carrots, goat cheese, Haifa oranges, parsley, black olives, lemon juice, Jerusalem artichokes diced, raisins for iron. She dug in. They sat against her bed, used fingers. A fellow from Rockford, Illinois, in a fox coat joined them. He wanted to find a Turkish girlfriend, for the safety.

Today I found the most amazing hill, Harlee said. I took the ferry up the Bosphorus, you know, three cents, fake student card. We came around this bend and I saw this hillside in the distance with a village of little white houses up top it. It looked so nice up there, kind of adobe houses high on a hill above the river. So I got off at the next dock and started climbing. The whole city dropped away, filthy air, noise. I mean it was paths through sheep fields. Lower down the people's houses were made right out of the earth and rocks they stood on, same color and rocks so you couldn't tell there was a house there. Brush fences, chickens scratching, kids holding their mommas. I kept hiking but the village wasn't getting any nearer. It just clung up there, like white flies. Clouds piling up, wind icing up. The river dropped way down, the running lights on the boats came on. I was wondering how they'd be. They'd flip out to see me. Crowd around, make a big meal, the women'd serve. The men and I'd be drinking raki and talking like, you know, men, arms around each other. Pomegranates for dessert. So I kept climbing, way past the last of the other places. And it was pretty well dark by the time I came over the last hump and could see the village well enough to see it wasn't no village at all—not your usual idea of one. It was a cemetery. Christian, Greek Orthodox. The whole thing was some trick of the light. Nobody invited me in out of the rain, that's for sure.

Yea, a fellow said, knocking his pipe on the sole of his boot. Right.

I've got to talk with you seriously, he said, lying with the weight of her head like a ballpeen hammer on his bicep. I think I'm getting things figured out. For example, here's the way women are, even in this day and age. They have this fondness for the ghost elements. In a woman it's like old malaria. She loves the shadows like orphans. She will murder solitude. She will turn on the light in a twilight room, she will talk, she will get knocked up. Do you think this is true, or am I just my old Tennessee grandpa talking?

Not true. I never talk. And I always travel alone, alone, alone.

Almost always.

Over the long run, always.

You ball like it's going out of style.

Well that's motion, and motion is everything there is and everything there needs to be. Making love is the best kind of motion because you go so far, so far, you dissolve through all the burned-out dimensions at a zillion miles per second.

Night with a streetlamp shining through the window turning every picture in their eyes into black and white, and she asked him what he was going to do finally with his ridiculous words and empty laugh. Tell me more things about you, she said, so there won't be all this terrific silence.

No, it's time for you. I'm not the silence.

Do you want to be a troubadour?

You.

I did already, making love.

Me too.

We're different. Very.

Am I supposed to sing better songs than Stevie Wonder? I can't see me making better poems, movies, better anythings. I've hardly got time to appreciate others' gifts let alone try and add to the number. If this radiator doesn't start putting out we're going to catch pleurisy and expire.

You never think, even, There's a fine looking woman and I'd like to take her to my frozen bed? I mean I do, about males.

When I try being conscientious, things don't seem to come to me. I can be somebody else, I can scheme like a President but usually I don't because I want things to know they can come to me, don't have to be scared of me.

You're saying you don't mind being a victim.
I can tell lies both directions from sundown.

Feeling better since starting the antibiotics, Ann was becoming
excited about the trip south. Glad I didn't get around to selling
off my tent, she thought. They could use his horse blanket beneath, her down bag on top at night. Harlee had a Boy Scouts
of America rucksack and was meticulous about provisioning it.
He had a slew of containers—film canisters, Greek baggies,
a bandaid can, two cigar boxes, an old Phisohex bottle. She
watched him bag raisins with a rubber band, intent. He put
matches and a strip of striking surface into one of her pill bottles. He cut the light off and she watched him take off his jeans
and hang them over the chair. They rustled a little because by
now they were completely soft and unresisting. Sliding down
into place he said, Those damn Levis are two years old and still
going strong. Yours are perfection. On each hip there's this
worn area about the size of a handprint. They rock up and
down. They're like a ghost played touch football with you
there.
     Don't be that way.
     What way?
     I don't think you ought to sell your blood tomorrow.
     I'm like a cow, I've got to be milked or it hurts.

Look, he told Jack baby, let's forget this weasel stuff between
each other and just be human beings. I need some money because I and a friend need to go down to the Mediterranean
where it's comfy. I copped a hundred bucks in traveler's checks,
easy signature. I'm asking you to help. That's the whole story,
I'm asking you to help.
     Okay, my friend, I give you Turkish hospitality. Next time
maybe you are doing something for me.
     I will, man, believe me I will.
     Jack took him to a room where there was a fellow on the bed
picking pieces of helva off a chunk but not having any. He gave

him six plaques, seventy-five grams per. In the cellophane they were like greenish gingerbread. Harlee rolled some between his fingers and nibbled. No fooling around, right? You cleared me with your buddies, right?

I give Turkish hospitality. Maybe when you are going she is coming.

Fine business. Now I hear you.

He bundled them off in a photo novel and that evening lounging outside the Tulip Pudding Shop sold them for twenty dollars each. He even sold one to the French girl, who mocked him while he mocked himself. For his eighty dollars profit in dollars and marks he got a hundred forty in lira. In the morning he sold the second third of the stones to a jeweler in the Bazaar for thirty-five dollars in lira. They still had the hotel to pay. He tried not to cheat people who gave you a room without bugs and with a shower down the hall, when there was water, for a dollar, also their passports were in the safe. Ann went back to the hospital for a checkup and more antibiotics, and that came to seven. Still, Harlee cashing in a last pint of blood, they were one-fifty-some to the good, two months in open air. The only problem was the doctor had gotten the idea she might be pregnant after all. And they found themselves denying even five kurus to beggars.

But their good fortune continued when Ann met a woman who'd just left a convent she had entered before their births and was looking for a good time in a Volkswagen. Drinking beer upstairs at the Tulip, Ann and Harlee told her everything they'd heard about the south and she wanted to leave immediately, not wait for morning. "Let's get the hell out of this hellhole. Dawn tomorrow we'll be hitting the surf! I'm going to live like you guys the rest of my life—I've paid my dues. No plans, no responsibilities, no hangups."

"We take life as it comes," Ann said.

Harlee said, "Back in India they started shooting at Wes and I, Pakistan jets, rat-a-tat-tat right down the road. So right off he dove in a ditch. But I just had to stand there, watch it come. It

was like this big sewing machine loaded with explosives coming. Shot limbs out of the tree next to me. I mean they weren't
after us, they were just popping some cows. One night we were
sleeping and the air raid siren went off. Wes jumped up, got all
tangled up in his sleeping bag, zipper and all. 'Look, we gotta
get out of here, mate—the railroad station is the first thing they
hit!' But I was having the finest dream, I couldn't leave it. He
came back in the morning. 'Look, we can't keep heading north.
There's a damn war going on. Come along to Goa, why don't
you, and wait it out with me?' 'Those mountains are wailing
me north,' I said. 'It's not possible to deny them a chance at
me.' 'Well then so long, mate.' That was as good a time as any
to split, I guess, though I'd love to climb in a truck some day
and catch him sitting inside in his striped shirtsleeves rolling a
cigarette.

"So now it's me looking to the coast. One thing I believe,
Ann's insides are going to thaw out once she gets under the
sun. And if it is a kid, I could see having it. I've got the name of
a man who runs fishing boats. Fishing is a trade I know. When
I'm glued in I can do it."

The ex-nun poured a look over Ann. Then she said, "Let's
get the hell out of this hellhole now. Surf City here we come."

But it turned out nobody could stand steadily and a while
later Ann had an attack, and they agreed she should stay in
Istanbul until the doctor could tell her definitely what was
wrong. Rain drumming on the window, unknown people yelling in the alley, unknown words, and he perched beside her
hours without the slightest sign of boredom, without much
sign of anything.

I don't want a banana split, I mean it. The woman with the
Volkswagen missed banana splits and Budweiser from Chi-
cago, so she wanted to stop at the United States base at Kara-
mursel. Also her sister and brother-in-law and little nephew
were there. I will not eat an Army pig banana split!

They're just fellows who it never occurred to there was anything that wrong with it. You don't have to eat anything.

I won't ride in a car with a person who eats Army fascist pig banana splits and drinks fascist pig Budweisers. I'll puke if I have to look at a person who has an Army fascist pig banana split in her belly.

We'll talk her out of it. We'll persuade her she'll like something else. That's not a radiator, that's a damn stalagmite.

Where did you go? I can't get rid of you when I want to and vice versa.

Finally he said, I'm right here at the window. He tried out his pointless laugh, neither one thing nor the other, on listeners below. Right here. Let's get up at dawn and walk the streets of Istanbul for the last time. Fare thee well, mother of cities. Godspeed.

What if Jack had set you up? Talk about fatcats, he's one. You'd suit that purpose to a tee.

I would have written you from jail, asked you to seduce him.

My pleasure. And what. Talk.

When he fell asleep wire his teeth, wake him up, say you'll plug him into the socket unless he gets the big man on my case.

A most workable plan.

Maybe I should hypnotize you.

The only thing I speak under hypnosis is Farsi.

He patted his stomach, looked back at her. Do you feel too miserable to make love tonight with someone considerate? Looking at you I'd really like to. It might ease your innards.

I'm not so sure about that.

Do you like to make love with the light on or off?

Yes.

Ha ha yourself.

It doesn't matter to me. I don't have hangups, you know. You like for it to be off, don't you?

Inside you in the dark is like being inside a rolling stormcloud. He touched the light, stripped, and darted into bed. Cautiously, in a pent up way that however was not an effort they made love, his anklebones popping loudly at one point, and then weighted with darkness fell to sleep in the position that had become necessary to them after even so short a time. She woke once but couldn't figure out why. She woke again, had to piss, and managed to climb over—he'd turned away from her—without waking him, a surprise since he usually slept lightly. When she returned—from down the hall, by choice over the basin in the room—she bridged him again without disturbing his absolute stillness. In the morning he felt as cold as air though he was under three blankets with her. To the region between her nose and mouth he felt like something cold on the beach. She wept without thinking, another surprise. She didn't want to have to tell anybody. She tried but couldn't stay under the covers with him, so got up, whimpering, bumping into things. Somebody knocked and if they had entered would have caught her standing with one leg in one jeans leg unable to pair the act.

She went down, intending to walk and walk but once outside realized there was nothing to walk to, only the same ashiness closing in—sludge, buses, raw, sour, damaged other people—and no way of stopping the engine roaring in her head. She walked past as if hurrying somewhere that was specific and intense.

When she came back as she had to there were others, because the cleaning woman had used her passkey. The manager lit his cigarette with a lighter, the French girl braided her hair, the Vice Consul hulked by the bed. He kept his left hand in his suitcoat pocket, and he filled the room. The manager, of course stooped, laden-eyed, looking as if he'd just caught a whiff of something mildly distasteful yet bracing even for him. When Ann came in, he flicked his head with his cigarette going obliquely so that the Vice Consul saw. Ann looked at the Vice Consul, who was only a couple years out of college, and realized he was shaken. "I didn't know what to do," he said. He had yellow hair, a potbelly, no doubt had been in a fraternity back at Purdue or wherever. "This is the first time I've gotten here ahead of the ambulance. I felt for a pulse. Tried to move his head but it wouldn't go." His cigarette looked like a toothpick in his large blond face, the manager's like a cheroot in his. "Christ, I just can't understand it." He took a drag. "Okay, I'm sorry, I don't mean to sound self-righteous."

She felt boxed in between him and the French girl. The strange thing about her was that even though she wore plain cotton and a Kurdish vest and plastic sandals her face was always made up with the shadings of a magazine face.

"What can you tell me?"

Nothing.

The French girl said, "I explained."

"What did you explain?" Ann said.

"I knew his habits."

"Why did you say that?"

She shrugged at the Vice Consul. In a way she was a flirt. "They're all liars."

"What do you mean? What are you talking for? That's completely untrue. You're the liar."

"Twenty-one," the Vice Consul said. "Sorry, I apologize again. I don't mean to spout the establishment line or anything. I realize you don't relate anymore to considerations such as not letting each other die."

"He didn't die the way she's implying."

"Then what?" The manager began to show a little concern over the Vice Consul—what might the Americans in the embassy subbasement do to his hotel? "This young lady says she saw him last night."

"Well she's out of her head."

With elaborate patience the French girl said, "What difference does it make? It happened I saw him last night in the lavatory."

"You little bitch."

"Why should I lie? What difference does it make?"

"Shut up, just shut up!"

"Young man twenty-one doesn't die of natural causes," the Vice Consul said. "He might die of getting more than he bargained for from his associates." He picked Harlee's shirt up off

the floor, a strain, tossed it to her and she opened it and saw
how it had been ripped. He kept standing too close to Harlee.
"Notice any discoloration? You slept through. Got up this
morning and went about your business."

"You actually believe you've got everything figured out. You
make me sick, your whole fatcat attitude makes me puke."

"Okay, miss, here's what you do. You write the letter to his
family. You write, goddamnit. This one was going to be a bit
harder because this time he's not simply a form on top of my
desk. This time I got here ahead of the ambulance. But this one
you're going to write, huh? Go on, write."

"I'll be glad to. Give me the passport, I need the address. I'll
write and explain."

After he was satisfied he looked away. "No way. I have to do
the letter."

"Then I will too. Let me see the passport."

"No, honey, you won't write at all."

"What do you mean? You don't have any right to not let me!"

"Well, I have every right in the world, and it doesn't have
anything to do with being a government official—I know that's
meaningless as well as anybody. It has to do with this one simple fact: If Harry had been my friend he'd still be alive."

She spat but it didn't reach, only sprayed across his gut.
"Well so would you!" Wanting only to be walking and walking
in the ruined streets never disturbed by a word she understood
unless in anger or the ridicule of desire, still she knew what had
happened to him. She'd learned that much about him, the way
he would die. She went to the window to the place where the
shirt had fallen. Its scuff was there in the dust. She had the gift
to erase the presence of fools in the same room with her. Pigeon
gray rising faster and faster off the stones of the street, she had
the gift to light in her own eyes exactly what he'd seen at dawn,
exactly.

Sixty-Three Questions

Do you ever hear him complain?

What does he have to complain about?

So he has to get to work at 6:30 A.M. to put the corrections through. So all day long he handles Customer Service—Customer Service means the people calling in bitching. So the department manager abuses him to the point he's developed a half a dozen nervous tics. So Composing Room calls him any time of night, calls Sunday, his one day off, calls him when he's just about coaxed his wife into a nibble of intercourse.

"Look, Pete," says Composing Room for instance, "we got a Mercedes here, 1963 220-SE convert. Says five-five-oh. Can't be. I'm buying the fucking thing myself for five-five-oh."

Like a number of perfumed tissues going back into the container Lelia retreats, pulls her nightie down. As Pete tells it, the events preceding her two pregnancies have been shrouded in amnesia. Pete says, "Is it 43 or 46A, Rog? Is it Automobiles for Sale or Parts?"

"Christ, it's 46A. Oh, Christ. Pete. Pete. Peter. Pete, can you find it in your heart to forgive me?"

"Don't let it happen again, Rog."

"No way, Pete. No way. Sweet dreams."

At least the guy said his name more times in one conversation than Lelia has in a year. Sure, let's try a few sweet dreams.

Pete has concluded that hypertension and assorted other medical emergencies aren't making him senile early but crazy late.

So he spends his days in an officeful of broads—and a few
men—having hot flashes—the men too—and stabbing each
other in the backsides. So he's been doing the same thing for
thirty-eight years.

So his son Gerry beat up a cop last weekend at Michelle's
Lounge, not the best thing he could have done on probation.

Do you hear him complain?

It's two years to retirement. You don't hear him pray and you
don't hear him complain.

The hell you don't.

Isn't she perfection itself?

Even wearing her headset, even wired to her telephone and
her IBM Selectric, Pam Theroux can knock you out, can't she?
That complexion of hers could be his nineteen-year-old daughter Cindy's complexion, creamy, firm, tastefully tanned. And
she moves like a nineteen-year-old.

For the eight millionth time in his career Pete Joslin is scanning the double line of phone girls, ad-visors, at their desks—
girls!: if those are girls Pete is a choirboy. Limber, that's the key,
she's limber. The other broads moan if they have to turn around
to yell at the supervisor. Lelia can't open cans anymore.

The twinned desks remind you something of a language lab
and something of a prison visitation.

What is she, thirty-two, thirty-three? She's the type that just
gets better and better with the passage of time.

Rich voice. A-1 sense of humor. Charm. Dependable.

A good character. Most of her nights she spends home with
her son, who's in high school. Weekends she comes into the
office to make a little extra for his college.

She lives with her parents a few blocks down from Pete.

Now watch this. Stu Chandler, the Classified Advertising Manager, the guy they brought in from the *Cincinnati Enquirer* the

second time they passed over Pete, has been doing the same thing Pete has. Only he's in a position to follow through.

He calls her on the inside line. She presses her hold button, limberly removes her headset—the other ad-visors usually get theirs tangled in their hairdos—and strolls toward Pete's end of the office. During remodeling his and Stu's desks are separated by ten feet of distance and a screen.

She slips behind the screen.

Everybody listens. Pete listens, Vinnie the outside salesman, whose desk is also at this end, listens, and Louise Pacheco, Stu's secretary, listens.

Stu, who considers himself a young-looking forty-five but who looks like an old-looking fifty, oils up his voice and says, "Your lineage dropped last month, Miss Bell." Miss Bell is her phone name.

"I think everybody's did, Mr. Chandler. It's sort of the fall doldrums."

"I'm interested in *you*, Pamela, and when are you going to let me take you out?"

Stu, whose usual idea of romance is to pick up a teenage professional in his Mercedes then show the Polaroids to Pete over coffee the next morning, has been trying the four years Pam's worked here.

"Don't you ever give up? With a son in high school I can't run around. Besides I still have my boyfriend I see occasionally who's the extreme jealous type."

"Somehow I doubt he can offer what I can in every sense of the word."

They hear the clip-clop of the C.A.M.'s lighter. The lighter, the Rolex send glimmers onto the acoustic tile over his desk. "Pamela, you're an intelligent young woman, don't think I don't appreciate that. You're sensitive, cultivated. You are, if you'll permit me to observe, a lovely woman. You're an asset to our team not only in the relationship you establish with customers—and I might add the contracts you service weekly all want to steal you from me—but also in your rapport with the other gals you're a morale booster par excellence."

"You *do* listen in on our lines."

They hear Stu's chair roll forward. They hear him say, "As a matter of fact I do, because nothing boosts my morale like the tones of your voice. It's boosting at this moment."

"Aren't you forgetting to ask me about my insertion average?"

An open hand hits a walnut-veneered desk. "I respect you, Pamela. Goddamnit I respect you."

Pete's tics get the better of him, but this time it's by way of applause.

IN MEMORIAM
RAPOZA, Mrs. Angelina
1890   1953
God saw you getting tired
And a cure was not to be,
So He put His arms around you
And whispered, "Your empty chair"

She stops at his desk. She's wearing a lime-green sweater and slacks—jeans, but on her they look like slacks.

Isn't that an absolutely perfect figure she's got. Perfect proportions. You can keep your top-heavy broads. Pete Joslin will take a woman with a touch of class, a smack of elegance, any time of the day or night. A woman you want on your arm as much as in your bed.

"Have a seat, Pam." The words cue a full performance of his tics. First the hitch of the right arm. Second the left hand clutching the right side. Third the huff of the chest, accompanied by fourth the grimace as if electrodes are being applied, and followed by fifth the downward twist of the head. And finally the right hand brushing the hair, checking the waves.

"You're gonna retract that offer," she says. In her not noticing his discomfiture Pam manages to signal, There, There, we've all got our idiosyncrasies. With her he cares about the tics but doesn't care. You could say he cares for her sake, not his own.

"Another deadhead."

"Worse. Composing Room screwed up this man's In Memoriam for his wife and he's been putting it in for twenty years and we screwed it up last year too and he's cussing a blue streak and bawling. See, they took half of the first line of the one below."

"What can we do, reprint the paper? Give him a deadhead for Sunday, with a picture, with a border. For his ten eighty he gets the forty-three-dollar treatment. Explain to him the scanner has a few bugs."

"Gee I don't think that's gonna make him feel much better."

"How about a personal letter of apology from the publisher?"

"That might help."

"First he sends one to me."

"Yea? What for?" she asks, smiling as if she knows what for. She knows.

You can keep your top-heavy broads, you can keep every one of the other twenty-nine broads in the office including the three in their twenties, you can keep Teresa Mendoza, the supervisor, unless you happen to be equipped with a diamond bit, you can keep Stu Chandler's date who posed for *Playboy*, you can keep the publisher's mistress and you can keep the Virgin Mary.

Pete Joslin will take any time of the day or night an elegantly proportioned woman who knows how to present herself. He'll take somebody he can talk to.

Sally Myrick, wearing Cuff-ettes, has been watching. She's been watching him for fifteen years, ever since the night of the Christmas Party, 1958. The credit girls are the girls closest to Pete's desk, and the closest credit girl is Sally.

Her hair no longer has the appearance of hair; it has the appearance of a poinsettia.

She smiles in that way she has, like she's just been slapped.

"Check some credit, Sal, will you?"

Blink. Blink.

Cindy's on the line, telling Daddy about Gerry, whom Daddy doesn't really care to hear about. At one time his son had a magnificent future ahead of him—ask any of the guys in Sports—but he pissed it away.

"So he's at the A.C.I. At least he won't be lonely for friends. He clobbered a cop, Cindy."

How is it a man can have a daughter who is the picture of everything a daughter should be, considerate, a beautiful dresser, married to a guy who's already pulling eighteen, whose company wants to send him to Harvard Business at their expense, and a son who's a hoodlum? A car thief. (Can't he steal furs if he has to steal?)

A football standout in high school like the school had never seen. Twelve scholarship offers, all of which he thumbed his nose at.

Tell him, where did this giant criminal come from? From the two decentest, dullest, normalest-sized parents in the state of Rhode Island? From a mother who spends more time in conversation with the saints than with people?

"It's lucky this time didn't send your mother straight to Russell Boyle's."

Cindy tells Daddy that she and Kenneth—Kenneth can't stand diminutives and with his salary at his age Pete's willing to call him Mr. Kenneth—Cynthia and Kenneth are going bail.

Pete says, "You know where he's coming the minute he walks out. You'll kill your mother."

No, no, no. They talked to him. He was blubbering like a baby when they talked to him. He wants to go to electronics school. The cop knew him, knew he was on probation and just kept needling.

They couldn't leave Gerald in the Adult Correctional Institute, they just couldn't, Daddy.

"Oh yea?" Pete barks into the phone. He has a phone voice, a well-tuned instrument of authority and decisiveness, the Governor would envy. Tics and incipient diabetes don't show over the phone. "Listen, you try to place one more of those bait-and-switch apartment ads and it's not me you're talking to, it's Edwards and Angell you're talking to."

Class. Cheekbones. There are the faintest lines around her mouth, the faintest lines across her wide forehead. There is a kind of intentness to her face but that's taken care of by the absolutely feminine way she moves.

Pete wasn't so bad-looking at one time himself, and he still has the hair (now white, naturally) and the face. A strong face, a good straight nose, wavy hair, an instinct for clothes, and the body of a twitching toad.

"I don't care if my balls fly off in the process, once is all I ask with her," Stu confesses in the company cafeteria. The company cafeteria reminds you something of a locker room for robots and something of a prison visitation.

"Plain donut," Pete says, biting in. "I've got a physical."

"You wouldn't have believed the two last night I picked up at the Ming. Scout's honor, I had nothing in mind but a little Poo Poo Platter and an early night, but these two . . . a bonafide seventeen years old. One white, one black."

"No photos, Stu? Are you telling me you experienced something like this and didn't take photos?"

"No film. I wanted to hit Stop-and-Shop but I was afraid they'd bolt if they thought it over."

Morning after morning for seven goddamn years Pete has listened to Stu Chandler talk about his crotch. He's entertained the thought this is what the paper pays him for, to decompress Stu, get it out of his system so he can start thinking lineage again. If so, they're getting a bargain.

"I'll wager you a week's pay, mine against yours, I'll have company when I leave the Scanner Party next week, the finest company in the building with one of the finest pairs on the East Coast. Granted they don't walk off with prizes in the size competition but the exquisiteness of the form is what slays me, the exquisiteness. Take a look when you go back, on my time."

Pete's right arm gives a hitch; he clutches his left side. ("What's that windup, Pop?" his son once asked. "You trying out for the Butler Clinic Dodgers?") Pete says, "You're on."

Stu says, "Your lineage estimate was off today. We had to drop half a classification. Watch yourself."

That was the other thing the paper paid him for.

IN MEMORIAM
BRUSCA, Giuseppe
1910   1973
(Newsstand operator, corner
Broad and Benoit)

A bouquet of precious memories
Sprayed with a million tears,
Wishing God had spared you
If only for a few more beers.

"You know, sometimes I think Composing Room has it in for me."

Today she's wearing a sleeveless. Today there are approximately—Pete's a whiz at this; this is child's play compared to calculating lineage—three hundred and twenty-eight square inches of skin exposed that were not exposed yesterday. The additional heat, the additional scent make his head reel but calm his nerves. Cirrhosis of the heart kills slow.

Blink. Blink. The switchboard lady rolls her eyes as she shoves the call through.

Sure, he doesn't mind. Sure, he'll grab something at Paul's across the street. It's Thursday—breaded veal cutlet, "How about a beautiful breaded veal cutlet, Peter?" Under doctor's orders he has to sit there and peel away the breading with his knife and fork. You want to feel old? Sit in a diner and peel the breading off a breaded veal cutlet with your knife and fork.

He can't remember if he asked how she'd feel peeling a cutlet. He can't remember much with Pam's bare arm so close.

"Out of the seven nights in a week she goes to wakes five," he tells her. "During the day she decorates, at night she goes to wakes. They don't declare you officially dead in the state of Rhode Island until Lelia shows up at the wake."

"Forever complaining about your rotten life," Pam says.

"I'm not complaining. I don't lay out big bucks for clothes. Somber's always in."

Blink. Blink.

Composing Room wants the lineage for Christmas Week. No problem. The President's Council of Economic Advisors can't predict the prime interest rate for tomorrow; all Pete Joslin has to do is predict the state business cycle eight weeks in advance, to the line, and how about the Jewelry Supplement?

"Get back to you, Rog. Rog, can you get somebody to proof the In Memoriams before he hits the sauce? We've got broken-hearted elderly calling every morning. The girls don't need this."

When he hangs up Pam asks, "Did he promise?"

Pete stifles tics one and two but can't keep his chest from heaving, his face from grimacing or his right hand from brushing. "Does the Pope," he asks, "use a plastic rosary?"

"Miss Bell." Stu Chandler's voice vaults the screen, the pivot in the vocal cords oiled so that it sounds as much fatherly as peremptory. He's in charge, but with appreciation of an attractive woman's place in the world of Piña Coladas and Marimekko sheets.

"I traded in my Mercedes," they hear him tell her.

"Oh, couldn't keep up the payments?"

"I traded it on a new Mercedes." Clip. Clop.

"I thought they lasted forever."

"Pamela, goddamnit I respect you. Are you bringing your boyfriend to the Scanner Party?"

"He doesn't like public gatherings."

"May I request the pleasure of your company at my table?"

"Just you and me?"

"You must know how devoutly I wish that were the case.

Unfortunately we'll be chaperoned by your charming supervisor Teresa Mendoza, Roger Bassey from Composing Room and Peter Joslin, our redoubtable assistant manager, and his majestic wife Lelia. You'll have to keep your hands off me till later."

"Well as long as Mr. Joslin is there it ought to be the most entertaining seat in the place."

Would Pete consider this last remark compensation for seven years of kissing the Russian-leathered behind of one of the most egotistical martinets in two-bit business, for seven years of being ridden so hard his physiology had rebelled by making him look ridiculous, for the taking away of the one puny ambition he'd nursed his entire working life?

No way. But it came as close as anything these days.

IN MEMORIAM
VALANTE, Dante "Danny"
1952   1970
VETERAN'S DAY REMEMBRANCE
Oh Dear Son, how we miss you
Since from earth you've passed away,
And our hearts are aching sorely
As we think of you today.
I remember like this morning
When we last kissed you goodbye,
How the tears fell like a warning
From the doubt inside your eye,
How your footsteps took you quickly
From your Grape-Nuts in the bowl
To the war that thundered thickly
Where we had no right to go.
I tidy up your room each day
Like you were coming back,
I even press your shirts and don't
Let Daddy sell your car and don't
Let your sister give your golf shoes
To the Salvation Army either,
Without you there's such a lack.
Oh, they took you to fight the battle
Of a sickie President
Who should've been put in an insti-

Tution with a rattle
Who didn't care what lives were spent
As long as he and his band of sickie
Wimps stayed in power crushing poor
Honest people who go around all their
Lives saying Yessir, Yessir because
They're afraid to speak on account of
Having a slight accent. Next time
You see God tell Him to give an
Evildoer what's coming to him for a
Change, and light a candle in Heaven
For

> Your loving
> Ma

There seems to be a finger stabbing toward him from the walk-in counter.

Pam is strolling his way. He ignores the finger.

"I need a policy decision," she says, sitting casually, causing tics one, two, three, four, five, and six. Today she's wearing a yellow sweater that clings like the down on a baby chick. She's wearing a cotton skirt with flowers. Must be a warm day out there. Indian Summer. Her eyes are off-green enough that they never unsettle you, just attract you.

"Mrs. Mendoza says we can't run an In Memoriam like this. But gee, I feel she really gets her feelings across. I know how I'd take it if my son had been creamed in that damn war."

Too bad they weren't drafting ex-cons, Pete thinks. He looks the piece over. "Pam, you let one crackpot in and they're all gonna be having a field day."

"This lady isn't a crackpot. We're supposed to encourage customers to write their own verses. Isn't that a way to increase lineage?"

She smells like soap, like nothing but nice soap. The other broads swim in perfume up to their eyeliner, and all Pam smells like is nice, nice soap.

"Whatever you say, Pam. Run it. I've got two years to retirement, they can't touch me. Nobody else can figure lineage."

With flourishes—or tics—he initials the top of the scanner form.

"Let me see that copy," requests Stu Chandler, he and his jocular-concerned voice striding over from Vinnie's desk. Today he's wearing his Stetson. If *Playboy* were to dream up for their advertisers the reader they try hardest to attract, it would be fifty-year-old, $38,000-a-year, Chivas-drinking, strapped-for-alimony Stu Chandler in his Stetson. "Miss Bell," he says, "I'm disappointed in you."

"I'm disappointed in you. Why not print an honest one instead of one more hypocritical piece of crap from someone who's glad the person's out of their hair?"

Stu and the Stetson shake their heads. "That's the difficulty in having intelligence to the degree you see too many sides."

"Do you have a son?"

"I have sons from here to Spokane but what I'm saying, Pamela, is that although there may be a thousand sides there's only one side I let myself see, and that's the side of the *Providence Observer*. Comprendo?"

Pam and Pete share a moment. It is almost as sweet as something real.

Stu turns. "Credit check, please," he orders. "Sally, would you—forget it, Sal. Edith, will you check this dame's credit for me?"

In seconds Edith, who wears surgical gloves, pulls out a stack of overdues going back three years and dated for every date even remotely resembling a state holiday, a federal holiday, a church holiday or a saint's anniversary.

That's Stu Chandler all over. If he can't get what he wants the first way he's got another dozen up his pantsleg ready and waiting. "Peter, by the way," he adds, "don't be too sure you can't be touched."

Another moment. A crick of the mouth for Pam this time, electrodes for Pete from top to bottom, as dreams flood the broad daylight of the Classified Advertising Department.

Ever been to a Scanner Party?

At the Providence Biltmore?

Classified is having theirs there, having more or less success-
fully completed conversion from hot to cold type (or as Pete
puts it, from words made out of metal to words made out of
rubber cement).

"It hasn't been easy for you gals, don't think I don't appreciate that," Stu Chandler, Stetson-clad, remarks, rising to his
own occasion.

The chandelier glimmers like the afterglow of a stale cigar.
The drapery, which reminds you something of a funeral home
and something of upholstery off a 1950 Olds, fails to rustle.
Among the ad-visors you see not only jewelry inappropriate
for office wear but a couple of plunging necklines—not important that they were sewn up three inches at the last minute.

"You gals did your homework learning the codes for the
type, spacing, kills, extensions and the rest of the bullcrap, and
to my mind you picked it up faster than any class of college
grads, and goddamnit I sincerely mean that."

Applause smatters.

Asks one of the ones in their twenties, "Mr. Chandler, how
come if we're doing the work of stereotypers we don't get what
stereos get?"

"Got, darling, got. They're receiving in Newsprint now,"
Roger Bassey amends, reaching into his goblet. The atmosphere is sultry but he can't remove the turtleneck because he's
only got a teeshirt under, as he keeps explaining to Pam.

"Field that one, Stu," Pete says. He hitches, clutches, huffs,
twists and brushes. He knows damn well Stu's ready but says
it because Pam is beside him, seated between him and the
C.A.M., and tonight she's in a red knit.

Isn't she an absolute doll? It's one woman in ten thousand
who can wear a knit and a strand of gold and look like she
belongs at a jet-set gathering instead of an office party in the
antechamber of the ballroom of a bankrupt hotel. Let's face it,

if you thought her lovely under fluorescent tubes, can you imagine the effect of soft light, flickering?

"If it were up to me, you'd get your wages *plus* stereotyper's, because you don't deserve less, but my hands are tied," Stu says. Stu pauses. "By the union."

"Cheap shot," pipes Pam. With the cocktails, the wine and more cocktails, people are getting fairly loaded. A residue of Tacky Finger keeps glasses in hand.

"However I don't intend to talk all night. There's something else I'd prefer to do all night." Stu glances you know where. He possesses the talent to carry off the mistaken gesture with the composure of a priest saying mass. "So I hand over the speechifying to the guy who rides shotgun, the guy who passes every buck, our ever-popular Assistant Manager F. Peter Joslin."

Stu sits, leans, whispers to Pam and whispers and whispers, from the chest. "Insertion average," the listeners catch.

Holding the tics to one and two Pete begins, "Maybe the food wasn't anything you'd serve home on an off night." Short and sweet, Pete tells himself, for her, into whose ear Stu continues to drop words like an ice cube maker cubes. "I've been at the *Observer* thirty-eight years and this is the second time the company supplied the booze. The first was when Eisenhower got in. I checked the caps. The Cutty Sark is the genuine article. I say forget the food, forget the speeches, and let's take our wages out in booze while we've got the chance."

The response thaws the bursitis of the crystals overhead. Pam puts her hand on him and says, "You're on the way."

The combo, a guitarist and an organist equipped with rhythm ace, slide into "Please Release Me."

Stu takes Pam to take the floor. At their example nearly everybody gets up, the women without husbands, the majority, dancing with each other.

Stu's bushings—Teflon transplants, is Pete's theory—glide so smoothly his disregard of the beat becomes a moot point.

From her table Sally Myrick has been disregarding Pete. The poinsettia is flecked with gold tonight. You think Pete Joslin no longer has any power? In an officeful of the constantly sick, an outpatient clinic for the female troubled, Sally calls in more than the rest combined. And if not on her account, it's her husband with the heart of suet. Pete has saved her job fifteen years.

He transfers tics to the tableware and converses with Teresa Mendoza about scanner's difficulty picking up corrections, until Roger mutters for Teresa to dance.

You want to feel old? Sit at a banquet table alone with scotch and some tapioca.

So he goes to ask Sally, also alone, for a trot but crossing the room—when a moment hits the timid, it doesn't fool around—turns and cuts in on Stu.

"Peter, I'll grant you a dance, but take it easy. I'm worried about your health in every respect."

Pete wasn't such a bad dancer at one time. He convinces himself she is dancing closer with him than with Stu.

She says, "Thanks, the aftershave, not to mention the topic, was making me queasy."

"What are you drinking?"

"Scotch."

He draws her closer yet. He throws some English on his moves.

"That s. o. b.," she says. "Would you cross the line if we went out?"

"Only when you're not looking."

She doesn't just hang there, she embraces. "Why didn't your wife come?"

"Too upset over Gerry, who I told you is out. She was so upset she went to a wake. Had to call everybody she knew to find one. She figures she goes to enough wakes he'll come home begging for another chance to change. He's not gonna change. We went to the encounter sessions when he was at Milestone Manor, bare emotions like you wouldn't believe. He didn't *change*."

"Anything's possible in human nature," she says.

Isn't dancing a wonderful thing for mankind? How else

would an old hypertensive with the body of a lamp from Wool-
worth's get to press his front to the front of a woman like Pam
Theroux? Maybe on a crowded bus—for a second, not for minute after minute. You can feel everything, the breasts, the pel-
vis, the musculature of the back, the arms encircling, upper
arms without briskets. You can smell the soap. The dimmest
imagination gets the full picture.

"You don't know dancing from hypnotism," Stu remarks,
swinging past with his secretary. "You're putting her thighs to
sleep."

Pam snags a heel in the carpet. Pete can't brace them; in his
case merely to stand defies natural laws. Only Roger's arm at
the last second prevents their crumbling to the floor.

"Back to drinking," Pete suggests, but with his mind on what
he has glimpsed.

What he glimpsed was her little move to regain balance, the
marvelously feminine way her leg flicked up, to the *side*, the
line of her lifted calf. Isn't it worth staying alive to see something like that? Don't his worries vanish in a moment like that?
Isn't it simple to ignore the laughter? Isn't he getting drunk?

"You've been staring at the carpet two minutes," Pam points
out. "There's hope."

"I'm watching this instant replay of your leg."

"Oh yea? Tell me more, Mr. Joslin." She definitely, no wishful
thinking, she deliberately takes his arm.

With fresh drinks they lean against the doughy wall behind
the head table.

"You notice I'm wearing an open-collar, Pam? Do you know
this is the first time in thirty-eight years I've come to the company without a tie? I sleep in a tie. At eight-thirty I fall asleep in
the lounger watching TV. I wake up in suit and tie. It's a brand
new color set."

"Are you telling me you feel naked?"

Would Pam tease?

Stuck with Louise Pacheco, Stu keeps looking over. To block the line of sight Pam steps in front of Pete, facing him.

"I've never said this," she says, "but I admire you. I mean you have one of the most difficult lives but you keep your sense of humor. Mostly. You know, you should remember it's not what other people do to you, it's what you do to yourself."

A-1 character. Mint. A collector's item.

"Let me show you my sense of humor." Yes, he's a little high and, yes, he's a man who has just danced with Pam Theroux, but he feels like a kid down in Circulation.

The combo breaks. Except for a clique of Holy Ghosters, people are returning to drinks.

So watch this. Pete saunters back to the microphone, tests it with his wedding band and requests attention. "There's another question I think we should ask our manager," he announces. Stu turns, smooth as oil, cool as a daiquiri, which for once is exactly how Pete feels. Not a tic in sight. "We should ask Stuart who owns the company that prints the scanner forms, also who designed them so nobody else can print them."

Pete sees his words emerge in seventy-two-point type on a field of agate, but they don't seem to register on anyone else, except perhaps Sally. The crowd thinks Pete is only joking around with his boss. Stu and the Stetson softly shake their heads, and wave the combo back to business.

Like a monk from a fleeting materialization, Pete retreats from the microphone. Pam murmurs, "You *are* naughty. Say something about that In Memoriam, will you?"

"First more scotch."

No sooner does she leave for the powder room (The day Pam needs powder is the day they put Elizabeth Arden under contract to the Berkshires) than Stu ambles over to invite Pete to the hallway.

The door raps shut on tackheads. Stu, who as a rule stands too close when he talks, moves to spittle range. "Peter, you're a

spunky guy, and I'm hoping in the cold light of day I don't recall
your little prank, because it betrays a lack of the esprit de corps
I've tried to foster. You've been valuable, and I trust my Grape-
Nuts'll make me feel rosy, but if I have the hangover I think I'll
have, and if Pamela's exquisite tits aren't there to comfort me, I
may be forced to reconsider the contribution you're able to
bring to your position at your age. Half-pension pains me. I
recommend you bundle home. You might catch Lelia in a pray-
ing mood."

Pam comes into the hall, hesitantly, only her eyes at full tilt.

"Miss Bell," says Stu, "may I have the pleasure?"

"I'm leaving. My son is picking me up."

"Don't break my heart. Call him, tell him you've got a ride."

"He's on the way. I come in early tomorrow for the kills."

Pete doesn't hang around. He heads for the doors he hears
opening and closing with the mucky rattle of a giant worn-out
ventricle. The scotch goes sour in his blood. His life bears the
sensation of a small box plunging down a very wide-diameter
drain.

The area around the Biltmore is one of those sections where
the articles on the pavement often cannot be recognized. Over
these and across the street in front of the *Observer* and around
the corner and across the street in back, eight lanes and three
parking lanes without a moving vehicle, he makes his way. The
pressroom rumbles and clacks. The air buzzes with the name
Pamela Theroux.

The car is at the far corner of the lot, out of range of the dents
Lelia fears.

Dents. Doesn't she make you weep? If only there was a car
bearing down; if only there was a mugger. There's nothing out
here but macadam sealed to the ground, lined, lighted. He's
showing up for his son's game the wrong night. The lot light
emits paste-ups of Pam's lifted calf.

He runs data through his personal scanner. This is Pete Joslin. This is Peter Joslin at the *Observer* in regards to the ad you

placed for your system for beating polygraphs, you lousy weasel. This is Pete Joslin making a beeline, the beeline of a gassed
bee, over acres of streets and lots. He's just left the Biltmore,
where he screwed himself so deep he has to look up to see
sewers. Pam!

He stops with the data and simply trudges, on the stubby
legs he passed on to neither son nor daughter.

This is Pete Joslin hanging by fingertips to the roof of a 1972
Ford LTD while denting the door with the key. Sure, he's drunk
enough to drive his wife to comfortable widowhood tonight,
like the admirable man Pam (Pam) believes him to be.

He wipes his hands across the wet roof and when he smells
them they smell like urine. The lot runs along the railroad em-
bankment. When the ten-fifty to Penn Station rolled by, he reasons, somebody was using the john.

He never went to the horses or the whores. Being intelligent
he sinned his life away without sinning. He is a kid again,
doing what he did again, ruining, this time without decades of
humiliation to look forward to.

And he taught his son how, and maybe taught his wife how.

Pam. Pam. Pamela, you made him do this, made him chuck
the one scrap of hope he had left . . . Pam, you stunning Selectric typist, you smooth-voiced headset wearer, you stopper
of the Section D run, you limber walker between desks, you
mother of a non-criminal, you understander of the soul . . .
You impeccable you.

Goddamnit he doesn't care. Dancing with you was worth the
ashheap.

IN MEMORIAM
JOSLIN, F. Peter "Spunky"
1910   1973
Dear Pop, hey aren't you a sight
You're nearly as bad as me,
Blown out in the nasty night,
Your face covered with pee.

Aw, that ain't pee and you ain't
You
Tho the memory lingers on,
You're still a fruit: Bananas
Over some young broad who took you
For a good long one
When all your rides were gone.
You gonna slobber over the angels?
Asks
                        Your horselaughing son,
                                    Gerry

Her footsteps, recognizable even at double time, dawn on
him.

Into his ear she observes, "At least I can say I was there."

The voice encourages him to fumble more.

"I told the s.o.b. I was coming out to send my son home.
Actually I'm sure he's parking down at Conimicut with his new
girl. Would it be too much to ask you to take me?"

"Does the Pope," Peter inquires, "puke in a trash can?"

"That's what I like about you, Mr. Joslin." She opens the
door, helps him in, cooperative half, bad half, and lets herself
in the other side. None of this are you sure you can drive bit
coming out of *her* cheekbones.

Starting, he feels very drunk and dead sober.

As they pull out and another car pulls in, a Pontiac with "desperate, posted overseas" written all over it, Pam says, "Whoops,
there's my son."

Pete and the kid, who looks like his mother but has wavy hair
he combs straight, roll their windows down.

"Perfect timing," Pam tells the kid. She's leaning across, her
head on Pete's chest, and her hair smells like nothing but nice
shampoo and contains nothing but hair, no gold flakes. "Mr.
Joslin is taking me, so why don't you keep the car? Be home by
one-thirty, that's all."

"Aw, that'll be terrific." He tests the idea on his girl, who makes a whoop-de-doo with her cigarette.

Pete tells himself nothing funny occurred to the kid seeing Mom with the old geezer. He reminds himself it shouldn't be occurring to him either.

He cuts—he sloshes, handling the car like a leaky cabin cruiser—across town toward Allens Avenue, which runs into his and Pam's street, Narragansett, further down. They surge past the hygienic syringe and catheter plant. Clearing the I-195 overpass Pete says, "You know what the brightest spot in life has been, the absolute pinnacle? Seeing you in the office."

"Get out."

"Knowing I'd see you in that hole kept me alive, to the extent I am. It's like a connoisseur. I'm a guy that to survive needs to see this particular work of art every day. It's like Gerry on the pills. I admire your looks, I admire your nature, maybe we talk, and I'm good for another twenty-four hours. That's the worst of getting canned, not seeing you."

He maneuvers along blocks that composed not a bad neighborhood at one time. He slows to see if Lelia's up. Drawn to the curb, he notices the living room light go off. "I want to tell her not to worry herself sick over my welfare." What he really wants to do is pick up a fifth.

From the walk, bricks turning to mulch underfoot, he sees a light open in Cindy's old room. Unusual, but not the first time for Lelia to be communing with the absent. From the portico he smells the house; smells like floorwax and an ulcer diet. But something else too, something out of the ordinary. Motor oil?

Definitely trick or treat night tonight. Before Pete can turn the key the lights are back on and the door is swung open—by his son, grinning, the large Peter Lorre of the hoodlums. "Dropped by for a few things, Pop. I'm moving into this house with a couple of the guys. The state pays rent." As a criminal Gerry gets more state aid than the Little Sisters of the Poor.

"Bastard," Pete says, going first, second, third, and so on. He recognizes Gerry's look.

Gerry waves down the remark, returns to the dining room with his usual tremendous grace, wearing bowling shoes and four yards of denim. In his hand nestles Pete's calculator for lineage. The TV console, a week out of the box, waits by the side door.

"Pop," he says. His voice oozes with compassion. "Pop, just to tide me over. Hey, how about can I fix you another drink?" He stoops and sweeps bottles out of the buffet onto the floor. He rolls them back and forth to check the labels.

That's what he smelled, his son. Gerry always smells like he's been working on cars although he never works on cars; he only steals them. "Hey, I don't appreciate your changing locks on me," he mentions as he uncorks the scotch. "You're gonna slow me down."

Pete grabs for the bottle but can't, in mid-tic of a new series, hold onto it. The scotch spins and glucks, dousing the Chinese carpet under the table. Pete says, "I'm gonna press the god-damn charges this time."

Gerry has to laugh, quietly. Isn't it a sign of something when everybody chuckles and murmurs as they screw you over?

"Mom's not gonna let you press no charges, get out of here."

Pete hears tires in the driveway but doesn't see lights.

"Pop, could you stand aside?" With a sigh Gerry smothers up his father in oil and sweat, carts him to the door, stands him on the stoop, says, "Don't worry, I know my way out, don't I?" and throws the deadbolt.

"Every charge in the book!"

Gerry makes a face out the bay window, but when he sees Pam coming up the walk reopens the door. "I gotta hand it to you, Pop. Press on me, I press on you." The door almost comes off its hinges as he and Pam give each other the once-over. "Here, I present you the calculator back as a token of my shock." He offers it, she accepts. His mellifluous tone now, the deejay of the hoodlums. "Busy tomorrow night? I mean if my old man doesn't wear you out? You work at the paper?"

"Don't bother," Pam says.

"Oh, but I shall." Tinkling fingertips, he eases the door shut like the lid of a lacquer box.

"You don't have the guts to rob strangers!"

"Dry it up, Mr. Joslin," Pam says. "Complain in the car."

Gerry cracks the door for another flash of meanness. Then all gentility he mutters, "Take care of my Pop, huh?" He closes up, pulls the curtains to.

Pam nods her shoulder to indicate the guy by the van in the drive. "Let's go for a nightcap. They'll be gone by the time you get back."

With even less control of the rudder than before, Pete plows into the wide wash of Narragansett Boulevard, trees on the banks. "You've seen it firsthand, my wife out at the wakes all night while my son burglarizes the place."

"Poor dear." She rubs his neck with fingers they never dreamed of at Swedish Sauna. "Gee, he's kind of attractive too. He has your features. You should drop by his house to talk."

Pete slides the calculator under the seat. He remembers forgetting his overcoat at the Biltmore and kisses it goodbye along with the TV, minimum. Would Lelia really believe Gerry borrowed the thing to watch Sunrise Semester?

So his driving turns the car into a Chris Craft with a bad screw, leaky seams and a sticky throttle. The point is he doesn't give her the opportunity to retract about the nightcap.

The bar of the Cranston Hilton reminds you something of a modern church and something of Howard Johnson's with the lights off. The waitress brings scotches. The bartender returns to his phone call, which has something to do with Vegas and something to do with Manton Avenue.

As for their fellow drinkers, if you ever wondered who answers ads such as

MARKETING: Dissatisfied? Growing concern
seeks aggressive self-starter, veteran, college,
married, own car, track record for proven ter-
ritory. Only high type need apply, in other
words fast talker with board up ass and ice-
water in veins to trample mother on way to
38K potential,

drop by the Hilton one night.

"Maybe I wouldn't mention this without the booze," Pete
says, "but you've had knocks yourself which you never delve
into. I tend to monopolize. I'll never get to know you, understand you, but you prove to me there are beautiful humans out
there. Personally I blew life, but I'm in the species. Believe me,
I wouldn't think twice about being out on my butt if it wasn't
for you."

There seems to be a finger jabbing from the bar.

Pam draws her stirrer through her lips while looking at him
very alertly. She always looks alert to every word. "I really am
gonna quit if he doesn't let that In Memoriam run."

"You'll never get the money elsewhere. Pam, could I take
your hand?"

She cautions, "As long as my boyfriend doesn't walk in. He's
jealous of anybody. He's sort of in the mafia, you know."

"Holy Christ," Pete says, and starts laughing. A car runs on
gas, laughs run on booze. On booze Pete laughs like a healthy
man. "Holy Christ, would that be a fitting wrap-up to the evening. Look, could he arrange things for a reasonable fee?
Lelia'd get the double indemnity. She'd get the full pension. I
can't face empty days without you."

"Joslin, I see you there!" says the finger's voice, Marty Pedrosa. "What do you mean I can't run ads without a license? I
ain't a dealer! It happens I'm easily dissatisfied with an automobile."

Pete ignores. Scanner, he asks you, is this the situation? Is
this Pete Joslin holding hands with the sheer loveliest woman
he's ever seen in his life, including in the movies?

Isn't this the situation, that he has nothing more to lose? She's seen him at his worst—in the hall with Stu, at the house with Gerry—and she's holding hands, pressing back, staying with him with her eyes. There's such openness to her look, such wit. She'll excuse a lapse.

The overgrown votive candle on their table shoots flames, the wise-ass before having stuck a book of matches in it. Pam lids it with the ashtray.

Pete says, "Hell, I'm taking a room here tonight, forget going home to hysteria. Take a room, sleep in, forget calling in the goddamn lineage too."

"I don't like the sound of this," Pam says. "You're not planning to do yourself in, are you?" She's giving him one of the first double expressions he's seen on her, wide eyes with a cast to them. Or were all her expressions double?

He hitches, clutches, heaves, contorts and smooths. "I'll lay out two days, fuck 'em. No lineage, nothing."

The wide eyes make no bones about narrowing to the exact calibre of suspicion. Still they also seem to be listening to jokes in the lounge. "Are you trying to seduce me?" He remembers her using the tone with one of the contract accounts.

"If I did, could I tell Stu?"

"No way."

"I take a solemn vow not to breathe a word to Stu." The situation has left him at the starting gate. What rental agency outfitted him with this mouth, and when did they slip it on, and when will the enormous charge be added to his Bank-Americard?

"If you aren't a hot ticket. I mean, do you really want to?"

"Does Bishop Gellineau take wine with meals?"

"I figured you all along for a romantic, in a different way." She had to figure. "I'd almost do it out of spite, combined with other reasons." Another double or maybe triple expression. The eyebrows rise. The lower lip crimps. The upper lip makes a hood. "It'd be extremely interesting, you can say that. I do have a weakness for wavy hair. I've never tried white."

At this juncture the agency repossesses his mouth, and once more Pete falls speechless in the atmosphere of ambition. In the way scotch has of illuminating old sayings, Scottish or not, it now causes Pete to understand what it means to Lose Your Tongue.

"I'm not making promises, but let's get out of here before my boyfriend walks in at this hour, okay?"

Never mind the rhetorical questions.

She pats his cheek. His tongue regrows. As carefully as a waiter he carries it to the bar and asks, in an approximation of his phone voice, for wine. The bartender's eyes remind him of his son's.

Marty Pedrosa keeps his mouth shut. Even along this bar, on the shoulders of people reincarnated once too often by computer error, heads waver.

A room in nylon and pressed petroleum, overlooking the parking lot, underlooking the strictly non-neon sign. Pete in his open-collar pours wine. They sit on the same bed, he looking at her knees. Her knees look like eggs over, in butter.

"Just pretend I'm your wife," she says, slipping off her shoes. "What's it like with her?"

"Not like this." In order to untie his shoes Pete exhales. "There were always more days when we couldn't than could. She scheduled our sex life according to the Gregorian calendar."

The moment he puts his arm around her, his left arm, she becomes the conduit for a violent spasm.

"You know, I bet your wife is secretly as horny as you."

"Our class didn't marry for sex, the meaning of life. I don't know what we married for, unless to overtake the Protestants."

He adds in case she's wondering, "I've got the psychological problems, I've got physical problems qualifying me for the Smithsonian, but for some goddamn reason it never quit. I don't consider it part of myself. I consider it a friend. I talk to the damn thing."

"You should try talking to Lelia."

Out of a file as thick as overdues at the credit desk, the question that punches in is, What would Stu Chandler do at this point? In front of the piece of furniture with the mirror Pete, pretending he's at the beach, strips to undershorts. Since he imagines Stu wouldn't leave his clothes over the chair, he takes them to hangers.

If the meek are ever to inherit, now's the time for the first deed to change hands, now as he turns back to her.

He doesn't look directly to see if she looks, but he notices she is adjusting the lamp. She's speaking.

"Pam, could you speak up?"

When he thinks he sees her pull her dress off he closes the distance.

"I'm modest," she mouths.

"I can't hear with the hypertension in my ears!"

By following her suggestion, pretending she's his wife, he reaches both his arms around her—around one thousand eight hundred and seventy-eight square, bare inches—and kisses. So now he's pretending that he is Stu Chandler kissing Pete Joslin's wife Lelia, at the beach. So at least a kiss happens, a kiss that opens and opens. He'd forgotten a kiss could have these additional openings. (Forgotten.)

She presses her hands to his belly, like a pleasant truss. She stops kissing, forms words.

"Can't hear," he moans.

His friend, however, accustomed to blood pressure, moles up through the elastic. Meanwhile his friend's friend, Pete himself, concentrates on caressing, because you caress with hands and his hands remain a strong point. For fifteen years he and Sally have shared Jergens, buying alternate bottles.

Each takes off his or her underpants and goes to the mattress.

Now, there's light from the sign outside. And it's sufficient for Pete, assailed by galloping glaucoma, to perceive what he could no more have dreamed of seeing than pitch for the Red Sox, the ultimate consolation of survival, the vision beyond vision.

Let's put it this way. If Michelangelo were to take out an ad in Class 90, Service Directory, reading

> CEILINGS PAINTED: Any subject, style, no
> job too big, reasonable, refs, call after 6

and the number, the relationship between that two-line ad in the *Providence Observer* and the Sistine would suggest the relationship between the sum of Pete Joslin's speculations and the reality of Pam Theroux in the raw.

Deaf, dumb and increasingly blind Pete waits for the blow, for referees to bust down the door, whistles blaring, for a hurricane to flatten the hotel, for his son to jump out of the closet with a flashgun, for the scotch to wear off.

She whispers something his eardrum decodes from the braille on the tip of her tongue. He and his friend weep a tear or two at the words, "Everything you needed since you knew me."

The unthinkable continues, right up to the phase where at last he believes there's no stopping, which is where she stops. He thinks she's stopping, when she pushes him to the side and raises a finger as if to say: You can look but you better not touch.

She taps his temple. His sight clears remarkably and catches every detail as she does to herself what he thought he was going to do, what he thought he needed to do.

He was wrong. She's right.

She shoots the works, front and back, top and bottom in a slow motion so slow it makes instant replay look like old-time movies; a ballerina in jello. Talk about limber.

And then she gives him one of her eight-level gazes and extends her hand toward his personal hold button. Closer. Closer.

And then?

Well, what can you say?

You can't say the plate glass window flew out of its frame sucking the curtains and pole lamp with it.

Nor can you say the room was transported to another sphere where life is ever slow and vibrant and at the same time gravity-less.

Nor can you say the sirens on Narragansett Boulevard started to harmonize Mozart.

Nor at the end could you have numbered any fewer than two distinct souls in the room (also the original count on the towels and pillows).

But you can say the traffic jams of blood in various parts of Pete's body caused no acute medical problems.

And you can say that at first he and she smelled like the party and then they smelled like flesh and finally there was the faintest whiff of sweat—wrung by remote control, granted, but wrung.

And you can say she wasn't so composed herself when she left. She drew him a hot bath, without his asking. But she forgot to look out the window and check the lot for her boyfriend's car.

So he calls in lineage.

(He woke and found himself doodling figures on her back.)

He calls it in forty-five minutes past deadline.

He doesn't pull into the parking lot until half past ten.

This is Pete Joslin locking his car and starting for the *Observer* building on an overcast yet rich with moisture morning. His cooperative half takes its time while his bad half idly assesses the prospects—idly, to emphasize, truly not caring which way events will turn. Let them can him. He and Lelia'll move to North Carolina, where she flies every year anyway for antiques. In the South you live on half what you do here.

(Wrapped around the calculator, labeled F.Y.I. the note read, "Before I left he warned me if I didn't go out with him he'd come down on you. This is to let you know I'm not going out. Miss Bell.")

Among the possibilities he weighs for parting shot is sneaking that In Memoriam in.

He wonders if they'll sleep together again, or however you refer to their activity.

He wonders about her boyfriend. Right here, right now as he steps off the curb a car may screech to a halt releasing a couple of goons—Gerry and a buddy, for instance—to pulverize his sockets.

You won't hear a whimper. In fact wouldn't that be a giveaway, a goddamn steal at sixty-three?

Borrowing

An hour and a half after sunrise I was down from taking pictures and my parents were in Virginia cloth finishing breakfast. They'd finished. They were having additional coffee, in boiling-point fractions of cups. My mother was wearing an apple-green dress of Virginia cloth with a pleated front, my father a beige shirt (and bowtie). He was dunking anise biscuits his sister sent.

By Virginia cloth I mean the fabric much clothing is made of in our state. It's a tightly woven cotton, very thin, very pliant. You imagine that after being loomed it's farmed out to people who hammer it, wash it in lye soap and hang it in the weather. It never appears in bright colors. Yet in the clear air among the greens and blues it suits. My mother's dresses and blouses gave the effect of leaves on a stream.

"Such ambition," I said, though they were always up at six. I set my camera stuff down on the mat with the garden shoes. I was nineteen, home from college for a few days in October. "The appointment's not till nine-thirty, is it?" My father and I were to go ask the bank for money for second semester. Out of the classroom now, he could take a morning off. My mother didn't work outside the home except at church, free.

She looked up as if licking a stamp. Her hair was still quite black. When it turned gray it would turn all at once, not one strand at a time. She kept it a little too short because her beautician told her that like pruning a bush this thickened it. "Do you want your breakfast first or your shower?"

"Yea, son, sit down, have some breakfast." My father, one of the last of the great eaters, always fit, crunched into another biscuit. He sonned his son and daughter-of-mined his daughter. She, Nan, one of the last of the great sleepers, was upstairs in my old bed, not due for hours. "We even have Earl Grey tea."

Abashed, my mother looked out the window, where the branches of the maple tree, my exact contemporary, crowded the porch.

"Yea," he huffed. He reached into the pocket of his sportjacket, which he'd hung, foursquare, over his chair. He shook his head vigorously. "Nine forty-five last night"—closing on their bedtime—"your mother got worried that we didn't have Earl Grey since you *always* drink it for breakfast."

"Oh come on."

"No, that's right." He pitched his voice lower. "So . . . race down to Kroger." Kroger stayed open late, on Thursdays. "Whew. I'm deducting the amount from your monthly check."

"Please, it's just that there's no way to get a real breakfast, so I do strong tea."

Now she turned her gaze to me saying with it: consider, consider.

He lit up his pipe, shook the match, and checking her for an interdiction lofted the first sharp cape of smoke, Blair House.

The night before on the way out of town I'd stopped at the Donut Hole on the bypass and spent a while watching the girl who worked there, exchanged a few phrases with her. On the one hand she talked very freely with the customers. She laughed pointedly. On the other she didn't seem to be exactly present. At the breakfast table I was thinking about her more than I had a right to.

"Lou," my mother warned. A bird's wings hit the jalousie like a wad of paper as the bird, a bluejay, came to the feeder, unbalancing it. When it took off the branch rapped the siding.

"Well, I wouldn't mind seeing Skip Terry myself this morning," she said. He was known as good-looking and was running for church council and school board at once, the steppingstones.

I said, "I was thinking maybe it'd be better if I went on and went by myself."

"Shoot," she said and rammed her chair back. She walked into the kitchen, clicked a button on the range, and filled my cup—our cups belonged—with boiling water.

My father brushed crumbs onto his plate with the bottom of his pipe hand. "Well, son, she and I agree, since I used to work with Skip, that might tip it."

"I was thinking it might be more persuasive to speak for myself."

She rang the cup of tea down in front of me. Its aroma, never more like rank fruitcake, overwhelmed that of the bacon. "Yes, my land," she said. "Great."

Later as we left she ran to the door and pointed out a late oriole picking up seeds frittered off the feeder. "Have you seen him before, Lou?"

"No, sure haven't."

"Well, he's simply amazing."

In the side yard my father had burlapped the fig trees, the only ones we knew of in the area, already. On the coldest days of winter he would stow an oil lamp inside with each.

The Valiant was of that year when the Valiant looked like a sculpture of eyebrows. Our road, lined with nice pines—also my age, the development having opened shortly before I was born—ran up a considerable hill to Lindhurst Road. The power company had cut the grown pines into wrench shapes. Virginia macadam is the blackest in the country, the dividing lines the whitest, yellowest. Lindhurst ran into Wayne, pure Virginia macadam, and Wayne, four hopeful lanes, into the downtown then out to the bypass. The macadam imparted no sound to the tires. Over level Wayne Avenue arched yellow-brown chestnuts all the way to the Post Office. The town paid a man,

Grady Clark, to edge and rake town curbs according to the season.

"Did you get the shots you wanted?" He rolled the window down a notch to vent smoke. "What were you taking? I know," he growled; he smacked my leg, "you can't talk about such things."

"No—just trying to capture a certain aspect." I would have had to explain wanting to show people in secret and that with a cold heart photography seemed the way.

"Yea, yea. Tell me, what aspect?"

My right arm lay across my lap, my left over the back of the seat. "That bare line of Loft Mountain, a lot of sky, just a couple trees, and then the glow. Not dawn. I mean right before the top of the sun emerges." I'd overexposed the pictures to have the ridge and trees appear ghostlike in a grainy radiance but I didn't want to explain that either. My father liked a frontal view of a person from the shoes up. He liked "Miscellany" at the back of *Life*, where, for instance, the lens made a horse appear to have eight legs.

He pulled into a space, got out and thumbed pennies into the meter. "What about your character studies?"

"This is a character study."

"Of who, you and Liz?"

"I guess, if you want to be specific." I imagined people left prints on emptiness, that if you shot a bedroom the disturbance in the sheets showed those who had disturbed them. This was a fad in the photography magazines. If you shot a mountaintop with a lot of sky you showed people who'd lain looking at the sky at that location.

"The studies I didn't like were the Du Pont workers with smokestacks coming out of their heads."

"That was intentional."

Because of the elevation and time of year the light lay pale on the sidewalk; the shadow side of the street was curtained in blue. A woman in a dress of Virginia cloth—a print like powdery wallpaper—and a sweater the lightest pink, crossed to greet us.

"Hey, Ruby, remember my boy?"

She pulled her sweater around. "He doesn't remember me."

I did remember her the moment I saw her husband across the street. The girl who had been working at the Donut Hole walked past him in medium heels and a suit, russet, a mature little package. When he crossed his arms watching her I remembered them from county teacher meetings I'd been taken to, the Aldhizers. The girl flounced more than I wanted her to, fussed with her pocketbook. She went into Hurst's Stationery.

Stepping out of the shadow Mr. Aldhizer crossed, fluttering his hand on his trouser pocket. As he shook mine he took stock, jauntily, through his steelframe glasses. Then the man we were supposed to see, Terry, came out of the stationery store. He and I noticed each other, recognized each other—he had had me in homeroom twice—but pretended not to. He put a hand to his tieknot. He put something in his mouth. He shook his suitjacket sleeves down. Looking at the jacket it seemed too large for him but looking at his back and arms they seemed too large for the jacket. His reflection shot ahead on the banked window of the next store then doubled back then went high into the corner behind him.

"I'd put something on the side of her head Ajax won't take away," Mr. Aldhizer said.

"John, how did the company decide on . . ." my father began.

Mr. Aldhizer looked back across the street. "They messed up on us pretty bad, Lou."

My father shook his head.

"We're enjoying your peppers, Lou," Mrs. Aldhizer put in. At the end of summer my father sent around jars of hot peppers from the garden, although the people here don't generally eat hot food. At someone's house once I saw years of unopened jars, the pigment separated out into solid plugs.

"You and Edna come see us," Mr. Aldhizer said. "And Glen if he's home."

As we walked up the block my father asked, "You're not nervous about this?"

"Really, I'm not."

Built of cement the color of the sidewalk and with flatly linteled windows and square columns flush to its front the First and Merchants didn't catch shadows except mornings that of the overhang of the Cline building roof next to it. The lobby went the two floors up; there were pillars and a mezzanine of glassed-in offices. The air was perpetually hazy, as if the Chamber of Commerce held smokers in there. Removing his hat my father stopped one by one up the line of tellers. "I wouldn't let mine in the house," Evelyn Armentrout said. An oblong of fluorescent light shone on the counter in front of her.

I said, "Don't worry, I walked straight off the bus into Shorter's." Donnie Shorter was the downtown barber.

"Your father's a handsome man."

"Oh come now," he said, rocking back, holding his hat in front. "Let's not get carried away."

She blew at the surface of her coffee. "I'm being perfectly serious."

Her intercom said send us up.

The office fronts were glass from the waist up, the doors full-length glass but frosted. The framing recalled cases for minié-ball and mineral collections. When Terry shut the door behind us with such care, however, it wasn't out of concern for its delicacy but to show what precision courtesy a big man in his mid-thirties was capable of, to the fingertips. "We look forward to your peppers every year," he opened with.

"Well, this go-around they're a disappointment, a little on the bland side."

"Lou," he said. "Lou," he stage whispered, "keep on disappointing us." He swung his arm around my father's neck. They went grin to grin. "Keep right on breaking our hearts, maybe we can eat a few of the damn things." He winked at me, he patted my father on the belly. That done, he waved us to the chairs while he sidesaddled the front of the desk. He was chewing Life Savers, Pepomint. His face was a bit narrow, his features a little bit fine for his size. From coaching junior varsity during his teaching stint and from playing golf he kept a tan, like a light woodstain, year round. His eyes were blue, his suit grassgreen. "Now tell me, y'all getting along all right?"

"Can't complain, as the man says. Wouldn't do no good to."

"Wouldn't *do* no good to. Nancy like Madison?"

"Very much, thank you, Skip. She's always had a good head on her shoulders. Yea, I guess one out of two's not bad. Just joking, son." He was sorting through pipe, foil pouches and lighter in his pocket.

"Right," I said.

"She always impressed me as a fine young lady."

"They both made it home for the old folks' anniversary."

"What old folks?" He looked back and forth between us.

"Okay, okay, cut the clowning. Frankly, Skip, that's the reason we're here. Having both in school is a strain on the finances."

"I'm aware of that, I'm awful worried about my own girls time they get there." One leg stirring, he asked me, "What do you expect from that sorry excuse for a football team y'all got?"

"Not a whole lot this year. At least they're not as sorry as some, U. V-a., some of those." I had yet to attend a game at school but did follow conversations.

"We'll see about that next weekend I reckon."

"You coming down? We'll see who buys beer. I won't bother bringing money."

"You better."

"Won't even be necessary."

"Bring your money, boy."

I said, "No point to it."

He said, "Well I'd like to sit yap with y'all all day but I reckon we ought to work around to the business end. Tell me your troubles."

"Actually, they're my troubles."

"Well, Glen, shoot."

My father dipped slightly away, while, on a sort of sine wave, bringing his cupped hand down then up in my direction. Frankly I cared less that Terry could give or not give money than that the girl in her suit had gone into Hurst's to meet him—what else would he have wanted in a stationery store at nine A.M., a nib for his pen?—to arrange to lay her love on his full platter: that power. He had had and would have it all his life. "It's not too complicated. I'd like to get one of those government-backed loans. I work—I wait tables—it's not really sufficient. I mean I don't need a fortune. A thousand." We'd settled on that figure intending to drop back to seven-fifty, five hundred.

"Can't do it," Terry said, plainly, as if plainly acknowledging the coldness he and I shared.

"That's what we came to find out. So thanks."

"We're not able to, son."

"Fine." I was supposed to mention the cars and homes I would finance with a B.A. but I avoided lifting my eyes.

My father readjusted himself, not for leaving, for staying, now that I'd had my fun. He set his hat on his lap, set his pipe, never having lighted it, no ashtrays, on the carpet against the chair leg. He became one of his students, in older flesh, ordered to the office. "Skip, as I understand it, if Glen runs out—and I'll have him thrown in jail personally, citizen's arrest—if he runs out you've got me as cosigner. If I run out, if I run off to San Diego with a hootchie-kootchie dancer"—he exhaled wetly on punchlines—"Uncle Sam makes good."

"Lou, don't you know we make twice as much on auto loans? I can show you this directive out of Richmond, tells us stop doing like we do. It's a hemorrhage on the books." He went behind the desk and flipped through papers in a coil. His wall decorations were civic commendations and a five-foot brown-tone of Natural Chimneys facing one of Monticello showing the pool.

Stop-traffic sign. "Never mind Exhibit A, so it's doing the customer a favor."

"We're not even doing Du Pont de Nemours no more favors no more. How about that?"

"That was pretty good."

"Not doing de Nemours no more favors no more."

"Just for the record . . ." The chair budged, tipping the pipe. "Oh my my," he said, or my mother in him. "Give me a scrap paper, I'll brush up this mess."

"Just leave it, Lou, no problem."

I said, "The bank is poor but they still have janitors, right?"

Finally Terry sat down behind his desk, taking a load off us all. "Time being."

My father was fingering the ashes into the pipe bowl.

"Lou, I'm asking you, now."

"Just about got it." He leaned back. "Edna and I've banked here twenty years, first mortgage, second mortgage—too bad there's no such thing as third mortgage—little loans here and there . . . she goes on the warpath for a bedroom suite and next morning I'm right here, signing on the dotted."

"And Frank Blakey told me do everything I can and don't you know if there was any way in this world . . . How's Edna's daddy making it? I haven't seen her to ask since we stopped coming to early service."

"Aw he's having these awful episodes, refuses to do right."

Fine, I thought, now we get out of here. I was sick of his sitting there so courteously amused, and in the Virginia cloth shirt, red bowtie, shoes polished fifty minutes ago. The way he sat there I saw his entire exile among the bland eaters of the Shenandoah Valley. I saw *his* father before the officer on Ellis Island, quenching *him*self, any price just to get into this land of the stiff-necked, the corn-fed. Then to elaborately say, "Come on, give us the darn loan and quit your fooling around."

"I could not ever justify it to the auditors."

Then, "I spent the best years of my life teaching history before they kicked me upstairs."

"Years well spent, anybody in this town will tell you the same." Terry was chewing further back in his mouth. He appeared impatient only to the extent he thought my father wouldn't notice. I could notice if I chose to, and give him credit.

"And I had a philosophy, a couple philosophies, maybe you don't agree. One was to make history vivid by matching it to the stages of my pupils' lives. The barbarians, that's childhood. The feudal serfs, that's the early teens. Then the French Revolution and so on and so forth." He rotored the point across, clearly loosening up. "When they went up to the Blue Ridge to make out, they were Transcendentalists. When they went to the drive-in, they were Pragmatists. Right, son?"

"I wouldn't know." I barely knew.

"No wonder you got through them farmboy skulls better than I could." The telephone buzzed, he answered, not grasping, balancing, the receiver. "Four o'clock would be fine, ma'am, meet you at the dealership. Not a speck of trouble."

"Another notion I stressed was how lucky they were to live in a small place where you know the individual histories behind the public events. For example"—he checkmarked the air—"when So-and-So Paving won the Route 340 extension: I explained to them, well, So-and-So, he and the highway department head are old frat brothers, they hunt together, this and that, la de da—So-and-So contributes, handsomely, to Harry Byrd: Who gets the contract? Then when So-and-So announced he wasn't running for city council, well, that was because the mayor got scared of him and dug up some of these funny bids. In other words, I told them to rub their little faces in the local dirt then apply it on the national scale. That's history. Do you follow me?"

"I'd love to sit down talk with you; I would." He hadn't quite let go of the phone. He seemed to be considering a new possibility, watchfully, as if having taken one drink but in no way intending to take another. "I seldom get a good conversation. Especially with someone who can bear on the European view."

"Dad, there's no reason to hang around. A bank's a bank."
Talking pedagogy to Terry.

"Keep your shirt on, son," he said, patting out restraint.
"Skip, maybe you don't follow this rigmarole, but I'm trying to
make a point, a couple points, that in a small town history is
your next-door neighbor. Do you see what I'm driving at?"

"Like I say, Lou, I'd love to delve with you, over a pitcher of
brew of an evening." Taking me off guard he flashed me some
charm, boyish, clear.

"Humor an old man. All I'm saying, first off, is my wife and I
have a history with First and Merchants, and I feel you should
honor that history."

"If you wanted a dormer window in your roof I guarantee
the money in five minutes."

"You want me to go on?"

"I'd be interested." He didn't give off impatience anymore.
He gave off a heightened nonchalance.

"I wish you'd reconsider."

"I'd be interested in what you have to say." He barely was
holding his eyes open.

My father put his chin to his chest, and from that declivity
looked up to the other man. "Well then, in the second place,
you participated in an act, a piece of history, not everybody
knows about."

That was one of the saddest things I ever heard him say. It
was the most unnecessary. There had been no need whatso-
ever for him to drop down to Terry's level—for me? for this, a
semester in college? I could have taken leave. If I'd been
drafted, I would have acted according to my beliefs and faced
the consequences, which I was capable of. My mother was
home at the table with Nan or in the yard waiting for us to call
but she was hardly liable to crumble at bad news from First and
Merchants.

Terry swung sideways in his chair, the bulb of his jaw working, standing out as cleanly as a frogleg muscle. "Lou, I'm as-

suming you're not referring to an incident dead and buried several years, might as well be a century. I assume you don't want to damage the opinion I have of you to that degree." Three years ago he'd resigned from the school. At four o'clock today he would pick up his new girl somewhere and take her somewhere and tell her about my old man spilling his pride in his office, her old history teacher most likely.

"All right, don't damage your opinion. Just sign the papers."
The affable growl.

"I am amazed by you."

"Okay, okay, we'll drop the subject. Let's go back to first base."

"I have no authority to contravene an order from Richmond."

"Come now, Skip."

"Pardon me," he said, swinging back. "Is Glen aware what you're referring to?"

"No, not from me."

"Really, I have no idea."

"What do you think of your daddy doing this?"

"I don't know."

He was at me—"What would you feel if he went to church council and made innuendos, ruined any chance of a future for me here, after I've worked to deserve that future again?"

"I think—that's fine."

"You think that's fine. For a thousand-dollar government loan."

"It's fine, I mean I'm sure—"

"You're sure what?"

"I'm sure he'd do the right thing."

Terry reached for the bladed pen in the holder. "You think he'd go through with it?"

"I have no way of knowing."

"Fine. Real fine. I'm going to sign this paper. You deserve it, you've earned it. Anybody that loyal to his daddy deserves a thousand bucks. Hell, how about a hundred thousand. Are you with me?"

"Yessir."

His restlessness, still-faced, was such that I wouldn't have been surprised to see him buck and to feel, with his weight added, the edge of the desk at my neck. But signing he didn't cut the paper but I cut it through to the carbon.

My father, dropping his pipe into his pocket, got to his feet. With his fedora he stood to, merely pleased and unconcerned, as if greeting people at the auditorium door after a band concert. "We appreciate this, Skip."

"Like I say, anybody that hews to the second commandment." He stood, offered his hand to my father, then me and I never stopped to consider not taking it.

Things were better outside. That's the advantage of our valley. I remembered in high school when a friend of mine was having trouble and we'd gone up the mountain to ride his Jeep coming back in the morning how good the light was, lifting, like a hydraulic lift, carrying away the noise of the gears, carrying away mistakes, floating us out black Wayne Avenue under the trees. My shirt collar—my father's roomy loaner, eggshell white (with a pattern, discernible under a microscope)—beat around my neck. Still at the corner of the drugstore I stopped. I struck the pose of the delinquent I never was. Giant faded Verichrome Pan boxes collecting dust in the window display. A pinging yawned behind my skull—spring in the arctic—he was rapping his pipe on the sash.

"Brrr, nicotine fit. Hey, don't look so gloomy."

"I'm going to tear this damn thing up."

"Aw that's just the normal give-and-take. What was I supposed to do, droop my head? You've got to get them where they live, as the man says. Come on, let's have some coffee and pie and call your mother."

"Couldn't you let him *be* a jerk, by himself?"

"There comes a point where you have to look at the other

fellow and think: As for you, buddy, you know what they say in Russia! Pie à la mode, then you can take the car to Liz's."

It wasn't easy to deflect his virtually triumphant manner. "You're wrong about everything. We don't see each other anymore."

"Well now you can tell her you've got money to get married on. Not much; a couple months rent anyway."

"Sir?"

"Or go ahead pay tuition, whatever. I just thought, your mother and I thought, the thing was maybe you wanted to get married."

"That never, ever crossed my mind." Which way it had changed them I didn't know. Two decades swathed in Virginia cloth and still my parents bore this low threshold of credulousness—believing in this instance that at my age everything went first for love.

We continued on down to City Lunch. He had an appetite.

What Do You Think About Three Times a Day

The Silver Dollar Man may have missed your town. There is the consideration that Dr. Pepper was more a regional beverage. But he came that dry December to the Valley. Low to the ground in a purple Nash he drove down between the blue shanks of the mountains and up into the towns that might have been nearly vertical but were low to the ground. In the valley he looked across the hard fields, the grayed-through woods. Near the mountain ran the windows of a train. Halfway up the mountain he stopped to rest the car at an overlook and looked down. He picked out the reservoirs. Even he, who fit his job like a glove, appreciated their partnership with the land. They were man-made but followed the natural contours. They were like silver dollars, melted down, spilled. He loved his wife Penny home in Richmond. He loved his girl in Staunton. He was thinking of the feeling when she seemed to fill his chest with flakes of metal and her head was angling away and the curtain hung so still and nothing else around them was very good.

In his work he wore a burgundy blazer, burgundy trousers, cordovan shoes. He wore a pink shirt with the collar slightly frayed. His hair was like stout polished twine and came to an edge along his temples. He was lanky but his shoulders were broad. In every town he made love with ten or twenty women. This is the story of his comedown.

It takes place in Waxboro, an incorporated city of fourteen thousand (named not for the secretion of bees but for the hopes of the founders). They had a Du Pont there and a General Electric because at the time there were no union shops. Still, wages were not bad and the people, a proportion of them, were more prosperous than in a lot of the communities.

When first arriving in a place the Silver Dollar Man registered at the hotel. Then he went to the bank and cashed a company check into twenty-dollar rolls of silver in wrappers of tarnish gray. Then he went to the radio station to buy time on the early afternoon show since he visited while the husbands worked.

In Waxboro the radio station was situated on Main Street above the cleaners. Stan Carroll, the afternoon announcer, sat next to him in green armchairs with a lamp between them and quoted prices. Fine, fine. Employed by an outfit that believed soft drinks could be sold in winter, could be marketed as a beverage to be heated on the stove, served hot, a poor man's or Christian abstaining man's warmer upper, the Silver Dollar Man had carte blanche. He bought every piece of time unspoken for and gave Stan Carroll copies of what to say, in capital letters.

The receptionist thought it intriguing to watch them. They were a pair of go-getters. Both had personality but when they used it on each other it snarled in midair, leaving the individual face blank. Around the office hung aerial photos of Waxboro, of fine enough resolution to identify houses, cars.

"I might add a couple twists and turns of my own," Stan said in his speaking not his radio voice.

Lingering talking with the receptionist about his grandparents' farm while Stan went on the air, the Silver Dollar Man explained, "I just can't work out of doors." A loudspeaker resembling what you bring inside at the drive-in hung above the soundproof window. "I was always sickly."

"You have some thick fingers on you," she said, not taking him seriously, typical.

"He has arrived," Stan announced a quarter hour into The Stan Thing, a program of Top 100 hits that ran from two to five, when Dinner Rhythms began. "The man you read of in the *Times-Dispatch* Sunday supplement. The man who wooed Winchester with winnings, who edified Edinburg, numbed Newmarket, cultivated Culpeper, crooned to Crozet. And he is coming next to: your house—yes ma'am—your house, to tally up the bottles of precious liquid on hand and award you a dollar for each, in Denver fine. You know what precious liquid I'm talking about?" He floated left the page he'd written.

The Silver Dollar Man tossed his head back and laughed soundlessly, though he could have laughed out loud and not gone through. Great, really great. The fellow didn't look like much, stringy hair, soft face, but he had the gift of gab. And a radio voice that resounded like an innerspring mattress. As the next record, a Bruce Van Dyke number, began, the Silver Dollar Man signalled Stan to step outside the booth. He asked his address. Stan merely assumed the Dr. Pepper folks liked to keep their announcers happy and the minute that flybrain pretty boy left called his wife to run out and buy more.

The word was out, so was the Silver Dollar Man, coasting around town in his Nash painted up with clocks pointing to ten, two and four and bubbles highlighted with thorn shapes. On the doors they had painted the trademark ellipse on its side, the illusion of a bottle on wheels. He got the feel of the city. He went by the Chamber of Commerce map but although he could guess where the different levels lived he liked to make sure. His prospects had been excellent but then he had wrecked his knee and made a mistake. This job paid a hundred twenty-five weekly and truly could have been worse.

The first house he tried, near the elementary school, attracted him with its brick. It was a specimen of that more-black-than-red brick that appears to have railroad cinder mixed in.

The courses of mortar might have been applied with butter
knives, they were so thin. An oak leached the soil to the nub in
front. In back the ground dropped off. Over the door the roof
rose to accommodate, he figured, a cozy bedroom. A widow,
he figured. Her husband was a preacher and at his passing they
bought her a domicile, in the church's name.

He lifted the knocker and the holiday wreath fell off in his
arm.

"Well I thought you'd never get here," the lady said, opening
wide, peering as he bent the nail with his thumb. "You don't
have to fool with that thing." She was handsome, full, her hair
had turned dusty but was still reddish, her skin was highly
freckled. Except the joints of her fingers, and the upsweep of
her eyeglass frames set with sparkles, there was nothing that
old about her.

"Came as quick as I could."

"Not always the best policy. Oh, listen to me," she said
cheerfully. She passed behind him, clamped the door shut.
"Isn't it just pathetic what becomes of a widow?"

"Not in your case, far as I can see, ma'am."

"Hurrah, you're a dream come true. Let me usher you into
my boudoir, which at this stage is my kitchen, you understand.
I've been frying chicken, polishing silverware and Babo-ing the
tiles. Sublimation, I believe is the term. Oh, I just—"

"Ma'am?"

She glanced over her shoulder as if the phantom of a daugh-
ter-in-law stood guard. She cupped a hand to her mouth. "Oh
I just have conceived a terrible love for Rémy Martin, isn't that
too pathetic? Of course, I was a Martin before I married." He
followed her back to the kitchen, which was yellow in theme.
A wide window gave onto descending barren hardwoods with
trunks as black as the black in the bricks and limbs messily tangled. An unspattered white radio next to the toaster carried
The Stan Thing. The Statler Brothers sang a joke, an ordinary
phrase that took on connotations of human love. As the blue of
afternoon deepened and the walls concentrated incandescent

light, it was possible to believe she and he dwelled in the sole bright box in the Shenandoah Valley. "Rémy and I, we have us a time. Loves to hear his momma run on at the mouth."

Chicken mounded counters and table, six hens' worth of leathery puffs on plates. The umber indicated a seal such that the intrusion of the tip of a tooth would fill the mouth with warm, slippery liquid. Necks, giblets simmered on the range. Pine cones, in pairs tied at the top with red ribbon that dangled down between, adorned the wall. The widow's apron enhanced the fullness of her bosom, an effect not lost on the Silver Dollar Man.

She took his hand and showed him in the cellar door. Along the stairwell ran a ledge on which were cordoned a galvanized pail and three cartons of Dr. Pepper. He made a notation on his clipboard. "Let me run out and get you about eighteen of them babies."

"Not so fast, Silver." She took his hand, drew him to the refrigerator, displaying in the door three additional.

"Make that twenty-one."

"How remarkable, just my age. Now, before you get back to business would you care to join myself and Rémy in a toast? Or is it against company rules?"

"Not a bit of it."

"Public relations," she suggested firmly.

"My specialty."

Two fingers of cognac each in cut glass goblets they sat among the chicken, he picking. She turned and stretched her legs out, hooking one foot behind the other ankle and attending to her hair with her free hand. Her legs were quite nice, smooth and substantial, grippers. This widow, he didn't know about playing cards with her for money. "Covered dish at church, that's why all this activity. I want you to know I'm not completely out of control." She leaned to him. "Not in the kitchen anyway. Just listen to me!"

The Silver Dollar Man could hold his liquor but by the same token it wasted no time on him. Once he and his wife, who

loved classical music, went to a symphony at the Richmond
Mosque. The moment the conductor raised his baton on the
upbeat he realized that was the way he was. One upbeat, he
was ready. "Was your husband minister?"

"Fifteen years. We waited and waited." She lifted her eyebrows, to which her glasses seemed attached. Suddenly what
she had said struck her funny and her being struck funny
struck him funny. Neither could have said exactly what was
funny but both knew what was and that it was the same thing.
"Oh my," she sighed as their laughter trailed off. "I told you I
was a Martin. He used to brag on my One-Hour Martinizing."

"No."

"From the pulpit."

"I believe *that*."

"He compared it to forgiveness of sins."

The Silver Dollar Man was ready. "I have a little boy who
brings home these old toothbrush paintings from school," he
said. "You know, teacher has them bring in a old wore-out
toothbrush and they dip it in paint and scrape it over a win-
dowscreen. You know what just occurred to me?" Her eyes
were no more trusting than if she'd ever known him. "I was
looking at the freckles on your legs and thinking they look like
my boy took his toothbrush and crawled up and sprayed
specks all up and down them."

"Oh." Without expression, pleased. She got up and cut the
stove off, strained the necks from the kettle onto a platter and
carried it to the table. "Well they say the legs are the last to go."
If Dr. Pepper made hosiery and he were in a position to, he
would have used her legs in the advertisements, in place of the
usual stalks. "I did have the veins pulled, as Rémy'd blab
sooner or later."

"Rémy," he said, toasting the bottle, "they did a beautiful
job."

"How are you at boning?"

"Expert."

She gazed at the platter of ridged, curving, steaming, sopping forms. Still he feared the matter hung in the balance, that any moment she might snap back to business, start bustling around the kitchen and behave as if he had lost his mind to pick at her sash then rest his hand on an eminence of buttock. "You've got some fine brickwork in this house," he noted.

She patted her sternum and killed the cognac. "Maybe we ought to allow them to cool first."

"You wouldn't want me appearing at the next house with blistered fingers."

"No." Very merrily her eyes kind of rose and died out. "That would not be the thing under the circumstances."

"Should I run to my glove compartment? I carry something."

"That won't be necessary."

The cozy bedroom upstairs was fluffy and as they said in magazines very oil of evening primrose.

Stan Carroll was right there, he really was, decided the Silver Dollar Man coasting around town listening to The Stan Thing. They had painted a big Dr. Pepper clock on the roof of the car. If he tried to run off with the dollars, he told everyone, they'd track him down from the air. On one section of the show Stan reported unusual items, events that were you involved might be disasters but to a faraway listener occasioned mirth. The gentleman out in California who forgot the relocation of his house to a mountain ridge and stepped out the back door. The lady who sleepwalking tried to press the wrinkles out of her husband's face on the linen setting. The gentleman in West Virginia who trained a rooster to play toy piano and when they ate him mistakenly shot his wife dead, case dismissed. Stan simply could *involve* the listener in his description of this old farmer dropping grubheads on the keys that make up a diminished seventh run.

Stan spoke about him too. "I want to share this with our audience. One time when the Silver Dollar Man and myself were eleven or twelve—this was over in Henrico, where we grew up—we went down to the river to ice-skate, you know. The ice was firm but it had slush on the surface. What would happen was, you'd be skating along fine for a while and all a sudden that slush'd freeze up on the runners, stop you dead. Anyway I looked and there was the Silver Dollar Boy skating right up to the edge of the dam and then at the last second he'd cut back around. Right *up* to the edge, cut back. He was the adventuresome one. Problem was, he was wearing his big brother's skates, size thirteen, lot of leeway around the feet. Well you can guess. I look and I don't see anything but a pair of iceskates poised at the edge of the dam, lonely sight, lonely *dam* sight you might say, and ten streaks of blood paying out across the concrete.

"I'll come back to this. First let me remind you just because he comes once doesn't mean he won't be back. No ma'am, huh *uh*. The Silver Dollar Man makes a practice of returning to check up, see if you've improved your habits."

The Silver Dollar Man eased to a stop at a green-roofed asbestos-shingled house in not the newest, not the oldest neighborhood, just small houses with a medium pine and a medium hardwood in front of each. The addition attracted him. He wanted to build an addition to his home for his boy. Last night he had dreamed of his wife Penny. Bending at the waist, and perky, ever perky, she was sorting through frozen foods. Someone asked where was her husband. She had no idea, she said, she'd lost him in the store. Lines of mere tolerance gathered in her face, as if husband loss were no less taxing but no less natural than a raccoon in the garden once again, once again. Spirit, sense, her hair would snap like carrots in the mouth. Peeking in the window, he saw a bookcase right in the living room, a map of the heavens above it, and figured the husband for a schoolteacher, liable to return. (It was three. The buses had been.) At the end of the dream they were home naked and he wedged her hands under the headboard and did something distasteful from real life shaming them both, ruining what they knew there.

He recrimped his violet tie and knocked. His features were exceptional only in that it was exceptional to see so many plain features together in proportion. When he introduced himself his wide mouth widened, his eyelids drooped, his eyebrows lifted like the windshield wipers of the Nash, from the center. When he relaxed you saw how strong the features were. His looks were like good teeth chewing evenly.

"I knew it," the lady said. Her son joined her at the door, looked at the man's face then only his middle. Fat, so poorly coordinated it was doubtful he would yo-yo by twelve, he couldn't hold a candle to the Silver Dollar Man's boy two years to one. His stance, flinching, asymmetrical, scaled him to middle age, one of those cases that ended up as salesmen for Dr. Pepper, all nerves and lard. The son was not the Silver Dollar Man's style but the mother would pass. She had whisper-fine black hair, which hung in a limp, fetching wave, perfect skin, a high forehead and when she smiled dimples the diameter of pencil erasers. She let him know he couldn't expect to get anywhere with her, son or no son home, but he'd met with the attitude before.

"Yes ma'am, your worries are about over."

"Well, shoot, I wish. I've never had an ounce of luck."

"Are you forgetting your appearance and manner?"

"Whew, bring me my boots. Come in, though I'm disgusted with myself. I don't know that I have a single Dr. Pepper."

"Don't tell me that. Don't keep telling me what you're telling me."

She squareheeled her way into the kitchen and he followed, noticing how nicely her skirt cinched the calf at each step. Because her husband was due she had dressed a little. At the time it was believed heels gave an extra range of expression to a woman, like the pedals on an organ. As she searched the refrigerator, her hair crumpled to her neck, strands sliding. There were three fulls, and a half throttled with a household syringe. He reached into his jacket and counted, bending the rules, four discs into the boy's two palms. From the radio, which occupied a shelf in the next room, came Stan Carroll reporting, on dolphins the Navy was training to deliver fresh tanks to divers.

"Did you hear that?" the boy said, not to anyone in particular. She should send him straight to Ingleside, company sales school. As soon as he could get a permit, fourteen, he'd start making *money* talking to himself.

"He's something, ain't he, boy, old Stan?" Deaf to direct address.

"I'll see you to the door," she said.

"Do you mind if I peek in your addition?"

"It's not much."

They stood in the bright little room, louvered jalousies, Christmas cards down the post between, a dinette set with a copper-bottom lamp on the table and books, between bookends, published by Ginn and Scott, Foresman. She stood with her feet together, insteps actually touching. "I admire y'all for building on," he said.

"We've gotten a lot of enjoyment out of it." She was altogether shyer showing the addition, or else subdued over not having stocked up Dr. Pepper.

"I'd like to add on to my home."

"Would you do the work yourself, or hire a contractor?"

"I'm allergic to outside work."

"You sure you're not just allergic to work?" She liked that, retained its essence between her teeth like a Sucret.

"I bet you're more of a summer person," he said, because she held herself aside from the glare pouring in through the bare limbs of the tree in the side yard. When he saw hesitancy he pretended the opposite, in order to appeal to the truer nature of the woman. "I can see you at the park, feeding the ducks, wearing a halter top, the sun bringing out the auburn in your hair."

"I enjoy the seasonal changes. I'll see you to the door."

She hardly needed to, since it was but eight adult steps from addition through kitchen across living room to doorjamb. The boy patrolled him, if what she had gotten qualified as boy.

At the door she gave him a smile as if entering a great space where at an earlier time a bracelet had slipped from her wrist and only now was she realizing how futile it was to have come back to search.

On the west of town there was one place to get six-four beer, the Shamrock Lounge. On the east there were two, the High Hatter and Jack's. That night he visited the latter and had Chicken in the Rough (man, he was going to start clucking any minute now) and ran into the receptionist from WAXB sitting at the bar uncomfortably. He asked if she'd care to help him finish, as he hadn't realized the jumbo portion would prove so actually jumbo.

"Second time's the charm," she said. "I was wondering how many nights I'd have to sit here wait."

If he wasn't mistaken she had frosted her hair since yesterday. She had puffy little arms, a sure sign.

She lived not far away, across from the brass foundry where they cast the eagle in the form of having been blasted, neck broken, wings pinned, above your door with number nine shot. She lived in a mobile home with immobile furniture, and it turned out the same applied to her. Her husband had left her with furniture that were she to try hauling the mobile home down the road would drop through the floor and with a body that although it lurched and swayed did not budge. Rarely did. The Silver Dollar Man didn't feel it his place to dwell on the matter and perhaps as a result sneaked her around the bend, and left rolls of spending money.

For lunch the next day he picked up a souse sandwich at Dairy Queen and drove to where the Stan Carrolls lived, Cheshire Shores. The ebony, acoustically absorbent road wound toward the river from the ranchhouses along the golf course. The streets were called Lanes. He gargled from a pint of Listerine and aimed one perfect squid-sac out of the car window into the clay. The lower half of the Carrolls' was brick, pink crumbly brick, the upper half aluminum siding. The house topped its trees. Their lawn needed resodding. It was quiet here, even for Waxboro, where the building code stipulated that with a dance band inside no leaf touching a house may tremble.

Their car was a 1955 Thunderbird, cream white, the fender-skirts abraded as if somebody enjoyed driving through barbed wire. The straw-colored light as he looked past the front of the house over the hedge (broomstraw now) to the river down at the end of the road offered that valley echo he enjoyed. That is, the conditions but nothing echoing. He was strange, when he thought of himself. He could have stood there and whistled, not cared until the song was done. He could have whistled to the bird teetering by the dryer vent and broken its little bird heart. The job had advantages.

Mrs. Carroll opened the door and leaned back against it. She might have been in the midst of a conversation too fatiguing to continue. She was the prettiest woman he had met in his work. She had the looks of a Miss Virginia, a county Miss anyway, the picture of pale yet rakish, big-headed, somewhat wobbly beauty. Seldom had he felt so foolish on the doorstep. "Good afternoon, Silver Dollar Man dropping by to see how many you got."

"Two. Two of everything. Are you considering New Mexico?"

"I've been considering regular Mexico." The company was advertising in this month's *National Geographic*, which featured that country. By a fireplace blooming a giant tulip of flame (inked red, as was the logo) a ski party were shown with their Dr. Pepper toddies.

Her eyes sank in acknowledgement. "Let's discuss that. Not argue, discuss. Shoo," she said but that was only a sound. She had on a green terrycloth robe, her hair was wet and combed back in quills. What disqualified her from notorious beauty was that head of hair, which was pure gray at, as nearly as he could determine, age twenty-eight. Also, at the moment, her dopiness from bathing. He was strange in preferring women not at their best and admiring oddities in them. He had tried to explain to Penny but she remained presentable, sound as an offering plate. I'm just me, I'm just Penny, was her refrain. She even had the boy saying it. I didn't mean to, Daddy, I'm just me. "Lock the door behind you, okay?" Mrs. Carroll asked, skulking away. "These neighbors out here. They'll all come back as bees in their next lives, and be happy. Little honeypot buzzbombs. Such fun. Don't you agree?" Fingertips lighting centripetally on the back of the lounger, she turned.

He stuck to his work line. "I've got the money, if you've got the Dr. Pepper."

She smiled, an effort. "Oh great, we're doing this. Okay, let's. What's your name?"

"Bill."

"Bill, you will find me in possession of five full cases of your all's carbonated prune juice. Which I purchased just in case. Get it?"

"Where are they?"

"You won't take my word."

"I'd love to take your word."

"Uh huh, it's definitely the end of the road, Bill. But it's interesting, it's truly fascinating about the end of the road? The person is there, no choices, they can be deaf, dumb and blind and not miss it and still you have to lead them by the hand." She took the stairs up to the kitchen, barefoot, though heels wouldn't have surprised him, heels in the *tub* wouldn't have. At the time it was thought desirable for a house to have several levels on the ground floor, like a train wreck. In the Carrolls' you went up to the kitchen, down to the dining room, exercise at mealtime. She posted herself at the doorway; walls and doors were furniture for her. Going past he brushed the terry nap on the uplift of her belly. Her soap was strong, smelled like plants.

The kitchen was coppertone, all electric. The oven had a window, the exact style he wanted to buy Penny with his mileage check. The refrigerator, sponges piled under, did not go with the rest, nor the dish mess. Occupying the table was a plug-in football game, two felled teams. By means of wafers on their feet they moved to the vibration of the board, mystifyingly in the right directions. She pointed out the Dr. Peppers. "Dah *dah*." He pitied her. She knew the trick of casting a seriousness that was almost a depression when you looked at her. As if he could not have counted from a standing position he knelt by her knee and touched each crate. Her legs were like her nose, slender and tucked in along the length, Colonial. On the cold floor her feet rested to the outsides of the soles. The nails of the big toes were rectangular, beveled. He lifted the top case, set it to the side, lifted the second, set it on the first, then the third, the fourth. "Just making sure," he said, not feeling like any jokester.

"I'm offended you'd think I cheat."

He would look only at the Dr. Peppers. He felt a kinship with the schoolteacher's son, a being averse to strong sights.

"I'm so honest I'll tell you my husband works for the radio station. Tell you what you already know, huh? But we're doing this, aren't we? I'm ineligible for your silver dollars. I'm as ineligible as a soft drink machine, except in Las Vegas."

"We're not being sticklers."

He stood. She lifted her hair off her squarish temples and walked over to the table, extremely self-consciously though what else would anybody be conscious of, her included? Her hair took on fullness and undertones as it dried. Her robe, like husk, loosened; fortunately her breasts took that nice swing to the sides.

"You must have a boy a couple years older than mine." Throw kids in, he thought, clear this up. Her way of speaking, the free and musical qualities fairly undermined by her lips being drawn back alum tight always, was not going to clear up anything.

"Let me tell you about this little set-up. Stan, my husband, well you *know* Stan, is a very gifted person. Moody, moody as anything. You think I have moods! I only have one mood. More. That's my mood. Full of doubts. Full of ambition that he doesn't even recognize as such. He wants a big job, on a big station. That's his. Big."

"He'll get it some day."

"If doubts don't get him first. He works like the loveless, twelve hours, sixteen, practicing on the tape recorder in the garage. Making up his cute news items. The pay isn't anything."

"He makes them up?"

"Stan cannot be spontaneous, which is hell on sports. He runs out of things to say, like when the team's in the huddle? Or he says the same thing the same way over? Anyway he thinks he can't get a big job unless he's the complete broadcaster. So what we do—"

"I follow you."

"I need to *tell* this. We sit at this table and I run these toy football players around and he describes the plays. All evening, every evening. At least I'm free to injure. You ought to see me melting thighbones on the stove element." She raised a few linemen (the pinned-over figures) to their celluloid feet. "Drop by at two this morning, bring pompoms. We'll be here, making believe these little fellows are in high school." She did have moods. Suddenly she was standing there daring him to express *his* opinion. Nerves, that was his frank opinion, yet they were becoming, around the shoulders, like flakes of metal drifted down.

Maybe she'd had no other intent than to win the kitchen audience of someone she didn't know from Adam and due out of town in twenty-four hours. Most likely he would have listened anyway, without her flirting. That changed. She appeared to surrender a dimension, to flatten back, her posture, the darts of her face, even her breath flattening back and in the same stroke loosening. "Young and old in Waxboro, everybody only talks to theirselves," he said.

"Did you play football?" she asked, shameless.

"Played at football. Baseball was mine."

"I can see that. I really can see that. You appreciate perfection."

"Too bad my boy's not here. He loves to dry his momma's hair. Loves to go to town with a towel on his momma."

"We can't stay here, with this buzzing all around the windows."

"I don't take a woman to a motel," he said, all controlled.

"Something you have to learn," she said, no older than he, "perfection isn't surrounded by perfection."

"I stay in the home."

"I'll dress. You drive. We'll each do what we're best at. If there's any comment, I'll say it had to do with the radio station."

In his mind he always had been faithful to Penny. As part of this he did what many husbands did when they slept with another woman and made love only twice, which at the time a man could do without betraying his wife. But that afternoon at the Valley View Cabins near the ridge of the mountain when they could have just lain there, done on either side, he became unfaithful. The upper branches of the hickories visible out the window were casting around, with the snap of horses pulling up. Nearby a trunk cracked, sounded near. He didn't know yet why certain trees cracked in the cold. Cheryl (that was her name, Bill Coyner, his) was, in strong fact, perfect. It wasn't that she worked hers harder or that her skin was Du Pont nylon or her muscles the surprising fish he had heard of, never found. She hardly tried at all. The moving trees, forward of a bank of taxidermied pines, brought to mind boat masts and that brought to mind the last time he and Penny had driven to the beach: the gray days, a vacation of gray. If he were to drive to the beach with Cheryl, be it midwinter, the days would glisten like postcards. Why? No one will ever know. She simply lay there pale and untangled with that fact inside her, humid and spacious with that inside, and though she in no way invited his return, she gave no sign of objection. Their unit, the end unit, woofed in the wind.

His hand on her underbelly, wrist over one knob, fingers reaching the other, he looked out the window. Two thoughts different from any he'd had before came to him. Surveying the ridge from rockslide (only very gradually sheening over, leak by leak) to the antler rim of trees above, he thought, Part of me is over this ridge like the sky. As he went back to her (this was stronger) he thought, Thousands do what I'm considering and thrive afterwards. He remembered seeing them places, ordinary times, rounding the corner of a building for instance, a lone person, emptied, momentary, gracious, delicate, hot. There was fear in it. There was not caring.

"Where's my hundred and twenty dollars?" she asked. "Don't let me interrupt, we only slept together."

"A hundred, that's the maximum. Your husband keeps omitting that detail."

"Did you ever consider washing the present down the drain?"

"I was just."

"I suspect Mexico is talk." The third time her inkstroke face misaligned, grew angry, old, quite suitable to her hair, which itself grew bristlier, streakier, like beautiful sauerkraut as prepared in the Valley. She slabbed on weight. She made him believe of their sensation as much as he was willing to.

Then when he discovered the photograph she left on the car seat, he determined to have nothing more to do with her.

"Big winners, the hundred-dollar kind. In fact I'll let you in on the secret. It's the big winners that generate the publicity, dollar to a dime. Like I say, he'll give you a handful to make a believer of you, turn back around with a bushel the next day. It's not his money."

Out of the blue he'd receive a letter from his girl in Staunton, a graduate of Mary Baldwin, common-law divorced. Concocting parts difficulties, he'd drive to the Valley. This was prior to the silver dollar promotion, when he rode around repairing trucks.

After leaving Cheryl downtown he drove to Staunton, the next town west, picked Paula up and took her to the Chinese restaurant, her favorite, always ordered duck morsels with water chestnuts. Since age twenty-three (she was twenty past that now, his girl) she had run the county agent's office without receiving credit. Tall and shallow, dressed for the sudden earnest cold in a plush coat with rabbit hem, she waited on her porch, at a tilt, her purse to her leg. She greeted him with the usual bemusement, short on touch, long on some joke never to be shared.

"I had a shock today," he said over the meal. "I gave a lady her dollars, a hundred. And I had a call of nature. And I guess while I was in there she snuck out to my car, because when I drove away there was this picture on the seat. It was her naked. Not only that, her husband was in it and he was naked."

"Bill," she said pointedly.

"Yes ma'am, I sat at the stop sign a long, long time. Cars pulling past. Nobody honks in Waxboro."

"What did you think?"

"What would you think?"

"I'm not certain."

"One time, I want to do the right thing that will make you, I don't know, I'm whipped, it's been a long week, that'll make you open up and talk to me."

Rubbery skin, sheaths of fat, she sucked everything down and went after odd bones. She was different with him. He could see her at one of her Ruritan banquets picking at fruit salad with a two-tine fork but not cracking bones with her back teeth. "Is it you're smarter, or just older that you don't trust me?" She bought suits in March to wear the next winter, as she wrote him one season to bed him the next ("Till autumn then, Kittydog," typed). He could give her earrings tonight (not that he'd bought any to), not see her ten years, she would wear them on the date and not think it worth mentioning. "I have no idea of your daydreams. When you get the kids sloughed off to college, you want to run out, go to another country with me? I don't know what you *eat* when you're not eating duckmeat. What do you fix of a schoolnight, liver?" He meant to be light now, as he generally did when he liked someone. But she was watching her plate. Her eyes filled. Being Oriental the waitress gave their table a wide berth. The fun of having acquaintances see her with him had gone bad, perhaps irremedially. He waited (here it came) for her to chew up her weakness, swallow it and raise the view of cheery resolve she might use coasting to shore after a boat ride to shake hands with Democrats. "You never can tell the truth," she observed brightly. "That's how you're young. I'm not saying that with malicious intent."

"You want us to be one person?"

"I construe the meaning differently." She relaxed, needling the oilcloth, tears or duckfat glistening on the knob of cheekbone turned to him. "I've heard better dinner addresses, including in the category of fertilizer."

"I believe we should forget the thing."

"That's certainly appropriate to this evening."

"It suits me." It did too, because he felt thin where he should feel stout and was worried.

Of course in the end they gave in.

He carried her up the stairs to sound like one pair of feet, though both kids were into growth spurts and reliably etherized through to breakfast, when they would discover their mother's friend under, nearly dressed for work under, chaste percale on the sofa. They went back to his putting words in her mouth for the occasion. He was all right after all. By morning they were glued fast, trusty, groaning in the single pelt she spread.

"I was telling you yesterday," Stan Carroll reminded his listeners, "about taking my pants off to save the life of the Silver Dollar Boy clinging to a rift in the concrete of Charles River dam, there at the stoveworks. Did I mention the award I received from Dr. Pepper? First in Heroism, a year's supply of Dr.

Pepper. Second was two years' supply. You know I'm just fooling with you.

"But *he*'s not. He might fool around but he doesn't fool. Not the man who harped on Harper's Ferry, who defied Fort Defiance, was a royal pain in front of Front Royal, harried Harrisonburg, made the sons of Madison mad, set Strasburg on fire, committed more crimes in Crimora than, huh uh."

At Maupin's Cash & Carry he was speaking with Merle Maupin when he overheard a conversation. He had stacked three hundred cartons of Dr. Pepper in the soft drink aisle, a ziggurat, a Babylonian hanging garden of liquid nickels. Atop the display went a poster of a family nearly buried in silver, Saint Bernard plowing through, not brandy at its neck. Strips of Du Pont mylar scrolled back as cartons were removed. Now he was an aisle over with drymopping Merle.

A boy's voice: "If we think he'll come again he won't?"

A woman's: "Think how we'll feel if he does."

"I know."

"I'm not giving them the satisfaction of my standing here all day deciding."

He recognized them, the teacher's wife and son. Understand it was no great trick to talk with Merle and listen both. Merle was ranking on A & P, had his version of what the initials stood for. In so many words the Silver Dollar Man said Cash & Carry in comparison to the bright and cheerful chain store looked like the inside of a tractor trailer.

"Momma, how much is a hundred five centses." The boy knew the answer.

"Yes, oh sure, somebody's going to walk in lay a hundred dollars on my table."

"I guess not."

"We're not going to win any vast sum. We should settle for what we can and enjoy that."

"Fifty."

"My life is simply too short for this."

Overhead hung dusty banners encouraging the customers to buy Standard Brands. His mind was made up, he realized, and to the contrary of yesterday. It was made up of Cheryl, private areas, likenesses so clear he could go over them with reading glasses in his memory (thigh area, that was one, enough space when shut to pass a wallet). For today at least, they seemed equal to the black-and-white she had left to torture him, par for the course.

The lady: "Set two more in for me."

"Maybe if we go to extremes it *will* make him come."

"Shoot on that."

Leaving the store just after them he caught her eye. She was wearing a forest green overcoat and a felt, rather churchy hat at an angle, both of which set off her color, and a trace of lipstick, pinker than red. But first the boy caught *his* eye and stared, dreadfully reading his mind. Then Merle loading the trunk (couldn't expect the youngster to), she saw the Silver Dollar Man and smiled, a quick, premeditated smile, that of a girl whose hand has just been taken by a sailor at Ocean View who will not take no on the subject of the Dragon Coaster.

She met him at A & P, where for unspeckled lighttubes and one cent an item the people were indeed deserting Merle. She folded up under the dash, placing her white straw hat, her unseasonal reminder, on the seat. That car siphoned stares out of even the wells of inattention Waxboro citizens walked through their city in. They stayed on the bypass. The last Phillips 66 was *like* Mexico, perfect orange, perfect blue, snow dirt on the tiles. As airily as anything he could have passed a hand over her and she would have been naked, the trees flickering skimmilk light down to her from the perfect blue sky. Neither did he mention the photograph. Make love, he was thinking: then.

Up at the Valley View he told her about the conversation in Maupin's and instead of sneering, she applied it, as he'd hoped, to them. Surely they were strong enough to follow what was obvious to the conclusion. From the beginning nothing had seemed brand new. It only seemed this old thing they had never known had come back, or never hoped to know, or never knew to hope to know, or known and forgotten. The gas heater made them lightheaded. Through the window they saw cars, no drivers, rounding the curve (forget any valley view), and each time they looked the window had moved farther off. A woman with eyebrows so black, with a brush so stiff always smells this way, he thought. How could I forget. A woman with a mouth so thin always breathes this way having sex, beautifully like a file on standing plywood. He believed he'd forgotten these things, that they were true, and that also true was the foreknowledge (not Presbyterian essentially) of them.

What he now thought of as Chinese restaurant smell rose the length of them as they rested, throbs of blood winging off like birds out of an abandoned cottage. "I'm running through a matchbook," she said. "One minute I'm going 'I just *want* to catch on fire.' Next minute I'm going 'A person *can't* just catch on *fire*.' Next minute I want to throw myself at Stan's feet. I worry you're not built to last at this rate. You'll go sentimental on me. You'll call the Triple A. God, who *can* keep track? I'm just rattling. Say anything but don't lay back looking or we'll end up where we started, back at the end of the road, down in the valley so low."

"We're already up the mountain."

"Keep looking and see."

"You're bossy."

"I worry you can't live the way you do when you sleep with me. I worry you're another who won't wrap me in furs."

Not many called women chicks at that time but he'd heard the term around the plant, and now understood it. There was a way to span her back with his hand so that her bones felt as delicate as a hen's, lovely twists, strung for occasional flight. Today he found the second lovemaking as strong as yesterday's third and was concerned about tomorrow's first. In three hours they grew thinner, in four so raw it no longer made a difference whether the bedclothes were over them as to the clarity with which they saw each other's forms. A kiss could eat through cloth.

"See, mashed prunes," she said, "your lips are made out of mashed prunes."

"Terrible. Gives me the runs just to think about it."

"I guess you never tasted yourself, although you should. You should." She was going over him pretty thoroughly. "Lime juice on your shoulder. Gonna tell on you."

"What's in my armpits, please? Stop. I was fooling."

"Dillweed and Lucky Strike. That's where that darn flavor is." She was proud of herself going over him this way. "Down here in the navel region I hit the molasses."

"You found my bubbles yet?"

"I found the secret ingredient."

"That much I know. Chitlins. You won't believe this but they introduce a couple drops of chitlin juice in the vat at the very end. Mr. Rudy told me that one." His boss, who watched him like a hawk, triple-checked him all up and down the line, and whom he would entertain royally when he got back.

"Believe it? I can't get the taste *out* of my throat. Kiss me, you can taste it."

"I don't really have the appetite."

"I'm not talking about arsenic, I'm talking about you. French kiss, hurry."

Then when it came time to bring up the picture he hardly could, such a long-ago souvenir, now hidden in the spare tire well, where Penny wouldn't sniff it out. (Oh that isn't nothing, sweetheart. I was just me, they were *just* them.) It didn't count anymore, like nailbiting or a drinking problem that meeting him had broken her of. She had tucked against him unnaturally still, expecting seriousness. But the curtain was drawn (though enough sun passed through to light the lampshade beside it).

A chill sized the room, the paneling. Tips reddened, went out, among the heater's little cones. How mean could this be? "You know what, what about that picture you forgot?"

"I didn't care how you came, just came back. Mad, flabbergasted, I did not care."

"What else? I don't want to tell you the things that went through my mind."

"First, my love for Stan is unshakeable."

"That didn't."

"It should."

"You'll never leave him?"

"I won't talk this way."

"Are you all a couple of operators?"

"I'm doing what I have to for the time and place. Waiting on him. I meet a lot of people through him. I have plenty of time to think. You'll never know how much work it is to start age twelve and make yourself what I am. You have that too but you didn't have to *do* it too, to the same extent, and you're not at the phase I am."

"Quit pulling rank. Who says you have it to pull?"

"I'm at the phase of using what I've made." They were lying serene, blankets to the ears. "Could come crawling back. We could both come crawling back. But we'll never think of that. I mean we won't think of not either. Just be looking one day and, damn, here we are on hands and knees crawling up gravel to the Blue Ridge, wondering what hit us."

He ran the flat of his hand down her back in a stropping motion, what Penny did to him if he'd have thought. "Let's jump in the car."

"Not even think about the car."

"Who took it?"

"No one. It was a self-timer. Setting on the railing of the lodge. This is what he was afraid of, it circulating, although he couldn't have predicted the circumstance."

"What's a self-timer?"

"You set it and when a certain time has elapsed it clicks the shutter."

Minds might lie but bodies, at the time, did not so much. It was believed God gave us bodies to make our minds aware of danger and shelter and sustenance and so preserve us. Lies and truth walked. The physical self gave the sign that no matter what had gone before the fact was here and the fact was now and you could follow if you were alive or hang back the rest of your days in shadow. The Silver Dollar Man couldn't take his eyes off Cheryl Carroll as she strode about the unit dressing, never faltering. Her nylons whistled, her hairstyle, a sort of flip, sifted through the brush like very fine sand, she put on the straw hat indoors and the brim undulated, her fine Virginia profile expected any moment some intriguing if not grand suggestion from above eyelevel.

Contrary, he asked her to again. During it she stuck her fingers in his mouth, clamped the heel of her hand under his chin and shoved him around. Whichever direction she went she shoved him the opposite way, like shaking off a dog, though that wasn't it.

She put her grandmother's tiny pearls back on, the one possession she would not risk. Good. She finished re-dressing, smoothed her skirt, straightened her stockings, which had seams, waited for him to catch up. His shirt was soiled, wrinkled but his putting it on sharpened it. Good, they were doing good. She walked out with the Silver Dollar Man and their legs took them to the car and his hand opened the door for her. The icy seats trued them. The clouds raced but not a tree breathed as they descended. "I'll tell you," she said, "I know what I know."

"I know what I know," he said. Where the trees left off along the left they saw down into the valley, and could make out the chimneys of individual houses smoking. The haze was not of woodsmoke, however, or humidity or imagination. The weather was dry, she applied lotion to her hands as she looked out the windshield but the valley glared. I mean that they sat in the purple automobile curving closely down the blacktop through the forest, which where there were no breaks allowed long sightlines in, and these statements didn't sound the least bit mysterious.

The Silver Dollar Man was overdue in Lynchburg but the home office when he called in with his tremendous reception in Waxboro voiced no objection to his staying the weekend to work the smaller outlets. He gave a glowing account of Stan Carroll's abilities, suggesting they use him in shopping centers at a high fee. Mr. Rudy may have had an idea of the situation but played along.

Sunday when he called the Carrolls' the right person answered, wrong. Addressing him as Connie, she went on about Stan being home all day playing new records, writing bridges, while she cooked for the somebodys. That did it, he went to church.

The Baptists had a big brick and blond church, clean as a whistle, with Colonial molding, human-height Christmas wreaths, unstained windows, altogether a bright and cheerful place, a solarium for the Lord. The Silver Dollar Man's work clothes blended better with the ladies' outfits than with the men's. He entered the pew of the late pastor's widow. She, vigorously rouged, turned and shook his hand, howdy do. He turned and shook another's hand, which gave him a visitor's card. Handsful of prelude commenced. Children stopped talking. They looked at each other over the pews then didn't look at each other anymore.

"Are you lost?" the widow asked.

"Trying to get my bearings in the bulletin here."

"One fifteen. That's the number of the responsive reading."

"One fifteen."

She protruded her lower lip and glanced around. "One fifteen."

"Thank you."

"You are welcome."

He arrived not a minute late.

"Well, of course," Stan Carroll said, coming a fraction of an inch closer to the microphone and looking down upon it as you might on a wayward child, "I'm not setting here poking fun at the misfortunes of others. You all understand that, I know you understand that. Every now and then I receive a letter, 'Stan, you shouldn't be encouraging laughter at sad cases. Shame on you. May it not take a tragedy in your own life, Stan, to make you see how thoughtless you behave.' To those who've written, I just want to say this. And I'm being serious for a moment if you'll bear with me. I want to say this. Yes, we take a bit of amusement in these reports. But we take them to heart too, don't we? At the same time we are chuckling are we not, on a deeper level, reminded that these misfortunes do befall many a soul? Are we not reminded of our duty to be always ready to reach out with any aid we might proffer? I think so. I know so. Certainly that is my intention.

"Before we turn to our last report, about a lady over in West Virginia who thought the train coming was nothing but her husband wearing a carbide lamp, I ask you to look at the clock on the wall—that's right, the plastic apple with the little hand and big hand—and notice what time it's getting to be. What do you think of when you see four o'clock? If you can't answer right off let me call your attention to a couple other hours of the day. Ten. And two. Now what do you think of? What do you think of three times a day?"

Once burned twice smart. It was believed that saying the opposite of the truth would make it true. He had made his bed now he had to lie in it. Visiting homes on the southward route to Lynchburg and Roanoke the Silver Dollar Man began falsifying entries on his clipboard. If he gave seven dollars to the James Mosers in Piney River, he wrote twelve. Fifteen to the James Redds in Clay he entered as twenty-three. Fifteen to

Mrs. James Roadcap, with tufts of hair like herbs on a winter porch, of Bedford, thirty. By the end of the first week he had stashed an extra salary, one hundred twenty-five, by the end of the second, three weeks'. Mr. Rudy would catch up with him surely, as assiduously as he went over the slips of salesmen and drivers, but this was promotion, the more paid out the better, right? In the long run Mr. Rudy would nail him (there were follow-up letters, there were phone calls asking would the family mind appearing in an advertisement, although these featured the hundred-dollar winners, on whom he didn't, couldn't, cheat). This way lay free room and board, no doubt about that. But he didn't need a long run, and was avoiding the sheer disregard he had fallen into once before. Mr. Rudy too, handily, was avoiding his, the over-diligence that had shot his health, embedded the steel umbrella in his chest sprung to open at any hint of rain. He made no secret of liking Bill Coyner. He valued the young man's friendship, his stories, particularly of the ladies, above any other aspect of this present job. Time would tell. The shorter the time, the less told.

In a way too, the Silver Dollar Man earned the extra, for now he drove fifteen hours per day. If people in the Valley had stayed up all night he would have driven twenty-four but they didn't. At nine you might look across the long swell and dish of darkness and see one little barn light, like a frozen navigational mark. The taste of metal leaked from his gums. His chest bore in as if he had caught Mr. Rudy's disease, organs ballooning. He came down with diarrhea. He didn't remember much what she looked like. Her smell, the way she moved, the feeling of being bridled to her face, these stayed with him as distinctly as biting into wood. Who was Mrs. James Roadcap but a woman who against long odds happened to wear Windsong, Cheryl's scent, puffed it out of every tuft of hair? Sometimes he took the separation out on an innocent family, barging into a house that stood paraffin-still at eleven, triggering lights upstairs and down, potshots of electricity, causing the family to assemble in pajamas saturated with bedtime and stand dumb while he took apart their refrigerator, scattered the contents of their shed.

Back at the rooming house (he forewent hotels, motels, to profit on the allowance) he drank himself to sleep (even scotch tasted of chitlins, elixir of chitlins), slept badly, woke worse but by seven-thirty was behind the wheel again, revved to wield hour upon hour of courtesy and company coin.

There was her second gift, tucked into the seat, not discovered until he was on the road, a sheet of paper folded into a sailboat. Opening it he read "2-2-2" and, typewritten: YOU CAN GUESS. I LOOK AND DONT SEE ANYTHING BUT A PAIR OF ICE SKATES POISED AT THE EDGE OF THE DAM, LONELY SIGHT, LONELY DAM! SIGHT YOU MIGHT SAY, AND TEN STREAKS OF BLOOD PAYING OUT ACROSS THE CONCRETE. What could that mean but she was sick of the fellow, and ready, willing, aching for a change?

By the third Monday, when he called from Airpoint, south of Roanoke, he could not stand anything anymore. Some can last for years on a sure appearance but when trouble hits they overnight develop habits of those who have led nervous lives from age one. Calling from the Phillips 66, for instance. . . . Formerly he would have left the door open, stood bodily outside the booth, nodded to passersby. Now he slammed himself in, mashed his hand between his brow and the telephone's, covered his eyes, pulled his shoulders up like a collar. "Cheryl. How you doing?"

"Other than missing you?"

"Well, no. Other than that I don't care."

"We're fools to think we can keep something between us over distance. I'm not made to sit in a chair and think, 'Now he's thinking of me and I'm thinking of him so we're together in our minds.' "

"I'm turning around. You can've changed your mind for all I care. I'm asking you for one afternoon."

"An afternoon sounds like what the doctor ordered." In its coarseness that struck him wrong, but he blamed the connection. "Will you pay me for my Dr. Peppers?"

"I'm burning my bridges. They're firing up like matches in a matchbook."

"What?" Connection.

"Pack summer clothes in a box."

"Quit toying."

"I'm turning around."

"Be sure you know what you're doing if you do. Know for me, know for Stan."

His nerve failed, less at the thought of penitentiary than at Cheryl's nonchalance. Asking Mrs. James May, whom he gave ten (wrote twenty), to direct him to a colored fortune teller, he went to visit Miss Sonny Brooks, living in a cinderblock cottage on the ditchy outskirts of Airpoint. Miss Sonny said, "I see two women." Small, leaved tight to the stalk of herself, she sat at an oblique angle to him, in the attitude of awaiting another caller, one she needed to discuss fresher news with. Because of the chill of the house, whose inside walls were only the cinderblock sealed, she wore slacks, with a crease that would pare hard fruit, and a scarf. He pegged her at fifty but she was capable of sudden, spun-out, airy gestures.

"You haven't dealt the cards," he observed from the divan. Where were the curtains, the framed anatomy punctured with eyeballs, the charts of Aramaic, the dollbabies, all the certifying knickknacks of Richmond seers? No Jesus, not a trace of Jesus, and the week before Christmas. What did she tune in on that hundred-pound Magnavox, the Don McNeill Breakfast Club? Stan Carroll when the breeze blew right?

"You're double-sighted, see me pick up a deck of cards."

"No, ma'am."

"Next you'll be jumping your hands in my face." Winced at the thought.

"I just wanted to know the procedure."

Before the window on a maple stand were geraniums. She sat to the right, a cheval of poor mirror behind her. If she looked at him at all it was in there, askance of askance. He hardly recognized that blue-skinned man in there himself (petals as radiant as if hooked to a drycell, the plants were in flower, absorbing, along with Miss Sonny's hidden side, the foreground), that skulker in the back, that outcast. "I read," she said. "I see

two women, one good, one worse. Now I'll tell the future: I
was ignorant of my power till my children were taken. I regret
every wasted day. In the ground I won't be let rot for regret. It
mashes the breath out of me." What was visible of her in the
mirror showed more animation than that on the near side.
"You want to step in my shoes, suit yourself. How you paying
me, money or kindness?"

"It could be both, I reckon." He was relieved at his mind's
supplying the possibility, which it had been slow on, if she
meant by kindness what he did. Strokes of possession, the laying wide of her close limbs, that wasn't what he imagined.
Though he was thick with imaginings of women lying with
him, he seldom dwelled on that part. Hovering over the bed he
saw his own backside (not the prettiest sight in the world,
Penny claimed) and the snug black chevron of her legs hooked
over his and her impassive, conceited face with its straight
bangs, wig or real, and what he imagined was stillness, nobody moves, waters simply finding their own levels among dry
strangers oceans apart.

He was losing his grip. She meant nothing so fierce. She was
more like one of those colored nuns he had heard existed, living in a nun-scant dwelling. "Look in the other room and stop
thinking what you're thinking," she said, however, he could
have sworn, a hair jollier.

He went and looked. It was winter in that room, no less
shades-to-the-top than the front room, as much space clear as
if the pieces of furniture, all unbeveled maple, shrank from
each other. But he felt the gray weather at the window and was
aware of the reach of the land into it starting with the clods of
her garden and carrying back through the threads of trees to
the mountain, over which clouds were easing like enmeshed
coal. Looking at her bed he thought, If she sleeps, it's elsewhere, got to be. "Now," she called in, "can you raise that window for me which the painters painted it shut?"

He moved the night table (night when?) and strained until
the wood threatened to pull off. Then he ducked. Something

reared and lunged and roared out there and he ducked. Nothing but a backhoe sinking a line by the corner of the house. The body of the machine, and the driver, were hidden, the scoop had swung down out of nowhere at him. It deposited and reared, treading forward. Machines normally didn't faze him. This one, the raw lever in the gray sky, the row of pickaxes, the upside-down steel gut ratcheting over the landscape, did. It lacked a brain, but with one, or at least this was the instant's message, the quick fortune, with one would have felt this way: like *him*, such as whenever he pulled away from the Dr. Pepper plant onto Route 250 rolling quietly west to the Valley. It would have wanted to rip the very ground apart everywhere to the horizon but would remain too polite to, too clumsy. He and Cheryl together would not, theirs was not to by right. "I'm afraid the panes'll pop loose," he called back.

Her forehead was climbing and descending little ladders as he came back, and she was murmuring, "Hm, hm, hm. Paint your car and go then."

"I could stay a while."

"You and the water company's whiles. Leave a dollar and a quarter on the radio." She pointed, with a long reach and dip of her forefinger. "I don't drink your drink."

Even so he placed a roll of dollars next to the dome of veneer over the dial. He turned, perhaps unconvinced that the true woman here was the visible either.

"Paint your car and go."

A hesitant snow fell, the Silver Dollar Man's breath came sour and shallow as he left. The snowflakes seemed to evaporate along the paths where he rayed his eyes. Around back the backhoe kicked into high gear. Without stopping for his things, definitely without responding to Mr. Rudy's urgent message the landlady had served with breakfast, he drove through Roanoke and north to Waxboro, up to the Valley View, took a unit with kitchenette, went back down to town, bought two gallons of gunmetal gray at the auto supply, groceries at Maupin's, liquor at the A.B.C., flowers at the florist, odds and ends at Rose's and the pharmacy, returned to the cabin and phoned Cheryl to come for supper. She could, she said, as the statistician did not want to risk the snow in from Dooms and Stan had to fill in at the game. He pulled up a fire road and in two hours camouflaged the Nash, gave it a finish matted and pocked by melting snowflakes but not all that unsightly. Leaving he switched on the radio and just as it warmed up heard Stan Carroll say, "Don't do it, Bill." Then he heard him say, "And don't you do it either, Cindy honey. Or you, Melvin. Today's words to the wise, don't ask me where they come from, I use a Ouija board. Let's turn to a new release from Mr. Jim Reeves, entitled 'He'll Have to Go.' Try and follow the story to this one."

He prepared the dish he knew, pork chop casserole, set it in the oven ready, and fixed up: stood jonquils by the bed in a Rose's vase, attached holly to the ceiling light chain, distributed seasonal candles, cut, with a penknife, pictures of Mexico from the *National Geographic* the company had put in each employee's box and taped them up (cliff divers, dancers in the street in petalled dresses, loungers in a stream beneath weighty orchids), washed and dried tumblers and stood them with the whiskey, changed the bedside bulb for blue, the reading lamp for red, slipped lambsgut condoms to incubate under the pillow, set the table for two head and head and created a centerpiece of sweetheart roses fanned by cedar sprays and four hundred and forty dollars in rolls. He nearly regretted his laundry in Airpoint.

He was just dressing after his shower when the knock came. But he heard two voices, her jumpy thing, and another like a tractor in a dry field. No, it wasn't the manager showing her to the unit. With vivacity she was saying, "He was *so* glad we could come. I feel he gets lonely in his work, this time of year."

"That's not the car, is it? What in hell?"

"His is purple. Designs all over. I don't know whose piece of junk that there is. He's probably out buying something special. Be *so* good to him."

"Where'd you see his car? Oh, right, payola day, that'll be your story."

"And be true, Suspicious."

"I really messed up on the Community Bulletin Board."

"He's like you, on the verge. It's terrible to be on the verge."

The Silver Dollar Man was moving at truly top speed now. He snatched down the holly, snatched down the pictures, clicked off the colored lightbulbs, precisely, with the deliberateness of slow motion but carried out at top speed, arranged two extra place settings on the table, stuffed the condoms in his shirt and in tandem with the swinging inward of the door sluiced out the bathroom window in his stocking feet. He climbed the dead blue rockface to a little cedar tree, rooted right in shale, and fell behind it, chips carbonating down his path.

Keeping an eye on the unit's center rear window through the branches he tried to collect his thoughts. The snow laid on thickly. The snow suspended twilight. There were possibilities. But if Stan had shown up as she was leaving, why didn't she make up some errand, go out, call the manager to bring her regrets over? The other possibility he wouldn't let himself credit, not solely on the evidence of the photograph, them naked and as inviting to the camera as to a firing squad, which he had believed her about.

He saw her lean up against the window. He saw her narrow shoulders that he had held, that had bunched and risen up to him. She turned and glanced up into the woods, and turned back. Meanwhile, in an aura of gassy blue (*had* to find that lamp), Stan's form went back and forth, back and forth. His arm pointed there, there, there. Then he approached her with his right hand in the air, the fingers spread very discretely. For the time it took the Silver Dollar Man to rip the stitching from his cuffs and wrap his feet, then raise his shirtcollar over his head, the hand stayed upright. Then it came to the glass and came through, the pane issuing whole, not shattering until it hit stone. Back and forth again went Stan. No cars on the road, no breeze. The acoustics of snowfall tuned to the human voice.

He could hear them, at the edge of comprehension. Like the lines of fishermen standing too close the casts of their voices rose, knotted, fell. The hand lifted again. She went limp, dropped her head. Then a long underhand throw from her, and a stuttery, patterned reeling in. And laughter, plain laughter. Laughter filled the unit haywire.

The door slammed. Coatless she walked around back, matter of factly. This might have been her place and been for years. She looked creased, efficient. With a contented movement she shook snow out of her hair. She stooped, made a show of sifting the broken glass, stood, looked up into the trees again, overshooting him: three seconds: and went back in. Her form and the other met in the middle of the room. He lifted her sweater off, undid her. She gathered his head and rolled it between her breasts as if they were big all of a sudden and rock and she was trying to dash his brains out. They tottered to the left where the bed was. Tiny red glow. Darkness deepened. The illumination in the cabin took over. After a while she was walking unclothed to the table to fill the clean tumblers with whiskey, or the ghost of her as portrayed by condensation. She returned to the left out of sight. He realized he needed to take measures against the wicked cold. On all fours but face up, a lizard inverted, he worked himself to the top of the acclivity and scooted into the brambles. Finally relinquishing his view of the inside he knelt and filled his clothing with dry leaves, which there were plenty of, once he shook the little bit of snow off.

Seeing his way easily, the night setting space around the trees, he circled to the west to an outcrop by the road from where he could watch the front of Valley View. He shivered in waves that took away his awareness of anything else. Coming back he saw the cars still sitting there, taking, accepting, heard the grains of snow sifting down and saw Waxboro lights way down below, the southwest corner of the smeary mat of them. The automobiles seemed of an equal density with the air, liable to lift off. He collected leaves. He opened the condoms, wiped them down, and (the good strong veiny variety) tied them as garters around his ankles and wrists to allow fuller packing. He was lucky to be wearing stretch socks. Out of a condom and his handkerchief he fashioned a leaf-mitt for his left hand. The right he warmed between his legs. When the job was done he could have passed for a deep-sea diver. The woods crinkled like radio tubes coming on.

At last Stan walked crisply from the unit, a skinny snake or a very long nightcrawler in his hand. The Silver Dollar Man recognized it as the shower hose. Stan pulled the head off. He put one end of the hose into the gas tank of the Nash, the other in his mouth. Gas sparkled from his mouth. He coughed terribly, and filled the whiskey bottle from the hose and emptied it inside the car. He repeated this six, seven times. All right, the Silver Dollar Man thought, fair enough. If only Stan hadn't gotten into the car then and hadn't released the brake allowing it to glide down the incline and slam into the little concrete bridge over to the road. If only that moth of light hadn't pulsed. A flutter of light (the door opening, not fast enough). A contraction of night around the car. An adjustment downward of the sky. As a single piston the automobile pumped forth a cobalt radiance, a radiance that sank, pumped again, and pumped, the door slapping forward and back shut. A shadow appeared to vault into the rear seat. The blaze in the interior put itself out, overcame itself with smoke, and still the door wouldn't open. The hood rattled. The engine, or something, thumped. He heard liquid trickling onto the gravel and a moment later saw wispy flames touch down and there was a sound like somebody circling the car crushing cellophane bags. A breeze undetectable where he sat, or perhaps some invection of the machine itself, gathered small flames back to the undercarriage, which caught, skirting up yellow. Fire spread up out of the ditch. Last the driver's window shot flames, not blue but yellow flames that looked to have no substance or even heat, the prongs separating casually off. But heat was licking around the hood, steaming the roof, producing bags of smoke. When the

Silver Dollar Man closed his eyes, he remembered wash beating on a line, and July dust rushing to it past him.

The Valley View manager, yelling at Cheryl, who was leaning by the door of the unit in the Silver Dollar Man's overcoat, methodically and uselessly sectioned the drive and the automobile with jets of fire extinguisher.

"Up here!" the Silver Dollar Man cried, standing, receiving notice of what he had done to his feet, and she joined him and they lived in the mountains. She'd put her coat on under his, filled the pockets with matches, steak knives, a pot just big enough *to* piss in, and the rolls of dollars. They found they didn't need that much coin of the realm. They got rifles from a hunting camp. He did wrap her in furs. They met others and experienced the commonplace of finding civilization where you would least expect it. These others showed them method, how to pilfer greens from Howard Johnson's, which Park Service employees to trust, and told them of a man who bought venison for a lodge, drove a milk truck down a certain road and waited, never mind the season, another who traded in roots, another in antlers, which he pulverized for devil worshipers (believed *him*), many another with moonshine chores, quick drives in quick cars, these latter Cheryl's specialty, missing her T-Bird. They fixed up an abandoned hikers' pavilion for winter shelter. It needed a roof, they tried to cut shingles, gave up, traded game for tarpaper. Otherwise the structure was fine C.C.C. stonemasonry, nearly graceful, with fluted wood columns supporting the joists. They boarded up the windows, drummed them with hides. An unusually broadbacked ridge, as crooked in lie as a salamander, and gray with hardwoods, extended in front of the one they lived on. Close beyond that, all run together really, were two bunched-up rises covered with evergreen and gray together. Cutting south under the outcrops many hundred feet below the shelter then west by fits along the near slope and through the rises at its shoulder ran a stream, too deep to see but not hear. Its sunken trace through all obstacles carried the eye to the only sight of valley, the gap showing a slanted lake by a road on which they could follow the schoolbuses, and farmland to the point on the horizon where the mountains lay down head to head like dogs. The sun, raising these contours in reverse order, was no help warming the place in the morning but afternoons were a wood-chopper's dream. Sometimes they went down to the road and hitchhiked to Charlottesville to see a movie. (They were considered long gone by the police, whose theories in the weeks after the event they had followed on an acquaintance's citizens band.) The problem of blending in was more a matter of comfort than necessity. It became harder to blend because it became harder to tell what the people were like they were supposed to blend with. Those around at the movies acted jealous of their own body heat. Nobody just came out and told you you smelled.

They were talking about this the first warm day of March three years later. After a series of migrations they were back. Midafternoon, flaps up, the sun clocking the rock oak trees, the last blue snow trickling down the slope, the sound of the river coming up, sounding like an acetylene torch overhead. On the stone throne of a C.C.C. fireplace spaghetti and drippings, a great favorite, bubbled. He was failing somehow. In the middle of his sight there was a brown transparent leaf a yard high. He averted his face to follow movement at a distance. For close work he looked from the lower right quadrants. That close work was mainly furniture. In several Valley homes you would find their rough beauties.

She was leaning over her knee restitching a boot. He was trying to find a station on the transistor but the signals weren't making it over the mountain. "A lot of people prepare and prepare then never have. They don't let themselves have, because, Bill, they just don't."

"That's the reason."

"See ourselves as others see us, what crap. See ourselves as ourselves see us, equal crap. Show and tell, I mean they start in on us so early and it doesn't *matter*. Seeing isn't it."

"I may be able to testify to that soon."

"Quit." She knotted the gut, went after it with her excellent teeth.

"Was that Stan and my's problem?"

"You guys were, God, I don't know, what were you?"

"Not in love with you."

"That too. You didn't know the meaning of the word."

"Nothing like hindsight."

"Really. Really nothing."

"It's funny."

"It's something, I don't know about funny. Hand me that in your hand."

In late afternoon the trees on the broadbacked slope palmed off the sun more and more steeply.

"I'll tell you one thing, Cheryl. I wish old Stan was up here now. Or I wish we were all three you know where."

"That'd be great, wouldn't it?"

"I wouldn't mind seeing my boy either one time."

In the evening the dog nosed around, the fringe on his belly swinging, outside the soil continued to warm up and at last overpowered the leaves.

The schoolteacher's son and his date, who is farsighted, take a left off the road up the mountain and enter the quarry. It is twilight, a nice summer evening. Around them gather gouged and blown-out shapes the hue of cheddar cheese . . . cones and rubble, a sheared hill, self-interring skeletons of heavy equipment. Below them somebody is shooting. It bounces, then funnels back. He is speechless with luck, she with apprehension, not of him or them, both entities she knows too well, but of the place, so lambent with predictions of what may befall lovers there too young for a roof over their heads, a Simmons Beautyrest, a reading lamp. Marauders, mountain lunatics, wildmen, wild*women* drag them from cars, rob them, bash their skulls in but at the least take the car and leave them to trudge naked back to town, bipedal whippets of shame. Of course he and she, who aren't dumb, understand the impulse of these cautions in the collective unconscious of community standards. Yet a humidity of ambush hovers. She is prettier than she knows, older than he knows, having already performed the trigonometry of adulthood: state map, her place on it. She despises his equivocations but remains susceptible to these moron moments, in a *car*, though they exasperate her when she recalls how wasteful, how messy, how little was settled beforehand.

At a flat angle he sips from a can of Dr. P. She mentions the law of averages. Her fine, shallow-lensed, scant-lidded eyes check the top of the stone height and the prospect out the rear window. He stows the drink. They remove just enough. Even so, did he have a hundred eyes and hands, he'd have trouble dealing with this amount of beauty. He says, "I wish we could just disappear."

"Well we can."

"We should just plain run off."

"The thing is, I would, you never will. And I'm the stable one. That's why we're hopeless."

"Not do this again till we do."

"Oh yea? Okay." She moves to make herself decent.

"If it wouldn't sort of be like already risking our lives for nothing."

So they practice, to change beauty to a currency that may be handled with diminished attention, that may be married.

Like most prim, she has only the one threshold, past which is the whole works plain, and silence, and blindness.

Sudden sight, brought by a blow on the driver's window. The boy's head owls, the girl's drowns, taking in the huge, jumping, sprouted brow out there, the fissured grin, fissures everywhere, like tree bark that didn't dry right, a semblance exaggerated by the feeble last glow of the sky. Fortunately her muscles don't lock, which would necessitate a trip to the emergency room to pry him out. In fact the organs of love snap to rather promptly. Moving like an actual lover, somehow wired to the eyes at the glass, he rotates with uncanny deliberation, withdrawing his hand from beneath her, feeling for the ignition key. Red dot on the dash. "Okay," he whispers. "Okay." He completes the one-eighty turn and lies flat, looking up at the window and the sheet of paper smeared to the glass beside that face, pumps the gas, fires the engine. But by the time he is upright and backing, the attacker is behind, cellophane red, arms out in supplication. The attacker wears a cocktail dress, or the form of one, patched so thoroughly with hide it looks more like a martial costume from the Middle Ages. Broken-down knees, bare calves, bare feet. Worms and worts of hair. Peristaltic arms coming out of the sleeveless garment. The boy knows this much, that what he must do if he is to have a home with this girl one day is keep backing, ignore the crunch, or, alternately, jump out, grab the old hag, throw her in a deep quarry pool, whistle the rats on. But he just cannot. Too much responsibility, along with the general regard instilled in the Valley for any female whatever her present aspect. He zips up, rolls down the window. His date, her skirt by this time right side out, may not be paying attention to anything but a case of stomach cramps.

"I've been keeping an eye on you all," the attacker says, returning to his door but maintaining a distance, for their sake, it is clear, not hers. "It gets a little hairy up here sometimes. Here's a map." She steps across the footage she has elected, hands the paper in. "My buddy drew it before his sight went. And before *he* went, also relevant. I'd call that also relevant, wouldn't you?" She is capable of a certain giddy charm, which he recognizes from singing Christmas carols at the mental institution in Staunton, all the violence in the world in all the playfulness. "He liked your momma. A passing fancy but he asked me to pass this on to you. We lived all over these hills. This shows where the places are we fixed up." Her finger comes to the paper. A hank of gray hair comes in, smelling of iron and charcoal. The skin across the back of her hand smells like a drop of sweet oil. "So anytime, you can hike in, stay as long as you please, never leave. It's a whole new world and you never have to leave." Measured laughter, a curtsy and a stride (pouches beating) to the nearest upward path, and they're free.

The girl has been concentrating so powerfully as to wring flesh from bone. Finally it bursts from her, since her world lies closer to that one, where every life has a name. "Oh God," she cries. "Gravel Gertie!"

I Swear I Always Wished You Were a Possibility

You see my little books around here, particularly at Hattie's Restaurant, which I own. I'm not Hattie and neither was the person I bought from. I am Theresa Collins. Here's a poem from my *Spindrift Spinoffs*:

Wrinkled Captain on shallow sound
sighting from invisible to invisible marker
fell in love when
midway between unseen piney point and unseen shoal
he asked
You care to do like them divin' ducks
and the girl got out and walked home
breast-high

When I get two dozen I mail them to a printer in Elizabeth City who returns five hundred thirty-two-page books with coated covers, drawings by his niece. I sell them to friends, give them to tourists. I bought this place in ruin after the last hurricane and have built up to where I can retire in twelve years at age forty-three and live in Mexico. Hattie, a man, is long dead. I'm in my office surrounded by black-eyed peas I never ordered.

This isn't about me. The poem I'm working on is about my friend Christine Clark, who is leaving Water County, North Carolina, for Austin, Texas, alone in a hand-painted truck.

We're having a party in her honor tomorrow after closing, poem required. On both our behalves my regret is that she didn't leave sooner.

April before last. I pick up Glynda James and her, hitchhiking down from the Beachcomber, which has early happy hour, to Hattie's, where we have late. They are drunk but not sloppy. I've never seen Chris sloppy except once recently when it was touch and go between us. "Theresa," Glynda says, "may I introduce you to Crisco Clark, my long-lost cousin. She is Dick Clark's granddaughter and Fabian kissed her backstage when she was five and she's had amnesia ever since, haven't you, dear?"

"I. Have. Am. Ne. Shuh. Plea. Zuh. Hel. Puh. Me."

Being eighteen they think this is hilarious. I happen to notice that Chris is an attractive girl, with blond surfer hair—a false impression since she doesn't even know how to swim until I teach her—somewhat heavy features, a rangy body. I see one German parent, one Cherokee. She is wearing a plaid shirt with mother-of-pearl buttons, a bandana, and carries her pool cue in a pouch, so in rearing I judge pure District of Columbia. "Where you from?" I ask. I bang off into the sand to cut by tourists waiting to turn into Little Mint. She smells of lemon and Slim Jims. April before last she wears one piece of jewelry, a silver bracelet, and her arms show every muscle.

She takes a drag of her cigarette, a Lark—in my experience a brand indicating character. "I. Ca. Unt. Re. Mem. Ber." She keeps a straight face.

"I appreciate this must be difficult for you. But there is a final question I feel compelled to pose." Glynda, big-hearted Glynda, wipes her eyes with the heels of her hands. Sand blows across the road in sheets too thick to see through but I don't slow down. "You need a job?"

She raps her forehead against the dash, bounces back. "Jo. Buh. My. Mo. Ther. Fu. Kin. A. Suh."

"She means when does she start," says Glynda.

This is all right, I've been running with nothing but teenagers lately. Chris does work two weeks for me, one day out front until dumping softshells in the beer of a sport fisherman, the rest as dishwasher and slaw chef. She ignores directions, she oversleeps, she quits once per shift, but nobody wants to see her go. She runs through a half-dozen jobs elsewhere before moving up the list and landing the prize, seasonal clerk at the Post Office, where they issue clothes and let her stay. The clothes matter. She is aware how she looks in that P.O. shirt with three buttons undone at night and her yellow hair.

She becomes belle of the ball among the summer kids of Water County, N.C. No party starts without her. No third-rate band opens at the Casino—she loves pedal steel, will do anything for pedal steel, is moving to Austin for pedal steel—without her at the front table surrounded by beers she never paid for. The Miller man adds her and Glynda's place to his route, gives her her own tap for her birthday. Guys fall in love in an epidemic. They stop by the Post Office with shrimp, drugs and compliments, which is all right too, which is what they know. She reciprocates although with an unsatisfying, to them, impartiality. Here's a poem "Chug" from *Bridge to the Mainland*:

The boys learned
that
sudden acts
and a foul mouth
are ever
the true seducers

She stays through fall, when the hangers-on get serious about their partying, and on through winter. She and Glynda rent a cottage on the south road, wrap the pipes, mylar the porch, heat with space heaters, eat on food stamps, watch storms. She comes from six brothers and sisters, a periodically drunk father, a thoughtful mother. Never in her life has she been so popular.

It concerns me, this staying on of a young person who should have better things to do but once around isn't bad and I live for the nights she walks in here, hands in her hip pockets, P.O. cap way back, P.O. shirttail dangling, and takes a table as if not much caring for company this evening. Company. As others draw oxygen from air she draws company. Her style is to nuzzle you as she puts you down.

I could read this:

Sweet Crisco
your laughter in the smoky barroom
was to my ears the music of a hammer on a tin roof
On the other side it knocked all the billiard balls
          suspended on the lips of pockets
in

Stays on. This past August one afternoon I come over from fishing the bar off the beach across from her cottage, just happen to be fishing that bar—for exercise, no creature in August bathwater ever stirred for food. Chris is home driving the 1950 pickup she and Glynda bought for Texas. She is driving in the driveway up to the road and back, up, back, up to the lip of the macadam, back to the cottage, spewing sand. Red sun beams across the sound, across the marsh, across the bypass, into the cab. A tree of exhaust moves as the truck moves. I stand thumb out but she ignores me.

"Feeling good, honey?" I ask, jumping in between cycles.

Her face is like sandstone. She is loaded with bracelets, and rings, and her diver's watch from Snapper Griggs, and her turquoise pendant from Captain Sligo, whom she has never slept with though not because of his age or because he cohabits with his half sister. "Henry," she simpers, addressing Glynda's steady boy. "When do you want supper, Henry? *Wet Mama wub your wittle back Henwy.*"

"You don't need Glynda, never did."

"She's got the driver's license." Flying fists, blood, ten-foot waves don't faze Chris; driving does. Postmaster Saum offered

her a substitute motor route but even I couldn't teach her not to
freeze at the wheel.

"Have a sip of rum."

"Theresa, she was sup*posed* to be back this morning. We
were sup*posed* to go to Norfolk, buy parts and cassette tapes. I
know what happened. She married him. She married him and
they're screwing on his fish boat like it's a yacht on the fucking
Riviera, man."

"She has not." Of course she has, or near to it.

"She left Dinghy too and you *know* how I feel about animals.
She's a fool." Chris has a way of expressing this opinion once
and for all. "She could have traveled with me and she's gonna
stay here all her life and have kids and get disgusting and cook
suppers at five-fucking-thirty every fucking *night*."

"My, you do see the writing on the wall."

When she lifts her hand to take the pint the truck leaps across
the road, stopping, gearbox knotted, three feet short of my car.
"I've seen it," she says, reading the windshield, "and it says:
'She's dickwhipped. Glynda James is one dickwhipped little
girl.' "

"Chris, you want to buy fish at the store and cook them up?"
I want to touch her but one touch and she'll plow through the
Blazer.

Unfortunately for me and others, Chris has hers back home.
Not her first lay; that occurred at thirteen in Rock Creek Park
after school. Although I come from Spring Hope, full of grand-
mothers my age, I feel thirteen is pushing it but that caused not
a fraction of the harm David Gill stirs up at eighteen to twenty.
He attends college in D.C., has a beard and rabbit eyes and
stands two-thirds her size.

Intermittently she connives to get him down. She calls him,
from here since she doesn't believe in home phones. She calls
his friends. She calls his old girlfriend. She calls his father. If all
else fails she will go to the extreme of using the mails herself,
sending, for example, a cartoon postcard of the Wright Broth-

ers making suggestive remarks (Wilbur to Orville, "Reckon it'll fly?"). She buys the card over at Toler's, walks here, requests a pair of Millers—she likes a full in front of her always—asks not to be bothered, lights up, begins. If warranted she can talk quite intelligently. She reads books, and reads hard, like a contractor over blueprints. Still after two hours labor a card might come out:

> Hey Sweetie, I'm dying. When
> are you coming anyways? Glynda
> has this gigantic bug up her
> a— Theirs nobody. Got barred
> from 2 bars. I fell out. Only
> Theresa didn't. Sea is bee-you-
> tee-full. Get your a— down
> here boy
> > Hunka hunka,
> > Crisco

Then she heads up to the P.O., lets herself in, seals it in an Official Business envelope, and lets herself out.

Normally David caves in at a card, packs his anthologies, his fountain pen, his grippers and dumbbells and hitchhikes down for the weekend. When not even mail persuades she tries a last phone call, Thursday, two A.M. I am (surprise) in the office. She raps. I go open. She clomps in, hair wrecked, clothes wrecked, face shining in the peach light of the jukebox. "I am writing poetry if you don't mind," I say, even if writing Sandler Foods about an overcharge.

"Fuck poetry." A high note on fuck, low notes on poetry, a seagull followed by a foghorn.

"Really? Listen to this for my new book *In Honeyed Light and Other Dunesong*:

> Nothing is so like despair
> as the chalkwhite beacon against its field of blue
> nothing so like hopelessness, bad life
> as guidance in the dead of night
> Down in the black wreck what

weightless scuttle
what scaly secret joy"

"It sucks." Seagull, foghorn. "You're too good for your poetry, man. Would you please turn on the lights? I'm scared of
the dark."

"I can read by the jukebox, you can phone by it."

"Aw, Theresa." She squeezes my shoulders and raises her
eyes to mine, smiles and stops smiling. "Theresa, you dear old
thing, are you thinking I walked all this way to make a phone
call? That's awful, that's pitiful. I came just to see you, you're
the only one I want when I'm alone in the universe." This is one
of her best expressions, devoted eyes.

"I'm a vulnerable poet. You can toy with other people's affec-
tions, about three more years."

"Yea, whose speed have you been into?"

"Snapper's. You didn't screw him did you?"

"I *told* you I will not screw him."

"Don't. That's the beginning of the end."

"Well maybe I will call some *warm*hearted friend."

"Get your own phone. Mine'll be cut off with all your tolls on
it." Actually she settles every nickel including tax the day the
bill arrives, doesn't borrow either, attitudes her father taught
by reverse example.

On the way to the phone she stoops into the beer case, the
attitude her father taught by positive example. Of the kids he
chose her to drink with in the kitchen, his Gallo to her scotch
(grown, she drinks beer to reform). She fumbles in the holes
dialing. "He's no good for you!"

"You're telling me! Will you turn the lights on? What is
wrong with you? Will you quit staring? Davey?" A shade of
sweetness, the effect of two drops of milk in a cup of eight-hour
coffee, seeps into her voice. "Yea. So how you doing, sucker?
Hope I'm not interrupting you in mid-stroke or nothing. I
mean I hope I am. So you coming to see me this weekend huh?
Please? Pretty please? Glynda doesn't get rowdy anymore, it's

the Mojave down here. You're kidding me." Sheer scorn. I slip past to my desk. "Are you telling me you'd rather play lacrosse than see me? You can miss one practice, man, tell them you might pull a groin muscle." Knowing she prefers listeners-in I leave the door open. "Do you understand what's happening to you? You've got little man's disease. First you're into weightlifting, then cross-country, now fucking lacrosse. I *liked* you as a wimp. I've been in love with wimps before and they do just fine. Most of the time they do better. You're selling your soul to that school, man, and I'm your last chance for a pawnbroker." Listen, listen, hiss, hiss, slam.

"Give me a cold one, Theresa. Come out of there. Stand by the jukebox with me. Fuck poetry."

Mashing the right side of her hair to the back of her neck she stands in the office door while I write, two cases Gwaltney's links, two six-count key lime filler, one case Pine Sol, one cornmeal. She grins convincingly, the way she did coming out of the surf after swimming solo past the pier the first time. She droops an eyelid. I take off my glasses, go out and dig beers from the bilge. Now what light there is falls from the Old Milwaukee clock and lights her tee shirt like skin. "I've never seen anybody attract men and scare them off at your rate. Maybe Guinness has an 800 number."

"It's so simple they can't handle it. Aw I'm changing my fucking ways."

"What's that supposed to mean?"

"You tell me."

She gives me a glance of zero subtlety, generally my stock in trade but all I say is, "I dare you to repeat that," and hang my arm around her shoulder like nothing but a swim coach. "Your three years might be up faster than you anticipate."

"You wish," she says, and ducks. Luckily speed deadens everything but my brain.

Cards usually work. David, envisioning her sunk like a boat in solitude, arrives at the cottage, only to find it crawling—with

Water County friends, friends from home, friends' friends, *his* friends from school and how did they get here? Bikinis in the sea elder, speakers on the roof. People talking with sandcrabs, Glynda boiling shrimp, Chris on the porch swing with her legs twined in some guy's and Captain Sligo unconscious beneath, or not. "How you doing?" she calls, as to a neighbor passing.

She steps down to give him a hard, impartial hug. The guy in the swing sings along with Asleep at the Wheel. Toting a knapsack of iron in the September heat wave, David starts the reunion fight by comparing her loneliness to a germ's in a culture. Aw come on, man, she has no idea where these clowns come from, out of the woodwork. This is spur-of-the-moment to celebrate Glynda's breaking up from a guy with a serious personality and coming home. He doesn't care, he is going to the sound to study under a tree so he won't get tossed out of school along with off lacrosse. He'll see her at sundown at Hattie's, if she feels like it. Please stop casting shifty looks at the porch, she asks. That match went out before it lit. David asks not to be bored by her junior high affairs. He'll see her later probably. He'd better. The sheets are clean except for her own sweat, he still turns on to her sweat, doesn't he? Here. Get back. How's about some of this? Later, all right? There are chicken livers and shrimp, there is a fifth of Tanqueray tucked under the pillow, limes on the bedstand. He'll catch her later probably. He won't forget the Tanqueray? He'll try not to.

I make sure he doesn't—selfless me—listening to his troubles while he drinks more than he can, explaining—knowledgeable me—a woman's attitude toward *the* man in her life. "Your mistake is not appreciating how shy Crisco actually is. And how high her standards actually are, that's no act. She's not going to settle for any mere suggestion of a move. Something grand, Davey. Try something grand despite your generation." The waitresses are sweeping up and toking up, Chris seven hours overdue from a distance of one mile and a quarter.

"Yea, right, exactly, it's all gestures and maneuvers." He swirls his mug, hiking beer over the side.

"You are holding back, she can smell it. When you're ready for anything with her she'll drop these tourists."

Here's the start of "Postgirl," my country and western lyric (any musicians reading this? I don't *need* to be forty-three to retire):

> I didn't expect to encounter her at the counter
>   that day
> I merely thought I'd grab my mail and
>   slip away
> Then underneath a cap of blue her hair
>   flashed like a spark
> And put a tracer right onto my
>   missing heart
>
> She was a catalog of desire
> A warm letter from home
> An aerogramme from a friend so far away
> But as she lingered at my box
> I begged, "Don't touch that lock,
> You deliVER more bills than I can pay"

If only I can get another verse and if only enough show up to come in on the chorus; a stumbling block, convincing them to show up for her.

Shortly after that driving practice in the driveway there is one muggy Friday, one last stand, when she receives three proposals in a row, legal marriage. Four counting Sligo. (His is ongoing. He likens it to the Gulf Stream, which you can't see from shore but is always out there ever warm.) Chris and Glynda are throwing a party for their Texas truck, departure imminent— or so Glynda has promised, again, forsaking all others—guests to bring motor oil and wrenches. I come up from the cape, my team having placed first in the billfish tourney in ladies division. Instead of staying for my own celebration with yacht owners here I am driving inebriated seventy miles at twilight to a beer blast with teens.

A litter of vehicles noses the cottage. Glynda runs out in a white dress barely containing her. "You will not believe this, Theresa!" She is feeding bits of sandwich to Dinghy. "Snapper asked Crisco to marry him then Donald took her up the dunes and asked then Davey took her in the bedroom and asked."

I believe it. The only news that surprises me is of animals. If somebody raises turkeys with chickens I am surprised. "What about your nuptials, huh?"

"Theresa, I am not a kitchen appliance on an extension cord." Not her phrase.

The guys who want Chris forever are streaming sweat in the kitchen watching her fix seafood spaghetti by lantern, VEPCO having surrendered to air conditioners. Smoke rises from the lantern, pours off the skillet. Snapper, in sunburnt from a fishing trip (work for a change) lavishes Heineken and charm on me, his good offense since he owes me money on a certain transaction. He has another girl with him, with sunglasses in her hair. She is all over him, whose eyes are all over Chris, who is running clam juice through a coffee filter. Sligo in double-knits kills a Blue Ribbon at the screendoor. Donald, one of Chris's oldest and dearest become drug seller up and down the coast, slices onions one slice per minute. David keeps his hand to his beard, doesn't want it to jump off. Glynda hacks a pepper to pieces, Henry smooches her neck.

Sligo says, "Chrissie, let's go, play diving duck, go to Justice of the Peace, go *now* I say."

"Build me a house."

Snapper hauls me to the living room, cinches me to him with useful arms for a change. "I swear I always wished you were a possibility," he says.

"Fifteen minutes under you might change me."

"You got that right, dream machine."

"It'll cost you four hundred dollars."

"I'm getting my checkbook."

Over the stereo I hear Chris's voice shift, hitting sand, from cruise to four-wheel traction.

"I'm getting supper," I say.

"I'll press your Post Office blouse, I'll fillet your flounders, I'll dust your albums all the rest of my days," moans Glynda, kneeling on the linoleum, hands clasped, as I walk back into the lantern light. "And we shall dwell in the house of the Texans forever, darling."

"I am not in the mood," Chris says. "I mean how many times did I ask you to remember the squid, man? You had one fucking thing to remember all fucking day, buy squid. I didn't ask you to drive me anywhere because I knew you wouldn't show. I hitchhiked to the grocery store, I hitchhiked to the A.B.C. store, I hitchhiked back with two armloads."

Glynda stands up, and, already a full-bodied girl, grows. "What do you want, blood from my tits?" she yells, then ruins it by sticking her tongue out—incidentally causing the legs of Snapper's date, clamped one over the other, to pop.

"Ladies," Sligo says, patting his clothes as if maybe he pocketed squid on the way.

"Really," says David.

"You all should pick on summer people while you have them," I advise. "I'm going for squid, back in a heartbeat."

"No way, you will not buy *squid!*" Chris glares at me, joins the kerosene glare. "It was her responsibility and her spoiled ass had better things to do all day as usual and that's just dandy and nobody cares anyway and just *forget it*. Fuck everybody. I'm going to Texas." She slams out the front as Glynda, flipping fingers in her direction, slams out the back.

On the porch Chris puts a kitchen match to her cigarette, slow to catch because of the air. In that air you can smell everything, the ocean and seaweed, the sweet pepperbush and asters in the sand, the oil on the stove. "Buddy Guy," she says, listening through the door to a radio. "So amazing." Either she wonders if I think she is losing her mind or she simply wants us to look at each other while Buddy Guy plays. Inside in the dark they hoot, ask about did you see that multi-limbed critter slithering under the sofa? Chris pulls her bandana off and shakes her hair in the breeze, much too slight a breeze to stir those wires. Her hair smells its color in the sun. Brine glistens in the vee of her federal shirt under turquoise.

I say, "In my opinion if she tries to stall this time too buy her half of the truck and go. I'll lend you money. I've seen it, people as smart as you trapped here, no future. The second winter is the beginning of the end. I'll take my life in my hands again, teach you to drive."

"I get too nervous somebody's gonna kill me."

"Not unless one of your heartsick fiances driving at you."

She touches her head to mine, jets smoke. "They always want to marry me. It's because I'd make such an excellent mommy, you know? They're fools. Snapper said if there's no other way to go to bed with me. 'That shows your mental age,' I said. 'If there's anything else I can do to not marry you, empty bedpans, join the WACS, I will.' Donald *swore* he'll sell only marijuana if I ride with him. He *knows* how I feel about the other shit. I told him, 'Check back in ten years when you're rich *and* safe.' Davey pulls out this Lancer's Bianco at sundown and drags me to the bedroom, gives me his retard smile. Move back to D.C. with him. 'I'm twenty years old, I'm a little beyond emotions and hormones, man, don't you think? You check back in *nine* years. If I don't have me a pedal steel man in Austin by then I'll be ready even for you. Don't forget now; do check back.' " She waits on me.

"You're a credit to womanhood."

"Thanks, you're my idol."

"Your face stands there"—making it up as I go—"your face stands there: a profile of the moon above a sea of wind: that pours off locomotives in another land: moon reflected in their windows."

"Cabooses."

"Moon shimmering in their cabooses."

She stares straight ahead, ignoring the actual horned moon high over the wooden motel over on the darkened beach. "I have *no*, zero, idea what I'm supposed to do with myself." She is holding her beer and cigarette in adjacent fingers; on the far side of the bottle her cheek collapses.

"If you're really ready to go, you wouldn't have picked a fight."

"She doesn't suit my needs anymore. She's *so* changed, beyond belief."

"You need to decide what's so great about your needs."

She folds down to the railing. "Aw I'm too depressed to, it's a vicious fucking circle."

"Oh depressed. Take courses at Austin Community College. Sell Amway."

"Can't fish. Is that it, Sweet Thing?"

"Hey Crisco!" Glynda comes bouncing around from back and, a feeble puff of white, climbs in the truck. She leans out the window, flashes the high beams at the porch and cranks, throwing the starter into a catfight. "Let's run to Norfolk, girl!"

"Forget it! Quit damn blinking!"

"Go see the Boys!" She means the Broken Mountain Boys, their favorites, worth any sacrifice of sleep and courtesy.

"For. Get. It!" Chris shades an eye with her bottle.

David and Henry wander out, and judging by calm appearance have reached a consensus on their girlfriends or puffed a Donald joint or both. David tries to take Chris's hand but she won't allow it. "Just remember where you got your real education, man. I was it for you and you know I was it for you."

"The Boys, fishface!"

"Stay here," I ask quietly. "Stay and talk with me. I did catch a blue today."

"Why?"

"Because I think we should drop this nonsense and speak with each other."

"Pardon me," she says, tossing the cigarette now and stepping over the rail, in five-dollar cowboy boots from Swan's Bay Thrift impervious to burrs (at the least).

"Think we ought to go after them?" David asks Henry.

Although he doesn't appear capable of going after conchs on

plywood, I say, "Stay where you are. It's none of your all's damn business."

"What in God's name do you mean it's none of my business?" Suddenly I have this hyena beside me, snapping, whipping its forelegs in the air, where before I had the rabbit version. "She's been my business for two years! I've put myself in incredible contortions for our relationship. I've given up everything at school, I've put up with every sort of behavior, sleeping around—by the truckload—everything. *I* want to know why *you* think she's your business. Tell me about disinterested interest. I have my own damn opinion."

"Break my heart, son." First I see Chris by the driver's window, legs wide, head back, like Sligo in his boat daring the man on the dock to offer a poor price. Second I see her slump against the door, speak to the ground. Third I see her just walk around and get in, and the muffler spits, the headlights wobble like doll eyes, the bed rumbles, and there goes Dinghy shoulder first down the road after the single, jittery, persisting taillight. I am left on the porch with a kid who needs sending to his room and with the affair I should be attending—damn the husband, we've lost him before—seventy miles away. I almost answer but don't, because I could care less what he thinks, because he couldn't comprehend anyway, because when all is said and done I own a good little restaurant I run on greased wheels and in twelve years I will be in Mexico living as I please.

Believing I use indelible ink I write her off. Of course the next morning Glynda, Henry, David traipse in here to worry over her over pitchers. Well, Glynda worries, not having heard since ditching her at a motel where the band took them to order records off late-night TV. Henry bestows worry only on tides and winches; he grows on you. David seems to have risen from his bad bed on the good side.

Unlike, I understand, most poets, I believe in writing a person off in person. "Anybody want to ride up the Post Office?"

"She'll never make it to work," Glynda says. "Anyway me and Henry are talking. Anyway not after what she said."

It is true that she and Henry are holding not only each other's thighs but a conversation. "She's there," I say. I know her equilibrium, that a lost night must be followed by prompt arrival at her government job, pension accumulating. David and I—it is true that in twelve hours he has turned life to a joke and himself to a worthwhile companion—drive up in the Blazer, one of those chilly eleven A.M.'s that foretell true autumn, the great blue desertion I, and stripers, live for.

"The same old story," he remarks, dry as history class. "Glynda wanted to get home in time to baste Henry's eggs, Chris wanted to slip into the other room with the pedal steel player. They argued. The usual names. Jellyfish. Spermicidal jellyfish. Groundhog-heart." The very bottom of Chris's list, groundhog-heart.

In 1955 the government airlifted post offices to the coastal towns, flat-roofed brick boxes with the locality in aluminum. Outside this one I run a comb through my hair. Inside she's there. Uniform wrecked, baseball visor low, she is in back dishing letters into boxes. David offers our gift, butter biscuits in waxpaper. "Care to try a few of these, Mr. Saum?"

"Believe it," the postmaster says, stacking kings.

"Hey Crisco," says David.

"Hey Proncho." Any expert on her could see through that airy behavior. I almost feel for her there in the federal hangover-punishment decor, but don't. Don't feel much of anything; I must have passed through madness to have. When she comes over to us, I see her plain, all twenty years.

"I don't care if you slept with the whole band," David says. "I'd be disappointed if you didn't." He doesn't care either if Saum tunes in, not to mention the other customers. One is Frank Willis, who sold me my place on decent terms on faith and is in collecting several thousand in deposits for duck season. One is Laura Pond, who works for the township, and her engagement ring, which Elizabeth Taylor wouldn't be ashamed to wear, to breakfast anyway, if she eats it. If they choose to wonder what these kids are to me, fine.

"I slept with no one." She props herself on her elbows striking her second-best pose, tacky desire. "I mean I did, with our *under*pants on. We talked about producing. There's a strong possibility they'll let me work with their producer in Austin."

"There's a strong possibility you'll take your underpants off next time. Anybody else like some?" He caters the biscuits around, tosses the wrapper in the trash and goes to study the wanted posters, particularly the female. Laura Pond can scarcely bear eating such a messy thing but does.

"Theresa, we told them we were in this movie about the submarine base, just in from L.A. to wrap up. Glynda danced in her slip. I mean we got college students to clog, we got Virginians to clog. Look, I been thrown out of better places."

"Way to go, honey." I hand her my sat-upon letter in the vermillion envelope. Her new belt spells out Virginia Beach in plastic wampum.

"Who's this to? Her again? Jesus."

"Just give me a stamp."

"And then," she says, "sitting in the motel listening to what's-his-face saw wood and staring over at Krispy Kreme till dawn, man. I got clear on people. I even got clear on you, you old rag doll." A switch—this is her workplace, the counter dividing us hers, and she adds to that the tilt that the visor requires.

"Congratulations. I am Windex on two feet."

"No way. You want people to think so but actually you're a mess. Like mailing letters to this turkey, at her *business* address. Come on, what are you scared of? At your stage in life this is fucking pathetic, Theresa."

The others conscientiously tend to their postal matters.

"I hear better lectures at college," David murmurs. The scales have fallen. He sees the beauty of murderesses, abductresses, any woman who strikes with criminal intent and crosses state lines. "Would I love to get involved with those thin lips."

"So really, are you sure this is the chick for you?"

It doesn't bother me, as owner of a going concern, what people think of my lifestyle. It's hardly news to anybody and check out theirs. But it bothers me, frankly it wounds me, that she thinks it will, wants it to.

"Chris, there are patrons waiting." The postmaster.

"Actually," she says, and turns, "I am waiting on our biggest patron. She patronizes my *existence*."

"Just cannot find help these days, can you, Saum?" Frank Willis. Due to the nature of real estate, he is an all-county gossip, but hell on channel bass.

Saum says, "No they expect the taxpayers to pay for their personal lives."

I say, "Oh Mr. Saum, we're buddies," catching him between this stage and the next.

"Seriously," Chris mutters. "I'm taking the coins from my own pocket, I'm buying the stamp myself. I just wanted to patronize her, you know? My opinion is she doesn't *need* this, this chick is *no* good for her, she doesn't *need* to keep getting jerked around by these married bitches!" No longer is anyone pretending to mind their own business. "Mr. Saum, this is the way we *always* deal with each other, we're tight. I'm gonna ask her for a loan next." Not a trace of expression, she adjusts her visor, works the tabs, runs off a meter strip for my letter. "Can you advance me seventy-five, Sweet Thing? That makes eighty-oh-three with the phone."

"Extra tight, downright snug." Frank Willis.

"We're just messing." However I stand there like a perfect robot, breathless. "You need it this minute?"

"Dump it in Glynda's lap and inform her she doesn't own even half a truck anymore. She's not even half-assed anymore. I'll wire the money from Austin. Texas."

"She's good for it, don't you dare give the child a hard time, Mr. Saum," I caution and on that note David and I more or less sweep out the door, past a Rock Church couple who eat at the restaurant Sundays before two and the mystified Laura Pond.

Wonderfully transformed, he holds the passenger door for me and takes the driver's seat, handles the transmission nicely and says not a word. I am thinking how practical a brick hut is for her by day; kelp-colored plate glass; radio waves barely making it to the set she keeps on the file scratching out country rock and roll. I give her credit for doing the necessary with all the tenderness at her disposal.

This fall and into winter you see her alone. Her, who once claimed she couldn't sleep without another body in the house, now without even the puppy, or live bait. The Miller man tells me she flung the tap at him, ran him off. Occasionally she comes here for breakfast, doesn't speak—still for no one else would Martha fix eggs at 2 P.M., for no one else bake biscuits special—eats, goes out, crosses the road, hair whipping, one hand in her jacket, the other holding a Lark in a split mitten, descends the hump of beach and reappears nowhere for a long time after. Occasionally, needing money, she comes in to shoot. She's improved. Where before, despite the thirteen-ounce custom stick, she never could put a whole game together, now the ruts appear in the felt before the shots, written poems she is only rereading.

I call David at school. He wants her to answer his letters but I explain she is deaf to me as well. He wants her to marry him and can back this up with a job at a private school.

After her honeymoon Glynda tries twice. The first time Chris simply hides. Glynda sees oyster stew on and waits until it smokes but nothing. The second time, Chris comes to the door but won't unlock. She tells Glynda to go home to hubbypoo and fuck herself and Henry fuck himself because they'll never fuck each other because they're too chicken.

New Year's Day following a night at the pier after hammerhead I swallow my pride. I am going to pieces—whoever intentionally caught a hammerhead?—and if I don't see her there won't be pieces left. I want to get out of the light, out of the

spray, sit in blankets, drink coffee with her and watch, as courteously as possible, her.

She throws the door open. "New Year's resolutions fucking
work." She is in cowboy boots and thermal underwear, the
shirt stained as if she's been leaning into the truck engine. "You
want a blood-and-sand?" She backs into the sofa, knocking an
ashtray, bearing a lighted cigarette, to the floor. She crushes the
cigarette, sending up a whiff of rag rug. In the kitchen she
scoops ice cubes from the tabletop into a glass. The place is a
disaster, oyster debris buried in vegetable ends buried in Wonder Bread wrappers. A piglet-size bird floats in the sink. Strings
of teabags hang down the window (Glynda's custom). "One-
third o.j., one-third cherry liqueur, one-third scotch, dash of
bitters. It's one of those drinks, man"—she collides with the
stove, spilling a good part of mine—"you can't stand for the
first two then can't conceive drinking anything else the rest of
your life. Vitamin C too. God, I'm glad you came."

"I'm hurt you didn't have the decency to include your old
buddy in the invitation."

"I didn't invite anybody. I'm into being pathetic." She
pushes up her sleeves, bobs the turkey. It sucks and gurgles.
"Actually I invited only you only I was too much of a wimp to
tell you."

"My land, but I've already accepted an invitation to the Governor's Mansion. They want to name me Poet Laureate."

"I sliced myself to ribbons shucking." She lifts her palm, a
dozen cuts. Her hand, all of her looks puffy, I doubt from lack
of exercise alone. "I'm inviting you to drink blood-and-sands
for seven hours and twenty minutes till the turkey's done, then
eat. Then you invite me, for a nap. Pretty please."

"You had tetanus shots?" Nobody ever accused me of lacking
sense, heart at the speed limit or no.

"Sligo gave me one last month. He keeps serum in his fridge.
I mean, he has this theory—I don't know, man. Are you avoiding the subject?"

In a damn tiny voice I say, "Aren't you going to Austin?"

"God!" She peels her forearm off the stove, every tin inch of whose exterior equals the four-seventy-five of the oven. "Blood-and-sands, ridiculous, fuck!"

I set my drink down—she's correct, it's revolting—wrap ice cubes in a teatowel and apply it to her arm. "Hold over the sink. Deputy'll be in Wednesday, we'll get your license. We'll practice at IGA."

She shivers. "Austin's a dreamworld. Don't teach me for there. Teach me for the Water County mail truck, which I'm gonna drive forever, and ever, and get wasted and drive the mail, and marry some congenial fool and be a fucking joy to come home to, doesn't everybody need a joy to come home to?"

"I'd sign away my business. Half." I stand attached to her, my arm grazed by her stomach in mesh. "What's this gut, Chris? Give me the date, when do you leave?"

"That's my *gut*. And I don't leave."

"That's not good enough."

"For *sex*?"

"Yes, for mere sex. I'm not interested in being a late-model Glynda to you."

She pulls away, wets down the burn—and the young tom beneath—with her drink, and shuts her eyes and opens them quickly. The sister rundown cottages out the windows are boarded up, with rundown boards. "Put your mind at ease, you dear old thing, we never came close."

"I mean another excuse to not leave. This is the critical period for ice."

She takes the poultice, staring at me as she would a tourist in a poor choice of swimsuit. "I'm not thinking in terms of some heavy involvement."

"Strange things happen."

"What's come over you to make such a big deal?"

"Lives are big deals."

"This isn't a marriage proposal!"

"This isn't nothing if you don't hit the road!" Then when I

say, "I'm driving to Spring Hope to eat with my sister, butter your arm at ten," I am reminded it is almost never right to go against body and heart. It causes her to wrench back, clear space. It throws a stillness I've never, maybe no one has ever, seen before on her.

Looking so still she says, "They can't stand you there."

The light changes, or we change the light. I am without will-power sober, she is without drunk. "You couldn't stand me either until today."

"You know, your self-image."

"Please, kiddo, spare me."

"Your self-image is so poor you're afraid somebody *will* want you. Your fake concern for me is because you're scared of your-self."

"No such thing as selfless love, right, Crisco?"

"Damn straight." She revives, standing in her thermals over that moldy truth as over a chest of doubloons brought up shin-ing from the depth of the sea. "That's your problem. Mine is I *al*ways end up bullying people into loving me then they resent it, *of* course. Damn it," she snaps (like wire, with a squeak) and, first making sure of the chair, sits down.

Suddenly I'm wearing out the linoleum.

"I've been reading the book you gave me," she says, "*Jude the Obscure*."

"It was patronizing. Matronizing. I want another blood-and-sand."

"Yea, they're—blackout guaranteed, the highest recommen-dation. You caught a chill. Keep this ice on me while I smoke. No, that book, I'm into it." I can believe the tabletop isn't hold-ing all that still for her. "Listen, would you care to take a fucking bubblebath?"

"All right." Sure.

Her idea of bubblebath is hot water with Vaseline Intensive Care Beads, we can't find a position, especially with her arm, and needing a blood-and-sand I remain so wooden it's a won-der I don't float. Finally I stand up—"My chill is gone but this is beyond me right now. Bed." Fine with her. Off her the water runs more slowly and in sheets. She reaches back over her head. The chain lifts her hair. For a reason unclear to me she is removing every piece of jewelry and leaving it on the rim of the tub.

Her bedroom under the roof, a window whose upper corners the gables touch, morning sun, postcards on the wall from all the fabulous resorts that Donald visits in the drug line, the rudimentary toiletries of the fresh, a clock radio wound in bungie cord and wired to an automobile speaker, a quilt upper, just the upper, no ticking yet, the Hardy and the Saint Augustine from her mother. Drafts but the stove feeds directly upstairs. "I've *needed* some relief," she confesses, on the side of the bed, hunched over the act of putting ointment on the burn. She swings up. "That guy from the Boys appears. Other than that. That first night he had on, believe it or not, this old Hattie's Restaurant tee shirt. He *plays* in that thing." Age twenty, she lets her hair fall forward of her shoulders, and weights her eyes.

"I'll be surprised to climb Monte Alban and not find one on somebody," I say, "or flying on a stick in the wind."

She flicks her head back with a sort of prizefighter reflex, meaning we can kiss now. At the start she holds her breath.

I'm not certain how well the normal are doing these days. But from what I see I suspect laziness, and poor budgeting of time. "B.B. King," she says, "the *chill* is over, baby." She makes herself comfortable, stretching out, waiting—which for the last two years has been her nature after all, though disguised. There is plenty of her, untended, uncomplicated and even where closest to the bone (only her face, stomach, hands have taken the new weight) really quite placid, no special thanks to bath beads. Her breasts though are moist from the bath. I lead and she's no slouch at following. "That in particular makes me crazy," she notes. "Aw Theresa anyway." She wraps me in four plain limbs. Our shoulders lock, the bottoms of our faces are wet—no revelation, that she is strong on mouth—and then in contrast, almost at a distance, the small rooting that is particularly making her crazy. A tang of her comes up. I cradle her as the person I sometimes ask to be cradled as. I live on for her enlargement, her easeful cracking, the glide of her leg from under me to the edge of the bed, where her foot stands free in the air.

"Covers," I say. "I need you in here, I'm serious."

"You are." Palpable shock.

"We have a long ways to go," I remind her. We go there.

> She left one day about as quick as
>   overnight express
> No special handling for me, no
>   forwarding address
> Egrets regret, the cane ain't able, gulls
>   fly gracelessly
> I swear that postgirl left her
>   stamp on me

> She was a catalog of desire
> A warm letter from home
> An aerogramme from a friend so far away
> But as she lingered at my box
> I begged, "Don't touch that lock,
> You deliVER more bills than I can pay"

After the party I'll send this to the Broken Mountain Boys gratis on the condition the next time they play Austin they play it to death.

Coldbeer at the Only

I was talking trash with the new mayor, the Honorable Dovey Gray, when this damn tourist family about poked my eye out. They were coming around the corner of the Only Bar as I turned to watch some strange going in the marina. If Trooper Taggart hadn't come along I'd have snatched that crabnet from that pygmy and broke it across his mouth.

"I'm blinded. What the hell you doing here."

"I heard you washed overboard."

"That's right. I drowned."

"Sea of strange," Dovey said. "What the hell you doing here."

"What would you do with it, old man," Taggart said.

Three of us watched while she windowshopped the tee shirts then the Honorable drove back to town to draw menus in his ice cream parlor.

"Finest kind."

"Yea heard you boys was grubbed up and sailing yesterday."

"You never had no strange."

"Never had no need."

"Who'd you marry, Catherine the Great."

"Liquor hadn't killed you, it would."

"She can take mine crabpotting after, believe that."

"Walk in the municipal office with me, have a coldbeer."

"I'm barred."

"Whole bar's barred."

"I do need to speak with the commissioner."

Buthrell's dog Jimbob was laying out under the bumper of the commissioner's Nova, big puddle of slobber under his head, a sorry sow-size half golden retriever half God knows, but no Lincoln Continental of Buthrell's that I could see blind.

"I love you," I said.

She draped her purse just right over her shoulder leaving. New tee shirt. Lovely aspirin tablets.

"You like them aspirin tablets."

"I appreciate them."

"I will lick you to the bone, I will beg for thirds."

"Lick. You're telling on yourself, old man."

"Thought you was buying me a coldbeer."

"You coming in come on then."

"I got business with the county commissioner, ain't I."

"I got business."

"You. You want a audience."

So I walked in with him, first time in eighteen months, twelve days, Jimbob shuffling and dripping behind us, eat-up heart playing a tune. Naturally there was the commissioner in powder blue trousers and shirt and tie and white hair, the whitest you will find in this world, at the regular table and there was a crew off the Cape May Bee in back and there was Jerry Combs sprawled slam across a booth. Jimbob went up to the bar and gurgled phlegm till Cammie drew a bowl of draft and set it before him.

"Clovis, another share of bribe owed here."

"Which," the commissioner said.

"Holiday Inns of America. Allowing them to build where turds float. Pay up or I go to Dan Swindell."

"We measured the water table."

"Used the metric system, did you."

"Yes I did," the commissioner said, tending his tie. "Damn if I didn't wait for a drought and a sandstorm too."

"Wouldn't bother you none them turds get up and walk," Combs said. I had thought he was out.

"Were they to hitchhike to Hyde County now. What the hell you doing here."

She was the steamer Mosetta T. Tattershall, one hundred and ninety tons, carrying two masts, out of Wilmington, under Captain Iredell Tattershall, and had outlived her economy. Having, over an excellent platter of eggs and roe, come to an agreement satisfactory to all parties, Captain Ange Buthrell and First Mate Roger Bone took leave of this same Tattershall and proceeded to the harbor, there to board the doomed vessel. A spectator could not fail to appreciate the contrast afforded by the aspects of these seamen, the mate in heft and wit the very embodiment of his surname, while his Captain typified that coastal heartiness no less fluent than authoritarian. Shoulders broad as a yardarm, carriage erect as the mizzenmast, torso stout as if encompassing a cask of Jamaica rum, the entirety of whose contents, it is true, did not overtop the good Captain's capacity, such were the physical traits which wed to mental acuity of the highest stood Buthrell as axis of all gyring planks. Yet such was his gaiety that ashore he was as likely to be taken for dancingmaster as seafarer.

Under cover of darkness he had caused to be transported from his covert storehouse a full hold of ruin: staved-in barrels of molasses and pinepitch, wagonloads of waterlogged lumber, bolts and bales of sunk flax and cotton. And at dawn, not to lose a freshening southeasterly, for the sheets at this stage of deterioration of the boilers counted as no mere poor relations, but brothers, in traction, Buthrell and Bone weighed anchor out of invisible Swan's Bay.

The commissioner hid a Roi-Tan in his mouth, tip and all, rummaged it around, shoved it out slimy. Up walked Combs and flamed butane a yard high. The commissioner took suck, flame jumping cluck, cluck, cluck. Combs sat down and then it was Buthrell himself slinking around from the back in Hollywood shades, Hawaiian shirt, flipflops, face looking like it'd been beat, floured and left to rise, hands doing the fly's wings.

"Gentlemen." He stood a fifth of Myers's on the table. Illegal to the end. "Would you object to my joining you."

"Your damn bar not his," I said.

"Five minutes yet. Cammie, bring these boys a last round on us."

"Let he who is without objection among you," the commissioner said.

Slue Swain came down the ramp in his fishtruck greens into the dark. "Ange, you could have rode that thing to Fulton Street this morning. My man waited."

"I crave punishment."

Swain sat. "Cammie, bring me one. Bring these boys a round."

"Sorry sucker. The one time," Combs said.

"Long as you're here, though, Angleworm, I might as well put in my license plate request. I want mine to read B.I.G.O.N.E."

"How much. It won't be cheap keeping in drugs up there."

"Brother, got you covered," Combs said. "Don't be worrying on that account."

"Cammie, don't allow no reporters, we're going to executive session," the commissioner said.

Buthrell looked at Taggart then and lifted his Tarheels sixteen ouncer.

"Taggart."

"Buthrell."

In the course of my analysis, it occurred to me that the name Buthrell might have a hidden significance for Trooper Theodore T. This suspicion was confirmed in conversation with my friend Blotto, an adept of the southern dialects. The name Buthrell is pronounced with the stress on the initial syllable; the final syllable carries the typical southern degenerative voicing of the vowel. Thus: BYOOT-rull. Byoot is phonetically equivalent to beaut, or the term which in the popular mind connotes a superlative example—e.g., that truck's a beaut. When we add to this an identification of rull as the degenerative also of roll—

e.g., the expression, gimme some o' tha' sweet jelly rull o' yourn, momma—the double entendre stands out clearly.

"Would you care for Myers and pineapple or you want a Blue," Buthrell said.

"Ginger ale be fine straight up."

"Woo, wee," Combs said.

"Man's asking you to have this one, this one with him and you tell him ginger ale, if you ain't sorrier than even I thought. How you feel tomorrow he rolls out dead in his bunk, windpipe and bloodclots."

"Keep coming, Slue."

"Man's ass ready to roll down the road might never come back, you tell him ginger ale."

"Didn't you never do nothing," I said.

"Never had no need."

"That's you."

"And you are going off the wagon for the occasion. Now that is brotherly love, Mr. Peavey."

"Right it is."

"Cammie, ginger ale for the officer," Buthrell said.

Just then Jimbob, both eyes glazed over bloodshot, huffed up to us. He was primed to take a hunk out of somebody and he was primed to fall out, a complicated animal.

"Been down to the docks lately, commissioner," Combs said. "Strange goings-on down there."

Buthrell tipped back and sipped and smoked and beat Jimbob on the head. Then if he didn't whip a letter out.

"Check out the stationery one time, Embassy of the United Kingdom of Great Britain and Northern Ireland, Washington, D.C."

"Strange on the tide, a nest of sneaky-snakes."

"I'm talking about the damn Queen of England coming for the Quadricentennial."

The commissioner held the letter before him like a hymnal.

' "The Mayor, the Honorable Mr. Ange Buthrell, Junior. The ambassador would be delighted to discuss the possibility of the participation of a representative of the Crown." '

"First thing when I get there I'll fire off a memo to the Crown."

"Don't let none of them see you," Taggart said.

Following the festivities of the 400th Pigpicking & Clog at the waterfront, Her Majesty met with local residents. The reception was hosted by the Only Bar, a local dining and cocktail establishment. Proprietor Ange Buthrell Jr. and staff transformed the dining area into an Elizabethan guild hall, or "gilde halle." The men of the community, as was plain to anybody stepping foot outdoors, grew beards. The ladies sewed colorful rayon costumes, those of the Fishpackers' Guild being especially ingenious as were the Cable TV Installers'. As the evening wore on Her Majesty's graciousness caused one guest to wonder if she were not truly the earlier, Virgin Elizabeth.

"You boys catch anything," Buthrell said.

"Dog feed," one of the Cape May Bee crew said.

"None of that hashish I hope."

"Well about nine hundred and ninety ton of that. That old trawler was offloading to us three days and nights."

Buthrell slapped down, cocked his head and shook his ten-pound-test hair.

"I worked, I schemed, I preached and I don't care what happens to me so long as this island gets put on the map."

"Why," I said.

"Cammie, bring a round to the fourtop and one here and that buttend, ginger for Triple T."

"No I'm fine, darling."

She unwrapped the roast, lifted it, made a face, got the beer and mugs and all, bowl of cracker goldfish, clean ashtrays my Lord, barrag, brought everything to us and went back behind without taking her eyes off the TV on the backbar. Wouldn't pass the time of day with the bossman. That gooey black slab never hit the floor just whuffled down Jimbob's throat and he stood rocking one paw to the other, more more. Cammie struck a match neat.

"I love you," I said, "I will give over my life and power to thee."

"Angleworm, take them shades off," the commissioner said. "We're both blinded. Them pole-toting tourists walk in here I'll smoke me some pygmy and some daddy."

"I'd like something else tourist to walk in," Swain said.

"Clovis'll get you a overnight release to rap with Her Majesty," Combs said, "won't you, Clovis."

"If the future was a snake this big around, Taggart, if the future of this island on this earth," Buthrell said.

"Don't be getting yourself cranked on any but the one sermon, which is the say-bye-bye sermon."

"Will I find that text in Revelations. Go, go, go, Little Queenie."

The Captain turned his ruddy, rugose visage, his porcelain-clear gaze to the incongruous horizon. His arms thick as juniper hewn at the prime, his legs vigorous as that cypress that stands to marsh suck, his heart of ironwood held the bow to rising seas, which striking gave the report of barrels of shot falling from a height onto tinder. The paddlewheels thrashed and screamed in the housings, the sails and masts keened their distress. Sensibly, the animal they rode was become a gelid thing, no more dolphin but reduced to nettledom. There was, incidentally, a young Negro, called Harlan Gates, companion of Buthrell and Bone, at this moment below tending the treacherous boilers. At sight of the lad racing up the orlop deck crying *fahty poand, fahty poand,* Buthrell wore the vessel around, the breeze having, as he had foreseen, transposed to the northeast, at one with him Bone and Gates setting the dissolute sails to gather every atom of it. The three mariners readied the launch, while around them rose the triple tempest of boilers, alarums, the precipitous sea. The ship's former master had guaranteed the pressure to fifty, yet certain rondelets of vibration, all too familiar, now persuaded her present, and hands, to abandon hope of orderly descent and hasten simply to disrobe, and leap.

"I heard something interesting about you and your daddy, had to do with the funeral. Do you boys know about Buthrell up at the home, up Spruill's," Taggart said.

Buthrell snatched the shades off.

"This isn't the time nor place."

"Old Jule Spruill told this one on him."

"I'm done for, I have surrendered, but bringing him into it don't cut it."

"You won't last long touchy. You're worried he's looking down. Most likely he is and what does he see, nothing he wasn't given cause to expect. I thank the Lord, he thanks the Lord for Dan Swindell. He shakes the Lord's hand for our district attorney on his own son."

"Talk tongues for us one time, Taggart. My sister-in-law can jump into tongue talk and roll, and damn if you're about half lit damn if it don't start making wonderful sense. No static," Swain said.

Buthrell smacked the Myers's down, brushed his hair over, raised his finger to his nostril. Jimbob hoisted up on front legs only. Cammie scouring nicotine off the mirror and the Cape May Bee crew, they were just hanging out.

"Swindell will do anything in this world to make governor, ruin a man to make a name in the northeast, I know it, everybody knows it."

"Man's had two coronaries," the commissioner said. "He lives hour to hour and gives fifty-nine minutes to the state."

"I'm giving a few to the state myself."

"Angleworm, if you ain't I don't know."

"Swindell's good as gold, I'm sorry," I said.

"He is right on," Combs said. "I liked that angina twitch talking to the jurors. Pops them little pills, slips them under his tongue, please don't notice me, y'all, I'm just dying in front of you up here on account of the law just hates that Ange Buthrell so goddamn bad."

"Buthrell's pernicious, like oleo," the commissioner said.

"Could you believe. I'm not even talking about, I'm not even dealing with the so-called investigation. The so-called handling of the so-called evidence. My Lord, I've bled your ears with that. Walk in, invite you to a drink, to a coldbeer, inquire after your loved ones, walk out. Maintain."

"Your daddy looked down and whispered in the judge's ear, Ventilate this boy but good. But I want to tell about up Spruill's."

"Cool out, Taggart, my Lord," Swain said.

"My old man was no less sorry than his son."

"One difference. He did damage only to hisself."

"Depends what," I said.

"I'm not dealing with it. I'll tell you one thing. He'd have paraded up and down Water Street with the damn Queen on his arm."

"Ange, I doubt we get the Queen," the commissioner said.

"Margaret be fine."

"Give me a emerald I'll get it on with any of them," Swain said.

Bulkhead bricks traversed the ladies' cabins and the parlor windows, copper hull plates parted company, lofty jets of spark issued from below, and smoke universally obscured vision. Bone and Gates had no opportunity to plot trajectory from the gunwale, for on an instant they were catapulted into the sea. Buthrell, engaged in his garments, was thrown to the deck simultaneous to the maintopmast's splintering and crashing, to rest not a hair's breadth from his burly skull. Before he could regain his feet, the foreyard broke in the slings, the starboard paddlewheel snapped away like so much confectionery, and there rose the percussion, which the bonafide Captain Tattershall, at the inquest, likened to that of a musket salute, of the deckheads plying free of the timbers. Decidedly aground, the vessel careered, and only by main force of his extraordinary constitution did Buthrell reach the rails and propel himself blind into breathless spray.

Through crushing seas, on isolate bearings, and at the last pulse of twilight, the three reached the skiff that they, customarily, had anchored beyond the breakers. Only occasionally, as

backs were bent to oars, did looks fly aft, to the Mosetta T. Tattershall as she subsided, hissing, the breeze picking the spars
of canvas, amber flickering in parlor glass as if phantoms now
danced where danced the Wilmington gentry in more buoyant
days (or such, indeed, were Buthrell's musings), upon the roil-
ing bar. They were away, their deed was done, they pulled for
shore: yet it was early to reckon gain and count up monied rest:
a lantern flash forestalled any such reveries. Athwart of Buthrell's calculations, which had determined a sinkpoint north of
the Ocomico scope, south of the Bodie, and escaping the par-
allax of both, sighted they had been. (The reader will recall
Buthrell's code—Rescue me from my rescuers, that I may
thrive among those who forsake me.) A boat of heroes plunged
toward them. The tone of Marcus Midgette, surfman, known
for eyes like a herring gull's, carried woefully to the salvagees,
charging the crew to stroke for their souls and the love of *Gawd
Awlmoyty*. First thinking to avoid detection by Baptist maneuvers down the two-days-unbailed keel, Buthrell secondly
seized upon a more prudent, however no less aqueous, course
of action.

"What do you expect them ladies drink."

"Crown Royal," Buthrell said. "Combs, watch after the Mark
IV for me."

"I'm not."

He shoved the keys back.

"You need something that moves. I'm not giving, I'm lend-
ing the bitch. While we're on the subject, borrow Tish too."

"Find her first, a big if," Swain said.

"We got to roll, gentlemen," Taggart said. "Cammie, call
VEPCO, call the telephone, shut down, lock up, report to food
stamps."

"Had to put that on her," Buthrell said. "How I know you."

"Fry in Cub Scout hell," Cammie said.

That little slip of a thing said that, and changed channel.

Jimbob sunk hamdeep in the hole poked by the pooltable

and we did hear TB ward at Sailor's Rest till Buthrell hoisted him.

"Look here one time, Taggart, check this out. Thirty-two years old, the same as you to the week, if you can believe. You had to wait two days for me. This island didn't give me up, I gave my ass up. Check yourself out, if the shoe'd been on the other foot."

"I could have plucked you out of that thing's legs anytime. I cut you slack."

"Oh naturally. You were cutting me slack. Oh goddamn, I just always wanted something else all along, people living together in some kind of beautiful damn—I don't know, some kind of new life on this sorry island. Connected, I'm talking about even you and me, damn especially you and me, each other and down through the ocean to whoever on the other side. But all right. Now I go ride my own spread-eagle body tonight probably and see what I remember."

"As long as you're not riding no slit, strung-up, dead damn body," Swain said.

"I'll think back on, I will long cherish the send-off my friends gave."

"You wouldn't look at your daddy's dead body up Spruill's. Old Jule has him a spyhole, to check up on the grieving ones, you know. He saw you avoid, not step toward, not peek in the old man's direction the other end of the salon. Stood with your back to the coffin the entire time, smoked a rum crook down to gunk, pulled back the divider, kissed people on the mouth and split."

"That ain't true, I saw him that day," Combs said, rocking in his charterboat.

"Yessir, shit-faced but respectful, what every man dreams of in a son," the commissioner said.

"I have this feeling I'll come out of there," Buthrell said. "And when I get back I'll take you, Taggart, and teach you the why of everything in my life, or slay you. Frankly, this'll sound strange,

I'd prefer to teach you. That boyhood stuff dies hard. But I will slay you if need be."

He threw the Myers's bottle against the wall, diamond jackpot. He threw his chair spinning right around once in the big booth, jackstraw jackpot.

"I heard it before. They all sound the same at this point."

Cammie climbed into Buthrell. "Don't wreck the place, even if it is yours to, was. I'll try and write."

"Try," I said. "She's the kind to set aside an evening weekly."

"I'm dealing with everything having been possible, don't think I'm not."

"I'd never."

Young and old left home up the ramp past Chas the Razz's model ship in the wall.

Surfman Midgette hailing the skiff discovered a lone sailor, Gates, the two he would have favored with recognition and speedy arrest lying some distance seaward upon a floating settee—upon, excepting lower extremities, by paddling which they maintained the back of the parlor piece to the inquisitor. Alleging the boilers had minutely destroyed the vessel and all hands save himself (though he could not speak with finality of Captain Tattershall, having been separated at the end), Gates was taken in and restored. Buthrell and Bone contrived to pass the night in the tide and wash ashore at dawn, subsequent to the turning up of the freshly watered Tattershall there. A month thence Buthrell made so brash as to attend the vendue at which the effects of the Mosetta T. Tattershall were auctioned, and to post bids on planking, for which he claimed consignment Up North. In time, having divided the receipt of Lloyd's, Tattershall embraced a life of leisure, Bone and Gates bought seats at East Lake, and their Captain took possession of a fishing schooner, on whom canvas was yet the fashion and whose nimble spirit he partnered to wealth and property, and marrying late, conveyed same to the stewardship of his son.

Blue eyebucket over a sea of hardpacked silt. The Cape May Bee crew orphaned up along the ditch, barefoot, getting smaller faster, stuffed with hundred-dollar bills. The commissioner of course ducked in his car and went, never gave traffic a shot to see him there, nor me a shot for money. Combs and Swain and Cammie and I stood a good distance from the car and a right good distance from each other.

"Fixed the car like the Chief's that time, did you, Angle-worm. Fixed the latches so he can't get out once he shuts the door. Well roll, brother. Tear up," Swain said.

"Watch them sneaky-snakes," Combs said. "They got the granddaddy of all the sneaky-snakes up there."

The girl went past the marina and combed her pretty hair in dragonfly heaven by the marshgrass. Taggart fired up, Buthrell put his shades on and dropped inside, reached to cut on music then remembered what he was in. That wasn't a cassette player, that was a police Motorola. He wanded his finger on us as the car wallowed around by. I checked the Only in the porthole. The chairs were to the tables. In back my eye shut and I put that thing out of his misery, which was what he was wanting.

The Love Letter Hack

His back to the water, the love letter hack manages to set up his typing stand at the stairway to the Galata Bridge without permitting a glimpse of the bridge to reach his eyes. The bridge floats, rises and falls in iron sections, and is the last thing a nauseous man needs to see at noon, waking. The vibrations of the ferry engines through the bulkheading are bad enough. The traffic is bad enough. Head bent, eyes compressed, he pulls a sheaf of onionskin from his inside pocket and secures it under the front legs of the typewriter, likewise a packet of tax stamps, and a flyswatter, which he hangs on the lefthand knob of the platen. He rubs and slaps his sinuses, ostentatiously enough that a simit-seller mutters to ward off the contagion of madness. He sits on his wooden chair and for a moment believes he catches the scent of Gaziantep.

Pain is a treasure, he repeats to himself, for within it are mercies shown. Along with his head, certain other organs ache, soreness flickering from one to the next, and the August sun like an incinerator flame distempers his eyes. The traffic howls, smolders. Hundreds of men wearing dark clothes pass his place of business, scuffing densely, obsessively, over this one more bridge to nowhere where there is ease or money. To his rear ferries shudder to and away from the docks, transporting hundreds of men wearing dark clothes. Salesmen cry taxicab trunksful of aluminum ware, Chinese toys, German condoms. He imagines a heap of condoms in gold foil to be doubloons and that the merciless nine-year-old approaching will bare a mouth of gleaming teeth, a purse of pearls.

He is dozing by the time the boy returns with the glass of tea and three sugars. In his dream are mingled smelts and anchovies grilling by the bridge, diesel fumes, cumin from the bazaar, essences which together plot the shape of a cypress in a grove of cypresses, weeks from water. The boy rouses him with abuse, saying he would pour the tea into his open mouth except that Allah does not wish to see drowned the flies on his lips. The hack responds with abuse, freezing, with Allah's indulgence, the boy's height at its present one meter, then gives him an extra twenty-five kurus. The tip reduces his assets to thirty liras plus the value of the typewriter.

At your service, gentlemen, gentlemen, at your service, cry the salesmen. Look how beautiful. And you, my honored lady, at your command.

Everything about the love letter hack at sixty-odd years is gray, his suit, his shirt, his remaining hair, the flesh of his neck and face. By night he bleaches himself with raki, the better to take the grisling dyestuff of the city by day. Raki is the houri of the heart, the gazi of the mind, the jinn of the bowels, he repeats to himself from this older brother Ozan's sayings. From the reservoir at the base of his brain he lets fall a taste of the liquor, one flake of anise, to his tongue, and feels the fumes rise to his eyes, descend to his liver. His wife washed the dead yet loved him still, didn't she? He winces. The heat renders the city. The hack never sweats.

Another nine-year-old, panting, scrambles beneath the typing stand and goes for his shoes with daubs and rags. The typist in dilapidated loafers brandishes his flyswatter.

The first customer of the day, whose intent the hack's sonar has detected well before he separates from the schooling passersby, approaches wearing a dark suit that exposes his socks and with cap in hand. His thighs bump the stand at the moment he says, "Baba, my selams, would you be he who could write a letter?" If the hack's features suggest—wrongly—a somewhat gouty Latin, the youth's are those of a somewhat ill-bred Mongol, a broad-shouldered youth from somewhere in the east, somewhere the hack knows. "Baba." He moves to block the glare off the buses. The hack looks up into his blood-thirsty, abashed face.

"At your service, my little brother, at your service. Already I understand you don't have much money, so first thing. . . ." First thing, what? he asks himself, sinking again into the after-burn of raki. "First thing . . . yes, I'm telling you the last price first. There's no bazaar-like talk here. Five liras for the writing, two kurus tax, twenty kurus postage."

"Agreed, efendim."

"What do you wish to say?" He feeds a sheet of onionskin, at a slight angle, into the machine, draws a deep breath.

"Beloved Hulya, my soul. . . ."

"Beloved Hulya, my soul," repeats the hack, typing blind but pausing to straighten the *a*, on which the solder has weakened, after each use. The youth's accent mocks him with its familiarity.

"Beloved Hulya, my soul, I wonder what the news is with you? Yesterday I went to Kadikoy and drank tea with my friends on the cliff above the Woman's Beach. We watched the swimmers swim and for the first time I spoke about you. I work seven days at the tinsmith's, make ninety liras, save thirty for our future. Very often I think of you and your family and our village. May health have come quickly to your father's kid-neys—"

The hack's kidneys quiver in empathy, beans in the same pot.

"—I kiss your mother's eyes. My selams. Adem"

The hack has ceased typing and with his palm to his sinuses, his lips rippling, awaits the request that will surely follow, no less surely than that the muezzin's catcall follows the very on-set of sleep.

"I wonder, my Baba," the youth begins. "My friend—do you

know Huseyn of Kayibkoy?—my friend said perhaps you would write something a little special. You've written for him. However, I'm not a romantic."

"Kayibkoy, Kayibkoy. It's not to be for five liras," the hack replied—of course it's Kayibkoy—unable to summon even his usual half-hearted conviction to the line. For fifteen years, until everything failed, he and his wife and their little one lived in, endured Kayibkoy. "The special is ten liras, the normal five."

"Excuse me, I don't have ten liras." The youth withdraws his thighs but stands as submissively and secretly unbeaten, as secretly beckoned to, as a war captive.

Lacking the stomach to prolong the ritual for an additional lira or two, the hack murmurs a phrase of abuse and rolls in a fresh sheet of onionskin. He wants only to dispatch Kayibkoy, before greater nausea gathers around the name. He gropes through memory, his shopworn catalog of phrases, bits of the odes and tales heard over and over among the dwindling caravan of his childhood, mostly from his father's lips. His index fingers work as fast as the heads of the pigeons on the steps of the New Mosque opposite, and with nearly sufficient accuracy to be read by his counterpart in the village, the hoca. The hoca, Fahir Bey's son no doubt, also will be a man of imagination. Let him earn his share. The hack pulls the letter from the roller, reaches into his coat for an envelope.

"Baba, will you read?"

"Naturally, if you don't trust me."

"I trust you as I would my loved one's Baba."

Surprised by this tremor of wit, the hack commences in what is for him an agreeable voice:

Beloved Hulya, my soul,
   For a thousand days and nights your stark-white and stark-black eyes, your hailstone-white teeth, your anemone-red lips I myself have not seen.
   Sus! my little brother, I must tell my heart, sus! and be still. No more of the girl so far away must you think. Time and distance have severed her memory of you. The lovely maid of Kayibkoy, no longer awaits she your return. Of what use is longing?

There are thousands of smiling women in Istanbul, there is one who will make me forget the girl of Kayibkoy, isn't there? No, Hulya, my poppy, it is not to be, for compared to these Istanbullus you are as a fleet deer in a herd of camels. Of the cities I have seen, the dust and thistles of

(With his pen the hack insets a third word, *stones*, at this point; he prefers to write in triads.)

the dust and thistles and stones of our village put to shame the gardens and treasures and carpets of Topkapi; in our village is you. Your steps, arrow-like, slipping to the market, I watched each morning. In this world nothing is more tender than as we pass your turning away.

Yesterday with my friends I sat at the teahouse by the sea. In the surf I heard your laughter, in the sparkling wavelets saw your eyes, in the anemone's hues beheld your cheeks. On the urchin's spikes was my heart impaled. I make ninety liras, would that I could save eighty!

The Poet says we must boil our pot by degrees. This I myself understand, yet with Mejnun-like sighs the hearts of the wild beasts I crack.

May time have passed quickly to the we-shall-make home for your parents and your saintly older sister

(The hack glances up for confirmation, which is given.)

and your beloved cat Ayse.

(Confirmation.)

To greet the morning with a cup from your hand, a smile from your anemone-red lips and cotton boll-like teeth!

May health have come quickly to your father. Care well for him, take him tea with brandy

(The youth seems about to speak.)

with brandy, and pilaf with meat and take him tripe soup. Ask where to press with your soft cool beautiful hands the secret pains of his weary, aching, peaceless body. Press your tender hands to his head, rub his fiery gums with oil of eucalyptus, talk with him of ordinary things and in his dark and tent-like chamber sing to him.

Hulya, my tulip, I would lie in your path that you might walk on my eyes, but I worry that my lashes will wound your feet.

To our future, my selams!

Greatest love,
Adem

The hack fingers two tax stamps from the wax paper packet—Gazi Mustafa Kemal Pasa's twin visage—licks them, anneals them to the foot of the letter with the heel of his hand, scratches his initials across them and asks, "Is this satisfactory?"

The youth's suit gives somewhere. A trickle of sweat emerges from his cuff as he reaches, hesitantly, staying his hand at the typewriter. "Baba, you have read my heart."

"I could have made it melodramatic, but I think this is what you wanted."

"Efendim, I'm no romantic. We ourselves are a modern couple."

"Naturally. You owe for the second sheet of paper."

"You're a great man, Baba, a reader of hearts. Always I will come to you here," the villager says, and finally raises the nerve to take the old man's head in his hands and buss him on either of his sapid, unshaven and anise-smelling cheeks.

The love letter hack shivers. Kayibkoy may it blister in hell.

The nine-year-old rouses him with abuse, saying he would pour the tea down his pants except that Allah does not wish to see drowned the lice living there. The hack responds with abuse, recalling the night he possessed, with Allah's connivance, the boy's lousy mother, sisters and great-aunt, then gives him another twenty-five kurus tip and brushes the stubble of his conical head. The traffic has stalled since he dozed off; he sees the same vehicles. Men in dark clothes jostle the stand. Steampipes sound.

He sees, or through his fumey vision and the waves of heat thinks he sees, his friend strolling from the mouth of the Egyptian Bazaar lifting a bowl—Alton Mallone, the American graduate student coming, bearing tripe soup. Phlegmatic himself for the last twenty years, the hack likes the lively, enjoys the sight of Alton crossing the square with this sloshing gift, dodg-

ing beggar children, the only bearded man in sight, the only
man in sight who bounces as he walks.

"At your service, my little soup-brother."

"My selams I do not give," Alton says in Turkish, his field,
referring to the disappearance of the Semitic greeting from the
contemporary tongue. He hands over the soup, leans against
the stair rail, wipes his clip-on sunglasses on his shirt, appar-
ently oblivious to the crowd climbing inches from his back. He
swims at Moda, past the Women's Beach, daily, and his hair
has reddened, which together with somewhat indefinite features makes it harder to pass as Turk. By virtue of a good ear he
used to sneak by.

The hack says, "Thank you, I suppose I did get rather
smashed last night." (Conversation between the two runs to
about one-third Turkish, one-third English and one-third
French, often switching from sentence to sentence or even
within the sentence.) Tutored in adolescence by an Armenian,
he believes tripe soup to be the only effective antidote for a
hangover, particularly when followed by a dish of almond
cream with nutmeg.

"I searched for you. They'd seen you at the Flower Passage,
so I figured you'd need the soup."

"I was with the gypsies." This is a catch phrase coined by
Alton meaning virtually anything. "J'étais parmi les gitanes."

"Business booming? Still selling illusions to the peasants?
Lovely, keep them in the chains of romance. Keep the sexes
apart. Modern republic, my ass."

The hack shrugs, shields his eyes. "People are just afraid,
why not?"

"You Muslims are to blame for romance anyway, you and
your poets, polluting the Middle Ages."

Alton's streak of pedantry amuses the hack, as Alton is
amused by the unflappable cynicism of the other, who says, "If
they pay it must be good."

"Look, men and women have to know each other for real."

"My little brother, what news from your girlfriend?"

"Letter today."

"Quelle surprise. I hope her health is good and she loves you still."

"Love is the wrong word. Love is misunderstood Muslim lies."

"Booming, not booming. I'm lucky the thieves didn't steal my typewriter."

"Our relationship is like a poplar."

"Masallah."

"Right, masallah. I'm going swimming."

The news from Alton's girlfriend back in the states has not been all that reassuring, and is one reason he turns back, against the tide flowing to the upper level of the bridge, to invite the hack to supper. Not that he wants to talk things over with a professional in the field of postal romance, not at all. His relationship with Darcy Hooper has zero in common with the love letter hack's hypocritical trade. He wants company, interesting company for a change. He's tired of the prissy academics he socializes with. Besides he suspects the hack can tell him more about transformations in Turkish since Mustafa Kemal Pasa Ataturk than anybody at Istanbul U. The man's present condition attests to his having lived a singular life. Alton usually finds himself more attracted to the ruin than the prime of singularity.

The hack gives a curt oblique nod, acceptance, drains the last of the gray broth. "I'll return this to Pandeli," he says—the bowl to the restaurant. "We'll see each other."

Alton doesn't really expect him to show. They're friends, have drunk together, eaten kebab and mussels, sung for each other, but they are not yet brothers for life. Turks take visiting a dwelling seriously. He could have asked him to a restaurant, but for some reason he wants him in his apartment.

On the way home from the ferry after his swim he buys perch, okra, pickled peppers, white cheese and melon, all cheap, and a fifth of Kulup Rakisi, the best grade; so as not to show off with the meal yet honor his guest with the drink.

He has the knack for finding on sparse funds delightful places to live, merely under trying conditions. His apartment on the fifth floor of a building pocketed among similar earthquake-prone structures down the hill from Taksim—that is, across the Golden Horn and around the bend from the spot where the hack plies his trade—raises water once or twice a month, has bugs, bad walls, floors and odors, a two-burner Aygaz stove and no refrigerator. But the view from the little balcony goes straight up the Bosphorus.

Out here overlooking Cihangir district and the spindly mosque, by Sinan, on the waterside, with a breeze unfolding and the channel turning smoky red, then gray, then blue-gray under the lights of crisscrossing boats, Alton waits. He waits, then goes ahead and opens the raki, pours a glassful over ice from the pudding shop at the corner and succumbs to the prospect of the night alone on this ledge above the humming glittering earth, the widening strait. The liquor clouds. He holds it to his eye to watch a ferryboat's lights through it. When he begins to picture Christmas trees he lowers the glass.

He is left then to think of his thesis—of remarks Professor Bebeyenalp made over kebab, of tightening the first chapter, wherein he compared Old and Modern English, sociolinguistically, with Old and Modern Turkish as devised by the scholars under Gazi Mustafa Kemal Bey.

But these thoughts are subterfuge. They've had their four hours today.

Darcy is what he's left to think of, his confidant and touchstone through so much time, for two solid years the stopper in the bottle that buzzes with the jinns of nothingness.

At the twenty-third hour he hears his guest straying up the stairway, dragging the typing stand with him by the sound of it. The love letter hack arrives at the open door offering a blown rose.

Dear Alton,

(So reads this morning's letter in Posta Kutusu 544, the chanting denizen of his hip pocket:)

It's seeming more & more difficult to write you, altho the waves of longing grow more & more intense. Alas, the paradoxes of the heart, no doubt. I keep thinking of facts & revelations & needs I need to write, but the adrenalin continually fizzles. Quite annoying. I've been marginally unhappy lately—diffusely anxious really—and this damn summer seems to stretch on so lengthily & emptily. Getting $ & getting tan, where does that get you?

I've been reading Force of Circumstance *(has the old Consulate library latched onto that one?) which may be partly responsible for my funk, at least that part which relates to my proliferating anxieties about time being wrenched from my grasp—getting older with such an appallingly meager output of good work to show for it. Tangentially, Simone's & Sartre's is an incredible example to emulate vis-a-vis other loves, don't you agree?*

Cries & *Whispers is on at the Dreamland but no one will change with me.*

Ah well, lots of fun tomorrow anyway—Darrell phoned to say he was coming on the early ferry to visit that dippy chick he met in Acadia, who's now waitressing at the Sandpiper. Most peculiar, his taste in young ladies, which may be one reason he has so many of them. Hopefully, at any rate, he & I can slip off on some adventure w/o her, exploring the moors or sailing Terri's sailfish or getting stoned on the cliffs & discussing how much we miss you.

Last nite I rode out to Cisco in the fog before the moon came up. It rose, a quarter moon, as I was riding back & even tho it was only a sliver and even tho socked in it lit up the rd. almost vibrantly, a spooky ribbon through the condensation. This may not sound like such an amazement, but at the time the effect was quite bewitching. I wanted to write you about it when I got back, but, alas, too many idiots hanging around the apartment.

I miss you, and miss rolling around in bed/you, to a degree that embarrasses me at every turn. Please send the 1st chapter as soon as it's in final form, tho I don't suppose they have xeroxers on every corner in Istanbul, huh?

> *Love and suffocating snuggles,*
> *Darcy*

As the hack's snooze descends into profounder trenches, Alton realizes he's been reading the letter aloud, and loudly, above the snoring and the sounds filtering up from the alleys and from the drone of the channel. He assures himself he didn't produce the letter until his companion had already passed out. He notices their plates lying clean as drumheads, their glasses empty, and sections the last piece of melon, pours raki. They've disposed of two fingers more than two-thirds of the bottle, a goodly amount. No wonder the Bosphorus looks so vast and grand and rich with danger. No wonder the lights on the Asian shore twinkle so lightheartedly. Lightheartedly. A half moon hovers in vapor over Uskudar. Existence can be so fancy, he thinks, in both senses of the word, so fine and fancy. It nearly can be kind.

Souls of warmth flow one after another into the night from his slumped but wonderfully potent body, carriers of love, winging homeward to wherever she is, whatever she is doing on that island where the sun is just this moment setting. Dot to dot, heart to heart, they are joined across the Pole of his formerly unspannable solitude.

(Off the coast of America, hoisting two broiled shore dinners to her wide shoulders in a steamy kitchen, surely Darcy Hooper feels a stirring.)

She loves him. The letter gives no cause for concern.

The hack rattles like a chainsaw running out of gas, rolls his head, takes raki from the bottle and says, "Who is this Darrell?"

"God, I'm sorry. I didn't know you were conscious."

"All the time I'm collecting."

"He's my best friend."

The hack murmurs, "Masallah," and re-passes out before his glass reaches the table. The glass suspends itself two inches above the surface.

"Yea, masallah," moans Alton. The word shakes him from the moment of self-deception, his glimpse of Darcy and of the bright and careless curve of feelings spanning thousands of miles intact. Like a balloon he collapses to a snarled remnant, then is pumped back up not with breath but with the gas of irretrievable loss. He is trapped in the bag of the earth with the presence of Darcy and Darrell by the sea, loving at last, abandoning him at last, fulfilling at last the forebodings he suppressed for months and opaque months. Their pumping crushes the breath out of him. They were the ones all along.

Wearing dark glasses, large dark glasses, and a scarf that veils what the glasses do not, a woman in cosmopolitan dress stalks by the love letter hack's place of business and in passing tucks a note into his typewriter. Quick as a cobra the nine-year-old teaseller snatches the piece of paper. Twisting the hack's ears to rouse him, he offers to ransom it for two liras or else set his lighter to it, as Allah in the first place intended.

The hack sees a man on the trunk of a taxicab cause a poppy to grow from seed to two meters before the eyes of the onlookers, interprets this as a sign the note will bring prosperity. With one hand he sprinkles invisible larvae over the boy's scalp while with the other renders payment, reminding himself that kadir, as guide, appears in many guises. The nine-year-old attempts to point out the lady crossing the bridge but to the hack the crowd remains an undifferentiated mass of bitter, futile motion.

Adjusting his glasses, scoured as they are, he unfolds the note, reads:

> *Efendim,*
> *At the 14th hour in the Gulbahce Muhallebesi in the environs of Taksim the kindness to meet me would you be able to find? For your service a fitting price I will give.*

Though the boy described a mature woman, the handwriting is that of a schoolgirl.

At the fourteenth hour, not before, he entrusts his typewriter and stand to his friend the seller of chilled plum juice. Anticipating the payment, and another meal at the American graduate student's—so what if he has to sit through a new letter from that girl whose English he can barely understand, that pigeon, who coos as she pecks? so what if he has to sit through it twice, as he did last night?—he hails a taxicab. He does not go to the dolmus stand to wait with the sheep-like ones to share, but hails a taxi, a 1949 DeSoto, of his own. He rides to the door of the sweetshop, on the way, for the driver's benefit, ascribing to each stain on the back seat a disgusting origin. For his part the driver puts his head through the tassles and curses other drivers.

He goes upstairs to the tiny mezzanine, seats himself next to a woman reading, or looking at, a magazine of large photos of love among cinema artists.

"Efendim," she says ("Efe—" rather, in breathless Istanbullese, as Alton would have noted). "At your service, I make thanks, at your service. I myself am married and in love with a man also married. This man believes we must stop seeing each other. He's from Bursa and has a conscience."

"Allah, what's his business?"

"Sells konfor." Konfor, from the French, is central heating.

"I'll write something a little poetic." Only a fool needs to see the eyes to understand the face, he recalls from his father's admonitions, studying the woman behind the black lenses she retains in the dim shop. A perceptive man may judge the soul by the nostrils, the nostrils if necessary by the elbow, no matter if it be wrapped in wool.

"In my view conscience is no big thing, I care for other matters. Don't waste time with conscience and poetry as he did. I came to you for help in expressing my thoughts. I don't want a standard formula."

Also, notwithstanding your up-to-date appearance, my honored lady, I am guessing you cannot write, the hack muses. I am guessing your daughter wrote the note. "Where there's a conscience, there's a poet," he tells her. He smooths out a leaf of onionskin, which then seems to disappear into the veneer.

"We've been seeing each other four months," she begins.

"Sus! Enough. Don't confuse me." He uncaps his pen, locates the edge of the paper with his fingers. "I'll be having coffee with cream and almond pudding with nutmeg."

Beloved Cevdet, my soul,
Once you brought love odes, now only regrets do you bring. The shepherd
flutes pipe me down the streets to the Square of Emptiness. With you the
hidden alley a tulip garden, the spare and secret room a harem,

(He pauses, straining to complete the triad.)

the street vendor's sausage a platter of tender lamb and pilaf and various
appetizers become.

(In the nick of time a waiter brings the pudding, which the hack
snaps down in three bites.)

Without you my clothes, my jewelry, my coiffure are but the rags of
a from-Square-to-Square-of-Emptiness-to-the-song-of-flutes-wandering
gypsy. By the side of the road the poppies change to flames of hellfire. It is
said pain is the seal of love and this I now understand, I understand!
Passion for your stark-white and stark-black eyes, your hailstone-white
teeth, your ebony-black mustache has emaciated me. The coins of Paradise
while continuing to tease my heart with your dance will you deny?
Is it possible your odes and regrets have been one and the same? The Poet
bids the lover bringing poetry to his beloved desist, and simply love. Love is
the matter of love, not odes, not regrets. The sun rising, the poppies do they
hide their faces?
Ah, Beloved, though the waves of longing grow ever more intense, it is
difficult to write the facts and revelations and needs I feel. In love-illumi-
nated eyes a paring of the moon the night sets ablaze!
Forever shall I open to you what is anemone-red, but to you alone, not
your conscience. One lover, if that lover is you, satisfies. Moreover the
afternoon sitter I shall not dismiss.

Greatest love,
Yesim

The woman's first response, after that of turning her nostrils
away from him, is to say, "He doesn't have a mustache."

"Well, he has hair then?" The hack amends the phrase ac-
cordingly.

"Yes that's just the tone, modern, to the point, not overly
romantic. I'm pleased to have come to you."

"Medium sugar, my sister, the way I drink coffee."

With assurances of future commissions, the woman presses

a fifty-lira note into his hand, medium generosity, about what he expected while hoping for more. After all, the taxicab cost ten.

She does order another round of coffee and pudding, and like lovers themselves they linger, observing the other couples, whose hands meet over glazed pastries of several layers. He finds himself desiring this woman, wishing she were lying back on her scented clothes for him. He pats the bristles on his temples, straightens his collar, posture and countenance. With the grounds from his overturned cup he prepares a paste of mock collyrium for her eyes, Foster Grants or no Foster Grants—Fostair, that is, as if from the French.

Before leaving he suggests, "Perhaps you'd like to make him jealous with a younger man, isn't this so?"

> *Dear Alton,*
>
> *Oh man, a minor adventure yesterday, last-minute rescue & all, Darrell having arrived, with ½ the Vt. woods, his new $-making scheme, a talent he definitely inherited from his old man. At any rate, I spirited him away from Kara or whatever the hell, that chick, and we took off in his jeep up Nobadeer beach. Everything was most pleasant, blue sky, big waves, but this fog swooped in & socked us in in a trice & suddenly we were to the axles in mush, forget the 4-wheel drive, tide coming in, yes? Prospects grim, I must say, altho we were so drunk it seemed mainly comic at first. . . . The decision was whether to maroon ourselves till low tide or go for help. Meanwhile the waves were hitting broadsides quite forcefully & we seriously considered the possibility the jeep'd roll. Buhhhhhhhhh . . . buhhhhhhhhh . . . (foghorns razz).*
>
> *Duh-duh-dah! The U.S. Cavalry, in the persons of this wonderful old couple, appeared in a monster Land Rover, Darrell hitched us on with parachute strapping, & with me & the old guy pushing—waist deep in the big sandy—we were extracted. Anticlimax. The day ends with us sipping quite potent rum toddies in the couple's living room—they're simply terrific, I can't tell you—which happens to be on the Cliffs. Altogether a trip.*
>
> *Now, here's a curious diversion, tangentially related to the above & partly, I fear, in response to your revelation of yr. latest encounter with the teacher at the American School. At some pt. during Darrell's visit I began to perceive this strange but really intense attraction between us, which I assume was some combination of being around ea. other so much &, strange to say, knowing how close you & he are. Does that sound reasonable? Let's*

see, to make a long story short, I really wanted to get into his pants, but didn't, & now he's off to Vt. again. Thus basically it was just an interesting interlude in my head. I'll let you know more of my inclinations when I sort them out, tho I suspect I know yours.

I love you so. There's still lots more circles to go in regarding sexuality but at least we've avoided certain dangers inherent in our original relationship. Advise me of any other projected or accomplished forays into the pants of young ladies.

Alas, have I mentioned that my tolerance for not rolling around in bed/ you seems to be about 5 da., after which I graduate into a state of suspended longing? Sheesh. A woman left lonely.

> *Into my cold sheets & unsettling dreams,*
> *Darcy*

N.B. God knows what my IUD's doing—last nite at work I started leaking profusely altho. my pd. was over 1½ wks. ago.

Well past midnight, slumped against a stucco wall somewhere down from Istanbul U., empty bottle between them, dogs clicking funereally past, the American graduate student and the love letter hack confront their unfulfilled quest—that of locating the house where the latter's sister was sequestered fourteen years. In the humidity the district, with its spine of domes and manufacturing hovels, goes to lifeless, glimmering gray, a coalslide down to the Horn.

"So my life is ruined," Alton gets around to saying. "So I've blown my one chance for full-blooded joy. God knows it's happened before in human history, individual and collective."

"Tomorrow perhaps we'll find my Zumrut's harem."

Obviously I deserve it, karma, Alton thinks, as much as she and Darrell deserve each other's impacted excuses for love. Their egos match; their bodies match. They are both such pretty specimens—she tall, smooth, danceresque, he blond and wiry, every inch the athletic intellectual—designed by *their* former lives to insure immediate, transseasonal allure, full genetic compliance, never a lonely night. All their kind need do is wait and sooner or later the floor will tilt, vortices form and every ion of sexuality fly their way crackling for attachment. (While over here stands Alton proposing a joke, pitting wit

against grace enfleshed, dribbles of ash against the spin and
heave of the species. Maybe he'll win an evening of guilt with a
teacher at the former mission school.)

Screw me too, he thinks, we've drunk too much raki and not
enough raki, enough to bathe us in bathos but not drown us.
Bathe, bathos, bathe. I do not deserve desertion. I have a two-
way heart, am not that ugly, I answer my grandparents' letters,
I have the gift for running into characters like this guy. Let Darrell scrounge hot moments here and there. Let him titillate the
publishing world with fodder for prep schools—"The Entropic
Vision: D. W. Griffith, Thomas Pynchon and CBS News," right!
Talk about your pork manure. Mine is lasting work, intended
to weave era to era, culture to culture, and to reach other deserted souls who sit with pen and paper before them in the
dead of night.

"My Baba, where is more raki to be found?"

"At this hour it's not to be. Now we can't find raki, my little
brother."

How come I feel so vicious? Alton wonders. A passing dog
shrinks to the other side, glancing over its shoulderblades,
which rub. She's advised him of the situation, analyzed it with
her customary earnestness, included not a word of love for
Darrell, not that love that connects man and woman and is as
deep as blood and unutterable as creation. They're the two
most important people in his life. Why should he to the marriage of their crotches admit impediments? Why so pinched a
soul, so niggardly a passion?

"Misunderstood Muslim metaphors," Alton says, using the
wall for balance to stand up.

The hack's head on his chest he starts down the stone passage which leads to another and another, down through crum-
bled civilization and job shops. Who does give a damn about
Turkish? Nobody he ever knew. He, Alton Mallone, idiot, ma-
niac—the most common epithets appropriated by the contemporary Turkish idiom, *idyot, manyak*—has palmed off illusion

on reality, bartered a woman's love for an inch-high stack of onionskin. If only he could take back the moment he left, if only tear up the ticket like the trash it was and return to their loyal Rambler and drive with her out of the cities, across the borders and drive and drive and eat what is delicious and sleep in woods. If only they'd constructed things together, a kiln, furniture. Darrell deserves her because he stays on the side of life and that's what people are meant to do: stay in their own countries and make things and talk.

"The irony is Muslims never crawled out of the trap either. They saw through it but couldn't get through it."

"We needed it, why not? We didn't have luxury."

"I need raki."

It takes seven days for a letter. If I write tomorrow—today— begging, she should get it just before Darrell, having finally figured out he will never, ever find another woman like Darcy, returns on expedition with his psychic sherpas in train, his confessions, confusions, weaknesses so ingratiating they become strengths, his schedule of broken bones. His winsome torment that compels him to search woman by woman through the Manhattan phone directory if necessary to bring peace to his brain and eyeballs. Isn't there one woman who can? Isn't there? Will you try? Won't you try?

All this and a hundred and fifty thousand dollars too, in his personal account this day, pending his old man's cornucopian demise.

"Sus, my little raki-brother, it is not to be. Come on, let's sleep on the bridge."

Which they do, lulled by the locomotion of the iron segments, among crates on the lower level near where the hack will set up for business in the morning and the Bosphorus ferries are twinned and tripletted for the night.

Buhhhhhhhhh . . . buhhhhhhhhh . . . the foghorn sounds from Leander's Tower at the crossing of the waters of the Bosphorus, the Horn and the sea. *Buhhhhhhhhh*, as Darrell sails into Darcy Hooper stretched beneath him and discovers at last what

Alton has known, each orbit and strength and smell and touching practice. Nor is she simply the latest field of pleasure, for
he takes pride in assimilating this one bit of life Alton has had
that he hasn't. To the newsstands with Darcy and Alton's secret
raptures! She opens like crazy, he tools with fey abandon, and
across the Van Allen belt shoots a transmission of her hair and
mucus as they cling and slide, cling and slide.

Nuri Deveyoglu (the suffix oglu means son of, patronyms
being another of Mustafa Kemal Bey Efendi's innovations),
who today earns subsistence on the streets of Istanbul as a
scribe of love letters, grew up far from this foul-stomached existence. He was born in a black tent pitched below a pass near
the present border of Iraq, then mere mountain Mesopotamia,
empire. Untimely, a second son, but welcome with the welcome due foals, poets, sons, especially to a man like Seyk Taner
(Tahn-nair).

　There were sheiks and sheiks, of course, some of nations,
some of villages, some of families, some of no more than the
idea of a family. Among these latter Taner belonged. Of follow-
ers he asked no kinship other than nerve and loyalty, qualities
as common among outcasts as legs and arms, minus the occasional hand. Behind his wandering from the marsh that was
his home lay teenage murder and the cowardice of elders, who
for blood price elected to pay with his exile, every coin of buried
and sunken gold, every reed mat, and a pair of girls, un-
touched. He and his bride fled north and west, took refuge in a
steppe village of poppy and sunflower growers who despite his
age honored him for his counsel, loved him for the poems and
fancies with which he filled their nights. They bore two children, Zumrut (Zoom-root, Emerald), named for the color of
her eyes, and Ozan, for the restlessness of his.

　In time they departed with a trader, a smuggler who soon
was slain, leaving Taner with three camels, five goats, a breech-
load rifle, a samovar and a journal vouchsafed by a dying En-
glishman, in transliterated Farsi. Taner proved astute. By the

year his wife died, pissing pure blood—bilharzia, jinn of the marshes—he had acquired both gold and reputation, so that offers were not slow in coming. He chose the daughter, the dowry, forty coveted longhair sheep, of the sheik of Kayibkoy, the village which had sheltered him and the first wife. Eleven months later, on a trip toward the border, Nuri was born, to his brother's baleful regard, his sister Zumrut's hidden and radiant heart. Taner brought the family back to the steppes. The camels increased to ten, then fifteen, light-colored, swift, disagreeable, including fighters for hire for weddings, when they were fed poppy husks and set, foaming, at each other, the only tangled movement in the landscape of chalk and beaten fields and hoarse flute notes.

When Nuri was eight or so Taner headed into the plains with twenty camels, transporting Martini-Peabody rifles, sixty to a crate, barrels down, the Sultan's purchase originally but since stolen, restolen, traded, retraded and destined finally to be used against him. Nuri's first full memory of his father crouched beside a narghile reciting—rattling off, gracefully—dates to this journey. Taner's every inflection shed mystery and courage and generosity; civilization, in other words, keen for blood. His accounts of lineage, war, chicanery and the slake of memorable passion constituted his fame more even than his skill at breeding. The instant the dogs caught the clattering of copper, the whine of camels a day distant, sweets and finery were smuggled from hiding and in the shadows the women's faces awaited their turns.

His renown preparing the way, Taner more and more was drawn to the west, across the plateau, by gold and by descriptions of Constantinople, where he divined a suitable husband for Zumrut could be had. Kismet decreed, however, that they enter the capital at the time of crisis. A German officer of missionary parents accosted them, ordered them to continue westward still, to Adrianople, there to join in hauling materiel. They arrived at the foot of the railway two nights later and were to make seven trips down the thorny peninsula and back, each grown camel loaded to a hundred and seventy-five kilos, Taner's legendary, flabby-footed steppers. Only nearer the fighting did they falter, only here were any lost, because they no longer heard the rhythm of each other's bells. Jale, Nuri's mother, loaded the carts the women drove to the soldiers on the slopes. Once when he went he saw corpses used to fill ruts but she assured him these were exclusively *alman*. The sulfur, the percussion reverberating in their innards mesmerized the camels, made them stand and shudder. Ozan was injured when a piece of shell, with the voice of a monkey, tore the leg off the camel—it was Haci—he was tending and the leg crushed his face, displaced his left eye so it stared downward. From then on he bled from the ear and kept that side covered. This and later work won Taner a score of decorations set with stars, crescents.

Near the end of the war they received permission to return to the steppe with the few animals not requisitioned, a slow journey during which Jale died of fever and delusions. Thereafter Taner wanted only the company of his daughter and to listen to saz. He became devout. They encamped under the tempered sun of Konya, where sometimes for days he conversed with a dervish in the rocks.

With the approach of winter in Nuri's seventeenth year, Ozan, to whom his father deferred, led this remainder south but strayed, falling into the hands of Greek raiders, who abducted Zumrut. Back in Konya, Taner experienced a vision of her in Constantinople, a merchant's odalisque, and to the city drove them again. He erected a tent outside the walls, renounced storytelling, vowed never break silence until his daughter was restored.

Ozan and Nuri took what work they could, as hamals, carrying camel loads on their own backs, as masseurs in the baths to provide the meager fare Taner now ate. Once Nuri delivered a writing machine to a glove shop in Pera whose proprietress, from Boston, befriended him, offering to teach him English. Since Taner would have refused the ensuing money, Nuri arranged to meet his brother in a teahouse every week to lose the amount playing tavla. By day he scoured the city for Zumrut. At night he donned European dress, insisting only on a green cravat, and exchanged a page of mastery in a novel for the Bostonian's wrought-up favors. Have you seen my beloved sister? he asked everywhere. Her eyes are stark-white and stark-green, emeralds in milk. Her voice is the music of water on parched ground. Her lips are anemone-red and in her walking you see a mountain deer in a herd of water buffalo.

The Bostonian introduced him to wine. Nights she found her rooms empty she took to bed to be waited upon by her red-haired Ferzan, who claimed to have lost her family in the Greek invasion. Eventually he returned, rosepetals and aloes in his trousers, bruised from fighting foreign soldiers who desired his countrywomen in Karakoy (Black Village), whores though they were. He taunted her with English phrases she did not know.

One night as he sat in fez and spats on their mattress the door slammed open and he screamed at the naked face that said, "Baba to me has talked." This was Ozan, in uniform.

"At this moment the Boston woman and I were finished," continues the love letter hack, squeezing lighter fluid onto the escapement of his typewriter. For all practical purposes he has moved in with the American student. They're both at their machines this morning, Alton typing, a letter to that goat-like—as common as she is nervous—girl, he performing maintenance. He should have left for the bridge by now, but his insides are dryer, fouler than dungcake. "I mean to say that very night I changed my clothes, put on salvar, went with my brother to our father's tent. On the last camels, Riza and Remzi, we took off, rode three nights, three days, maniacs. Dismounting at the battle we announced, 'At your service, efendiler, at your service. See, we're bringing ourselves and food too.' Riza and Remzi we butchered, we fought two months and advanced to the Sakarya and fought, and at long last drove them into the sea." Sunlight streams nicely, prelethally, from the balcony, making the cheese on the table sweat. Alton's machine would fit between the spools of the hack's.

"Four to six years later, after the Army, I returned to Istanbul to my father's, to search the city stone by stone for Zumrut. The government paid a small pension but he remained at the wall, among the crowding of more and more tents, and spoke only to gypsy musicians. Also I'd fallen in love with Ferzan, the Boston woman's maid, by writing letters to her from my posts. Naturally there came an evening I found her, the woman, upstairs in the darkness without other foreign women and surprised her with the news we were getting married. 'I suppose you were my last,' she said. 'I am grateful I taught you to disregard the primitive preoccupation with dowry and bloodline. That is not to say there will be no difficulty.' For the wedding she gave us a glove box containing hundreds of thin thin strips of silver."

> *Dear Darcy,*
> *For God's sake you're totally out of your skull if you think you can*

> *Dear Darcy,*
> *Please. Darling. For whatever our relationship does now & will in the future mean*

> *Dear Darcy,*
> *I can't believe you and Darrell—I take that back: I can believe anything of that spoiled-ass bastard*

> *Dear Darcy,*
> *This is by way of reaffirming, at whatever risk to my foolish pride, how much I miss you & how absurd this is, our being apart when obviously we're meant, as much as anything is in a cosmos of randomness, as much as gravity is more or less meant, to be together. The irony is, I used to think I couldn't focus on my work as sharply/you near, but now I realize I can't work my best w/o you. If only we could teleport to ea. other rt. this second so much misunderstanding & misgiving would be dissipated, so many doubts &*

(Uh . . . anxieties, no, too neurotic, he decides; insecurities, no . . .)

so many doubts & dejections. Appropriately, Temas *just hit the sinema—*
The Touch *to you no-speakenzies—& altho the audience last nite greeted it/jeers & yawns, the title anyway is what I need.* Temas.

 The old r&d goes decently enough, I guess, & Istanbul continues to exert its allure, which at full volume is yet a whisper to thine, & I've met an amazing fellow, an aging drunk who scrapes by by writing letters for the unlettered—could be a booming business in the states, what?—by far the most interesting & in fact most helpful to my thesis person I've met. He's an ambulatory, most of the time, compendium of tales & poems, speaks everything from Kurdish & Armenian to French. His ludicrously lurid letters to the lovelorn—am I not safe from Spiro e'en here?—are something you should as they say, git a load a.
 Which brings me—smooth, eh?—to saying I don't exactly relish the no-tion of you & Darrell in the sack. Don't know why I'm so uptight about a natural occurrence in the lives of the 2 people I love most, and wish I wasn't, but I wish you wouldn't. I still long for a world of utter sexual freedom, Utopia by any other name, but I have such difficulty keeping my heart up with my brain, or brane. Cela étant le cas, I guess I'm invoking that vener-able document, the agreement reached after our last respective flings, viz., wild oats is OK, even essential, but that there sowing of tame oats is too goldarn threatening, & there could be no oat tamer than Darrell.

(He reconsiders that, lets it stand, thinking, The rhetoric am-bushes the meaning but on the other hand makes it clear there is one person to whom the contradiction of Darrell's vaunted wildness does not occur.)

 Well, time to go fix supper for me and the letter writer.

(He prefers to give correspondence a nocturnal feel.)

 who turns out to be a bit of a mooch, but well worth it.
 Quickly write, reconfirm, continue to love me. I love you you know.

(What if Darrell reads this, in bed, smooths it over her butt and puffing a Balkan Sobranie reads this? He closes quickly.)

Yrs. fr. keeps,
All-tin

P.S. Maybe I'll get lucky & these martial law paranoids'll deport me imme-diately, to you.

The PTT (Peh-Teh-Teh, Posta, Telefon, Telegraf) is the danger. Sooted aluminum and glass between a document photo studio and a tripe soupery across from Istanbul U., it has become the most compelling piece of architecture in Istanbul, eclipsing Sinan's frivolities, in all Islam out-emanating the Kaaba. For a week he skirts its force field, shooting for fifteen days, the number until it must contain her yes or no or else, granting himself reprieve by refusing to acknowledge the possibility of earlier messages—side issues, teases. He times it so he's too rushed in the morning if he wants a shoeshine at the gate of the University, too late leaving at the twenty-first hour, when the PTT closes per municipal fiat. He mails at another branch.

The eighth night he cracks, bolts early. There might be a letter from his thesis adviser. His high school zoology teacher might be back in intensive care. His flesh trembling in swatches, vision pitching, legitimate symptoms perhaps of a disease no U.S. physician will recognize in time, he enters with seconds to spare, sets the number, cracks the little safe. McGraw-Hill. The Turk-American Association. Henry and Henrie at Indiana. D. Hooper. But thin, just one thin page, praise Allah in his omni-absence. She wouldn't tell him that on one thin page. He rips it open, reads line after line of affection as singleminded as if he'd penned it himself.

He jogs the kilometer down to Eminonu, past Sultanahmet, past the zoo—which either Crazy Ibrahim or Black Mustafa located next to the impaling pit to mask screams—crosses the heaving Galata bridge. On an impulse he boards the ferry to the Asian side, with the idea of visiting the teacher at the girls school or finding the hack, who is hitting the clubs of Moda with a friend, big man from Ankara, on Alton's money. On the top deck he notices an eye-opening (straight translation) woman his age, by appearance a bank clerk kept late, who doesn't spurn his glances. But he exerts abstinence, sympathetic magic, letting Darcy from around the globe eliminate another rival. Fat chance anyway picking up a Turk. He lets her eliminate the teacher too. The boat shuffles, gets underway.

Coolly he returns to speculations that before the letter were feverish. If he loses her, he loses not only his soul but the chance for excellent children, chance not lavished on a person like him. Three types of men father, goes the theory—the squinty and flawed, your regular grad student, susceptible to a delayed fruition but prized for safe surroundings; the punky, your hoodlum on street or quad when young, the darling of the insurance companies in a few years; the genotypical, who through a cancellation of recessives matures into the image of the ethnos. Slav, period. Wop, period. Connecticut-Prodigal, period, Darrell. Alton differs from the first in having a stronger body, from the second in possessing commitment, from the third in looking poorly executed, half Wop, half not, and thus stares into the face of an evolutionary dead end. Mother Nature has no designs on Alton Mallone.

But fawns on Darrell, the slut, even if his attractiveness is equal parts hereditary and calculated, at the service of a battery of desperate and imaginary needs. Each of his women is driven to cast her body against the stone of his eventual distance, not thinking she'll be the one, banking instead on the grandest rush on earth, the meeting of sluts, the being of sluts together, nailing metaphysics to the wall in sheets. With Darrell you can't lose. He twits Alton for over-seriousness, twits Darcy for deliberation, twits them both for getting wrapped up in each other, for how can they expect universality in their work when so provincial with their genitals? Darrell isn't just a slut, he's a didactic slut.

He's my friend, Alton reminds himself, my friend longer than Darcy has been my love. His character has reversed only in my brain in exile.

The strength of the Bosphorus shears the ferry. Two dolphins break water, sewing the slipstream, their casings glowing in the light from the lower deck. Simultaneously the truth of Darcy's note unfreezes in his liver, spreads to other organs, the reason behind such fluent protestation. Buhhhhhhhhh . . . buhhhhhhhhhh . . . the ghost of Leander, saluting to port. He sees the bank clerk change to Darcy, open her blouse, hitch back her hair and smother to her breast her baby with Darrell's scalding face.

Warily nearing the Kadikoy PTT, Alton buys postcards and stamps from a woman who displays them on pasteboard under the streetlight. Buys them, that is, after minutes of consideration and the seller's growing annoyance, which she expresses to passersby in the belief he doesn't understand. One last time he'll pretend it's not too late. On the first, a picture of tilted, turbaned headstones he writes,

> *Incidentally I'm no longer messing/that teacher, tho the pt. is she didn't mean anything to you.*

And on the second, a view of sheep among the crags of Mount Ararat,

> *How would you feel about homesteading in British Columbia?*

Twenty-two and a half hours, he calculates, minus six equals four-thirty in the afternoon there. Terrific, fine, that's some relief, a rag of relief. They're out sunning or boating or charming the rich. But then he thinks, When you first fall in love you make love around the clock. They haven't seen the sun in days unless occasionally it seeps through the window onto their wan, exhausted forms. At four-thirty in the afternoon they're squeezing some more in before she goes to work.

"Allah, Allah, in my father's tent, to the music of flute and drum, saz and poetry we were married," Nuri Deveyoglu recalls, refusing the offer of one of Alton's doctored cigarettes. The presence of esrar, not to mention leftist paperbacks, in Alton's apartment makes him extremely anxious. Constantly he chides himself for not straightening up and moving out altogether, not even visiting the place. Yet the elephant, he recites inwardly, finds it difficult to live without the fly, albeit the fly comprehends nothing of the elephant's essence. "We were married, we were happy, love was sweetmeats and incense. We persuaded my father to return to Kayibkoy to breed sheep. When he left the Army, Ozan joined him. Nobody spoke of Zumrut.

"I mean to say I was a different person, my little meat-brother." They've splurged on lamb for tonight's supper, which is cooking on the balcony. They float on updrafts of aroma from the pot, updrafts of heat from the dark alleys. The district has vanished in the time between the fading of skylight and the appearance of low-wattage bulbs behind curtains. "Thanks to the Army's influence, I was convinced of every liberal idea. First thing we moved to Ankara, we moved to Mustafa Kemal Pasa Ataturk. I made this and that translation for the government. In those days if you lived in Ankara you were young and crazy, crazy with hope for our country, maniacs. We stayed two years and when they needed teachers for the villages we volunteered for Kayibkoy.

"At that time in Kayibkoy, you must understand, our love began in earnest. We taught the alphabet to men and women who were grandparents when we were babies. We taught to remove the veil and fez, we taught hygiene, we taught geography, we taught to ignore the hoca. I'm speaking of the most difficult lessons. Naturally the hoca stood against us. But at first my father, whom the people honored, stood with us. Ferzan they were suspicious of. Her devotion to my father won many hearts but her hair being red was unfortunate. When she went into labor the only woman to help was from the next village, Devedikenkoy, with her amulets and evil concoctions, the old methods.

"However, daubing mud on mud the sparrow builds her nest. In the next several years we built a school with a tile roof and courtyard, we took in orphans, our love strengthened.

"A poster came from the Istanbul Municipal Committee naming Zumrut among women searching for their families because their husbands had died. Not true, the husbands hadn't died. Ozan and I travelled to Istanbul to the police barracks. They called her name, she walked toward us with her head down, very shy, very strong, very beautiful. Ozan wept at this mirror of his mother. His eye, which hadn't wept since the injury, wept. By train and motorcar we three rushed home to the village. My father came from his house but when he lifted her face he said, 'She must leave, there isn't any daughter with me.' I challenged him. He said, 'Don't you recognize the look of a woman who has loved? Kafir, kitapsiz (faithless, Bookless)!' 'He wasn't kafir. When he discovered I was Turk he married me also,' Zumrut said, but the words were tears attempting to melt rock. I told him, 'You're on the side of death now, well, that's fitting. What happened to the Poplar Bow? What happened to the Dawn Leopard?' Two weeks after, he sent her to a man in Baykal and we never saw her again. I left his house, forbade Ferzan from taking our son to him.

"Our Mustafa Kemal Pasa Sevgili died, Ankara weakened, the hoca revived. My father advised people not to let their children attend school. The village of my boyhood, the village of our hopes returned to the side of death, old methods. This regression poisoned our lives. Old methods means men and women can't love each other because they can't know each other, can't talk, can't see each other's faces. It's possible to turn dust to mud but turning dust to copper is not to be. In secret I began to drink raki—old methods they want, old methods they can have. Once when I passed out in the thistles the men took a retarded girl from our school to the public-house in Devedikenkoy, as was their former custom. We cursed them, we ran the streets cursing them and the next day we left, went back to Ankara. But there too discouragement, which doesn't care where it eats, ate the blossom of our love. During the war I made this and that translation until they discharged me for misconduct.

"Only one time after did we travel to Kayibkoy, to carry my

father to the mountains to bury, far from the village that killed his soul.

"Hearing of our difficulties, a friend called us to Istanbul, offering Ferzan the directorship of a Women's Institute. I assisted with musical studies. This lasted four to six years until they discharged us because it was said I attacked a student, a ridiculous charge, comic. We sank into poverty. When I was sober I sold things to English and French speaking in the Bazaar, otherwise nothing. Then our son was killed in Korea and that was the finish to finishes. I refused to do anything but drink. Ferzan went to Edirnekapi to wash the dead. Even there, despite her tragedy, the women mocked her hair, which she always hid in a tight scarf. I mean to say the new life was dead. Only the government remained. I didn't worry about these trifles, though, I worried about raki. Many nights I carried roses to the whores in Karakoy. I sold sweets from a glass cart, drank two bottles of raki every day. We lived in dens.

"Suddenly my wife fell ill. Always, you understand, she'd been the strong one, caring for me, and now she grew very, very ill. One afternoon after three months of sickness, she came to the door, leaned against the—"

"Frame."

"Frame, my little brother. I was in the street cooking pilaf. She leaned against the frame and a redness, much color, caught my attention—her hair, falling outside the door for people to see. I myself had never seen her hair in the light. Naturally, I took it in my hands when we were alone but my eyes had never seen it outside her scarf. It was like red willows, like a mountain waterfall at sunset, like. . . ." The love letter hack has to pause. "Allah, it wasn't like anything. It was her hair.

" 'Beloved husband, my soul, I'm going to bed, excuse me.'

" 'Go on, I'll bring the pilaf.'

" 'I'm supposed to go to Edirnekapi in an hour.'

"I helped her to the bed she didn't rise from. I asked, 'How has it been you continued to love me when I brought us to misery? Is it because I fought at the Sakarya? Night and day I trembled at the Sakarya.'

"She said, 'You never deserted me when they hissed *alman*! If you'll stay a short while longer, altogether we'll be even.'

"One month I am staying with her. I am not sleeping, I am not eating, I am not drinking raki. Only I am staying with her, only, only."

The main dwelling having been destroyed, the adjunct which served as harem for the love letter hack's sister Zumrut and her sister wives is now occupied by a teashop whose owner stands, sentry of a tall chrome samovar, assessing the two unusual customers. First the American stalks the place, conversing, while the old derelict with the accent remains seated, then vice versa. The American slides the photo of the Gaziantep soccer club to the side, touches the yellowed tile beneath, and looks to the one window, not so caked with soot that the ornate grillwork doesn't show through. Out in the heat the dogs lose their hunger.

"Twelve to fourteen years," mutters the hack. "Well, there used to be a garden with a mulberry tree, she told me. Evenings on the roof."

Alton tries to envision the merchant's entry at end of day, what was left for him to see, what hidden. He says, "All the goddamn signals getting crossed, they knew they had to change the language. But there's no way to start from scratch. Even if you could, how many years before a word insists on mysticism?" The owner misses this, misses the English, but understands the American's posture and expression, those of a public prosecutor.

"Sit, please," the hack says. "Tea, uncle! How much additional for today's instead of yesterday's? We're visiting the shrine where our beloved Zumrut Deveyoglu sang in a voice that silenced the nightingales. At your service, my little brother, talk business with me. What news from your girl-friend?"

"Very literally none of your business. I'm looking for a third sex that looks like women but is tenderhearted." Alton stands again, quiets his breath for the sake of the chamber, for the sake of the faintest echo of the sister's song. He hears the chant of an artichoke seller. He hasn't seen the hack this nervous before. "Are you asking me to finance an electric typewriter?"

"It's the love business I'm speaking of, since you've become an expert. For five hundred liras—one hundred mine—at the Otel Aksaray Palas a certain her-boyfriend-having-left-not-answering-the-letter-I-myself-wrote honored lady would you care to meet? She's eye-opening. She saw you with me."

The proprietor draws his hand across his chin.

"How to say, son of a quince, you're putting me on."

"Are you scared to try an interesting relationship? Elegant room."

"That depends."

"Yes, naturally, I've allegedly understood, it depends on the PTT."

Dear Alton,
In discussing matters/the I Ching, the Taming Power of the Great #26
Ta Ch'u popped up:

ABOVE, Ken, keeping still, mtn.

BELOW, Ch'ien, the creative, heaven

And I quote ". . . the hexagram has a 3-fold meaning expressing diff. as-pects of the concept 'holding firm.' Heaven w/in the mtn. gives the idea of holding firm in the sense of holding together; the trigram Ken, which holds the trigram Ch'en still, gives the idea of holding fm. in the sense of holding back; the 3rd idea is that of holding fm. in the sense of caring for & nourish-ing. . . ."

Pretty amazing stuff, huh? But here's the old clincher, the 2nd hex. which surfaces as a result of the 2 lower strong (moving) lines:

ABOVE, Ken, keeping still, mtn.

BELOW,   "   "   "   "

"... true quiet means keeping still when the time has come to keep still & going forward when the time has come to go forward. In this way, rest & movement are in agreement/the time & thus there is light in life. ..."

Alton, do you understand these are 2 sides of the same coin (rotten pun, I realize)? that our relationship will remain the mtn. of stability in our shifting existences? Don't under any circumstances get it in yr head to forget me if at times my relatively paltry quotient of mischievousness waylays me, & leads me to a confession that

His back to the stairway, where thousands of men in dark clothes are mounting and descending, Nuri Deveyoglu, the writer, orders tea and resumes a troubled reverie, diddling with his flyswatter. The limp and oily water of the Horn reflects alkaline flakes of light to his face. His internal atmosphere, anise-tinctured, is that of the dead rather than the living. His flesh is tallow. The nine-year-old dumps the tea into his typewriter. Nuri responds by swatting him, yelling that he's sold him to a Spanish pederast, cheap, swats again. Hamals toting file cabinets, followed by *alman* tourists on thick bare legs, mist the top of his head with sweat.

A ferryboat horn takes aim at his spine, fires interminably. As the boat pulls away from the dock, the screw propulses refuse over the bulkheading. He becomes aware of a customer bearing in rapidly, a young man who strides without a customer's customary deference, a troublemaker, dressed shabbily, bouncing as he walks even in compulsion.

"Wake up, son of an ass, before I throw your writing machine to the jellyfish."

The young customer who doesn't look that young and could never have been what the writer considers lively stands before him, slaps a twenty-lira note down, speaks with precision. "Baba, one letter I wish to send. In English."

"I was with the gypsies," Nuri confesses, raising his palms to indicate his condition, his eyebrows to indicate his regret. He has nothing he can offer, cannot bring a line from his catalog into focus or a phrase of friendship to his lips. To lift his hands is an achievement, to land fingers on the right keys beyond aspiration. Still he must say, "Agreed. Begin."

The customer reels off, "Darcy, you're afraid you and Darrell were overcome by mischievousness. Well, I'm afraid I mistook you for a real person, with real loyalty of a lifespan exceeding twelve goddamn weeks. I spit on your mischievousness. I wouldn't touch it with a ten-foot pole, let alone half a foot. Thanks for the stick figures of your privates. Privates, get it? Thanks for making it easy to jettison the both of you. Freedom from love is freedom indeed. I remain, sincerely *mine*, Alton Mallone."

"I'm writing this?"

"Right, only make it meaner, that's what I'm paying extra for. Put in Arabic curses."

Blinking back cinders, Nuri observes Alton's worn, fragile face and thinks, not for the first time, How is it we propose to ourselves too much to bear? Also how is it we are least able to help when most needed? He tries to divert his mind to coolness, to evenings on the steppe, but acid climbs to his tongue like kerosene up a wick. "My little confusion-brother, you type. I'll speak Turkish, you type. I can't spell English."

Alton swings the machine around, bends to the misarranged keys.

"You must type exactly what I say."

"At your service, efendim."

"Dear Darcy, my beloved soul. . . ."

"I told you what I want."

"Type exactly. Type! Dear Darcy, my beloved soul. . . ."

Alton types, eyeing the writer vengefully but willing to begin typing, willing to give sarcasm the benefit of the doubt. The *a* prints like a twisted hyphen.

Nuri closes his eyes, at last finds a few lines surfacing, the opening to a story of his father's that Ozan told in the mountain village where they buried him. One of many stories, perhaps the wrong one, but with no other choice he begins, "Darcy, there was a young wanderer."

He pauses, says, "Parentheses. This story was remembered by my brother Ozan, the wool of whose garment soaked up my father's words. Don't sheep have ears? Close parentheses."

"You're forgetting who's the customer here."

He continues, "There was a young wanderer who came to a certain village playing flute.

"Parentheses. My brother sits away from the light of the fire, not understanding that in repeating my father's gestures as well as words his disfigurement disappears. Close parentheses.

"This was many years ago, before any of you was born.

"Parentheses. My brother surveys the listeners, bringing his eyes to rest on the visage of the most wrinkled auntie. Close parentheses.

"I mean to say, somewhat after the oldest of you was born.

"Parentheses. The hag cackles, says, 'I remember that wanderer! He had a good one, a fez, not like you flat-hats!' Close parentheses.

"To the wanderer's amazement, you welcomed him like a sheik, with a great show of hospitality and well-being. Everywhere was music, dancing, feasting. Moreover he could scarcely believe it when, the day after his arrival, you let it be known your loveliest girl was his did he desire her.

"To be sure, no man could have resisted such beauty, a beauty not unlike yours, beloved Darcy-to-come. Her teeth shone like pearls of the White Sea, but tiny tiny, like kernels on young corn. Her skin was the white of mare's milk. Her movements in the selamlik—but that I must leave to the imaginations of the young, the memories of the old.

"Parentheses. 'Oh-oh-*oh*!' the men complain. Close parentheses.

"All right, she had a certain: twitch.

"Parentheses. 'Allah!' Close parentheses.

"In short, they fell in love, they married, and trouble left the village—you understand the welcoming festivity was a sham—as if winter had turned to spring overnight. Well, everyone knows of young love. It's like sweetmeats and incense and it's not anything like sweetmeats and incense. Occasionally the young man wondered why their house stood so far apart from the other houses, but such misgivings were dew on sand. What lover notices mosquitoes?

"Then one day a man from Kayibkoy came to sell chickens, saw the new couple, and ran, abandoning his flock. The young man chased him, caught him, demanded an explanation. 'Since I fear you'll harm me I'll tell you,' the Kayibkoyu said. 'Your bride is a jinn. At night she goes among the scorpions.'

"Parentheses. The listeners whisper certain names of the Merciful. Close parentheses.

"That night before sleep, after much love, the wife asked, 'My husband, my life, why is it you've brought the plowshare inside, dirtying the wall?' 'Bandits were seen at the pass,' he replied.

"Parentheses. My brother calls for a coal. Zeki, my father's lieutenant since before my birth, enters the light holding up two bloody fingers on his only hand, signifying the goats just born. The listeners are wondering if they've come too far. Sticks move, thistles moan, across the stars fly the condemned. Close parentheses.

"The husband pretended to fall asleep. After a time he heard a stirring. He peeked, and peeking saw a scorpion climb from between his wife's pearly teeth and leave the house through a chink. Up into her—please cover the children's ears—up into her womb he reached and scattered salt. Again he waited, pretending to sleep. It was nearly dawn before he heard the scorpion scratch back across the floor.

"As soon as the creature reentered his wife's mouth the husband rose and blocked the chink. He saw his wife begin to writhe. 'Go back to sleep, my husband, my soul,' she pleaded.

'Rest, you're looking unwell.' 'I have to milk the animals,' he said. She behaved like a person in a fit. After more than an hour of struggle she gagged a last time, fainted, and the scorpion climbed from her teeth and dropped to the floor, scurrying for the chink. Escape was not to be. From the scorpion's eyes the wife saw the plowshare descending in the hands of her beloved. He cleft her.

"Parentheses. '*Al*lah A*lah!*' both the men and women cry. The children shriek. Close parentheses.

"Black oily smoke rose from the wound, filled the room, filled the husband with visions. Yet in these visions he saw only the simplest things, the places and deeds of scorpions, with their peculiar beauty.

"You considered him a hero, but in the days of solitude that followed he came to see himself as the destroyer of the happiness he had traveled all his youth to find. What had it mattered after all? Sleep, according to the Traditions, isn't exactly living.

"He set off wandering, now without a flute, without water, wearing a coarse cloth, beating himself with a chain. His condition when we dismounted to attend him was this.

"Darcy, please, I kiss the eyes of your mother, the feet of your father. I am begging you, don't leave me alone.

"Greatest love, Alton."

Nuri Deveyoglu opens his eyes, a squint at a time, like a man crawling out of a mine. He has made it to the end. His lungs wring themselves with relief. Alton merely balls up a half page of typing, chucks it into the water, and stares his contempt at the writer.

Nuri grunts to his feet, nods, says, "Excuse me, I'd forgotten that instead of regarding themselves as human beings the young regard themselves as sultans." Then, without alerting his friend the seller of chilled plum juice, not caring whether Alton guards the typewriter or not, he turns away, down toward the docks for his stroll. He sees the haze between him and the cypresses on the outcrop below the palace and sees the water and the small boats on the water. The poets say boats dance on water and it's true. They dance! Nor is he alone for long. Indeed he chuckles at the hardly unexpected arrival of the companions who dog his existence, companions he's never seen, since they stay to the rear and besides are sneaky. But he feels their arrival and with them as entourage strolls down along the seawall, a shuffling, surefooted man, barely suppressing delight. The companions grin too, as much as their faces will allow, seven mutes with a silken bowstring.

Design by David Bullen
Typeset in Mergenthaler Palatino
by Wilsted & Taylor
Printed by Maple-Vail
on acid-free paper